Praise for the Novels of Kate Pepper

One Cold Night

"I was sucked into the book . . . and felt I was living each minute. . . . The story is full of nuanced characters that make it come alive. Add that to the jagged emotions, incredible tension, and gritty street feel and you've got a really good book." —*Rendezvous*

"Jam-packed with heart-stopping suspense, *One Cold Night* is a book not to be missed. Ms. Pepper has a magnificent way of bringing each character to life in this very fascinating and intriguing tale." —MyShelf

Seven Minutes to Noon

"In this highly suspenseful domestic mystery, readers are treated to the terrifying aftermath of secure and cozy lives gone chillingly wrong. Likable characters, plenty of suspects, and a relatively shocking ending that stuns and thrills." —New Mystery Reader Magazine

"*Seven Minutes to Noon* starts off running, and never stops until the end. A tightly woven plot keeps the story flowing. . . . You'll startle at every strange sound as you read Kate Pepper's second book. Best not to be alone when turning the pages." —BookLoons

continued . . .

HERE SHE LIES

Kate Pepper

AN ONYX BOOK

ONYX
Published by New American Library, a division of
Penguin Group (USA) Inc., 375 Hudson Street,
New York, New York 10014, USA
Penguin Group (Canada), 90 Eglinton Avenue East, Suite 700, Toronto,
Ontario M4P 2Y3, Canada (a division of Pearson Penguin Canada Inc.)
Penguin Books Ltd., 80 Strand, London WC2R 0RL, England
Penguin Ireland, 25 St. Stephen's Green, Dublin 2,
Ireland (a division of Penguin Books Ltd.)
Penguin Group (Australia), 250 Camberwell Road, Camberwell, Victoria 3124,
Australia (a division of Pearson Australia Group Pty. Ltd.)
Penguin Books India Pvt. Ltd., 11 Community Centre, Panchsheel Park,
New Delhi - 110 017, India
Penguin Group (NZ), 67 Apollo Drive, Rosedale, North Shore, Auckland 1311,
New Zealand (a division of Pearson New Zealand Ltd.)
Penguin Books (South Africa) (Pty.) Ltd., 24 Sturdee Avenue,
Rosebank, Johannesburg 2196, South Africa

Penguin Books Ltd., Registered Offices:
80 Strand, London WC2R 0RL, England

First published by Onyx, an imprint of New American Library,
a division of Penguin Group (USA) Inc.

First Printing, May 2007
10 9 8 7 6 5 4 3 2 1

For Oliver, Eli and Karenna
Always

ACKNOWLEDGMENTS

Many thanks to my editor, Claire Zion, whose insight, skill and patience helped shape this story from its inception, and to my literary agent, Matt Bialer, who met each new draft with sagacity and encouragement. Thanks also to Matt's assistant, Anna Bierhaus, who read and commented on an early draft of the novel; D. P. Lyle, M.D., for factual guidance on the forensics of blood; and friend and attorney Michael Fay, for throwing legal documents my way in the hope that I might actually read them. A very special thank-you to Jessie Lief, whose input was invaluable, as was the hard work and dedication of the talented staff at New American Library and Penguin. And, last but not least, I owe special gratitude to my husband, Oliver, who listened, advised, read and commented throughout the entire process of bringing this novel to life.

PART ONE

Chapter 1

Sunlight poured through our front door's stained-glass window, splashing the floor with an impressionistic rainbow. My two large suitcases sat at the ready; everything I needed for the next few months was in them, plus various sizes of clothes for Lexy to grow into. I stood there, stunned by the reality of what was happening. I was really doing it: I was leaving my husband. Stood there, in this moment that felt too heavy and too long, torn between letting my baby daughter finish her morning nap and waking her up and leaving.

I decided I should wake her or we might miss our plane. And, truthfully, I was afraid of another fight with Bobby. Our arguments at this point were just filler; we had been through this for months already and nothing had changed. But before I reached the bottom of the staircase I heard his footsteps, steady echoes from the direction of the kitchen, and I turned to face him.

"What's this?" he asked.

"I can't anymore."

There he was, my handsome husband—sandy brown hair still unbrushed from bed, plaid pajama bottoms and an old T-shirt advertising a dentist in Oregon, ocean blue eyes searching my face—stricken that I was making good on my threat to leave him. There was a smudge of newsprint ink on his cheek; he had been reading in the kitchen. I wanted to cry, but didn't. Bobby was the love of my life and even now, in the middle of this stalemate, I wanted to move in his direction. I wanted his hands on my skin and my nose in his neck and his breath in my ear. But he was having an affair with some woman who was just delirious over him; he was wining her and dining her and gifting her in a romantic torrent he had not afforded *me* during our brief courtship. All on our joint credit card, making it so obvious he might as well have brought her home to dinner. He'd denied the affair, disavowed all the unimaginative charges (books of poetry, flowers, candy—not an original gesture on the list, but even so . . .). I had wanted to believe him—I *tried*—but if it wasn't true, why had the charges started up again on our new cards even after we'd canceled the old ones? And why had *she* written to him again, just today?

"Annie, *please.*" He stepped toward me, but I shook my head.

"I want you to read something." I opened my purse, balanced atop one of the suitcases, withdrew the e-mail I'd printed out that morning and handed it to him. He disliked computers and rarely checked his e-mail himself; lately, since all this had started, I had taken to checking it for him.

I watched him, now standing in the colorful puddle

of light, as he read the letter. It was without a doubt the most painful one yet, describing his body in accurate detail, the way his collarbones seemed to spread like wings when he was above you, making love. The first time I'd read it, *seeing* him over *her* brought such crisp pain I'd had to look away from the page. By the third and fourth readings, I was stoic, and by the fifth, in my imagination I saw him fly away. She began the e-mail using his childhood nickname, Bobbybob, and ended it with a flourish of intimacy that nonetheless concealed her name: Lovyluv.

His hand, and the letter, fell to his side. "I've told you so many times: I don't know who's sending these."

"I never thought you'd lie to me."

"I'm not."

"So all those love letters are fictitious?"

"Annie, *please*—"

"And all those credit card charges?"

"Why won't you believe me?"

"I've been wanting to ask you," I said, "and please tell the truth: Would you have even married me if I hadn't gotten pregnant?"

"This is exhausting, Annie."

"It would help me to know."

"I didn't marry you because you were pregnant. I married you because I love you. The pregnancy just sped things up." He stepped toward me and reached for my arm, saying, *"Don't go."*

Reflexively, I moved away, tripping over the nearest suitcase and falling against the door. My sweater-clad elbow pressed into the bottom edge of the stained glass and the first thing I thought was how soft it was as the lead seams bowed under pressure. The next thought: *Who would know how to fix such a window?* I regained my balance and stepped away from the door. Fixing it wasn't my problem anymore. I was leaving.

"What about Kent?" he asked. "When are you going to tell him?"

Outside, a bird sang a sudden, tremulous spring song. I kept my voice low and steady because I knew this information would convince him I was serious: "Bobby, I already quit. I called Kent this morning at home. I've been thinking about this for a while. I have another job lined up in New York."

His face, already pale from last winter, went ashen. Bobby was nineteen years into his career as a physical therapist in the U.S. Public Health Service. In one year, he could retire with bounteous lifelong benefits. Me, I was just two years in and I didn't care anymore. After Lexy was born I'd had only six weeks off before jumping back on track, and our workday at the prison began at seven a.m. I didn't want to drop my baby off at day care in the pitch-dark morning ever again.

"Annie, don't leave me." The strain in his voice, the regret, the *yearning*, were painful to hear. "I'll find a way to show you you're wrong."

Then show me! But I didn't say it, because that plea had been my mantra and yet—nothing. I was finished waiting. This latest e-mail was the last straw. Lately I'd wondered if he had met her while I was still pregnant with Lexy, toward the end when we weren't having sex anymore. Julie, my twin sister, had told me that was just what happened to a friend of hers: a loving marriage, a wanted baby, and then the husband couldn't tolerate a couple months of abstinence and he "roamed." Like he was a cow who'd wandered through a broken fence. I'd never thought Bobby could do such a thing. *Never.* Julie's friend hadn't either—but then you never do.

"I'm going to wake her," I said, "or we'll miss our flight."

"Where are you going?"

"To Julie's."

His face seemed to clamp at the mention of her name. No surprise to me. I'd always figured that, deep down, he was jealous of the closeness I shared with my twin.

As I walked toward the stairs, he followed me. "Annie, please—*please* don't take Lexy away from me."

"I'm sorry," I said. And I *was.* Sorry. Sad. Out of rationalizations. Finished with begging for what he couldn't seem to give me: the simple truth and an end to the affair.

I went upstairs to get Lexy. Quiet footsteps on the pale carpet Bobby and I had chosen together, an impractical but beautiful shade of champagne. He would be lonely by himself in this house. (Would he bring *her* here?) I could feel its emptiness and I wasn't even gone yet; I was still here, Lexy was still asleep in her very own crib, I could still change my mind, we could stay, we could stay . . .

Lexy's bedroom doorknob was cool in my hand. It clicked when I turned it.

Morning light edged the pulled-down window shades, creating a silvery half darkness. Lexy's breaths were long and deep and her room smelled baby-sweet. It was a good-sized room, with butter yellow walls trimmed in white. Two built-in corner bookcases held whatever things she had collected in the five months of her life. Dolls, books, colorful objects that made all kinds of sounds when you moved them.

On a high shelf of one bookcase was the collection of tiny handblown glass cats and kittens from the summer my parents took us to Italy, when Julie and I were seven. It was the July before they got divorced, a final and typically dramatic try at making their marriage work. It was a fun summer, though; Julie and I played happily beneath marital thunderclouds inside the ancient stone walls surrounding the Florentine rental castle where we stayed for four whole weeks. We were the kind of kids who didn't worry about things unless we had to, believing that our twin bond protected us from hazard (we may have actually still believed this, now, at the age of thirty-three). Being together always felt like safety in a storm.

The way our parents finally broke the news was this: Dad left the house and Mom sat us down in the living room (we were still in our matching pink nightgowns; the new school year hadn't yet started) and said in her cheerful way, "Daddy and I have decided that enough is enough. There won't be any more fighting."

Their divorce was final before Christmas. Under the tree that year my mother wrapped my glass cats in purple tissue paper with a green ribbon. Julie's cats were wrapped in green paper with purple ribbon. We had watched the glassblower make the tiny cats and even tinier kittens but never knew, until we received the gifts, that our parents had gone back to buy them for us.

Now I wrapped my glass cats in tissues and eased the soft square into my sweater's pocket. Well, Julie's sweater—she had forgotten it on her last visit, in March, and I was wearing it to return to her tonight. (It was a wonderful sweater, an expensive Oilily with pink and orange flowers shifting dominance depending on the angle of the light, creating a hallucinogenic effect. It reminded me of the old Cheerios boxes Julie and I would stare at during childhood breakfasts, shifting our gazes to catch another invisible, floating O.) I noticed that one of the sweater's six large, distinctive flower-shaped buttons had fallen off—and for a moment I panicked. But I had no time to search for a button now.

Lexy was asleep on her stomach even though I'd left her on her back; she had only recently started turning over. I ran my hand lightly down her back to let her body know Mommy was there, then carefully picked her up and positioned her over my shoulder so she could keep sleeping. Her eyes fluttered open, then fell shut again. I detoured to my bedroom for one more glance to make sure I hadn't forgotten anything and discovered that I had: the novel I was in the middle of reading. *The Talented Mr. Ripley* had been keeping me up nights, distracting me from my troubles, and I needed to finish it. Steadying Lexy, I dipped at the knee and took the slender paperback in my free hand.

Downstairs, I transferred Lexy to Bobby's shoulder so he could hold her while I put the suitcases into the trunk of the car. I figured I owed him that. At first he wouldn't follow me outside into the bright morning, instead staying in the front hall with our baby sleeping floppily over his shoulder. It was the week our cherry tree was in full bloom, with a few pink petals on the dappled shadows of our front lawn, and I got the feeling that the perfect beauty of the tree and the clear sunlight would pain him more than he could handle at the moment. I did feel sorry for him. But I had to go.

"Okay," I whispered. "I'll take her now."

He didn't move. I could see him drinking her in, smelling her, feeling her. I gave him another moment before slipping my hands under her arms and shifting her back to my shoulder. This time she woke up. She took a deep yawn and settled her weight into me.

"I'll park in Long Term and leave the ticket under the mat so you can get the car," I said.

"How will I get to the airport to get the car and then drive it back? I'm just one person." His eyes teared up and for the first time I saw a fleck of gray in his left eyebrow, just one lone hair. In the past months he had sprouted silver at his temples and his face had become a fretful map. He had twelve years on me—he would grow old first. I'd always known that and it had never bothered me. I wondered now if his affair was some kind of midlife crisis. Was *that* what this was?

"Oh, Bobby. You'll figure it out. Ask someone to go with you."

He knew who I meant. *Her.* The mystery woman. *Lovyluv.*

"You're making a real mistake," he said. "This is a marriage. We have a child."

But I still believed that if he really wasn't having an affair, if the love letters and credit card charges were really part of some hoax, he would have found a way to prove it. I kept hoping he would. Even up to the last minute, after I'd strapped Lexy into her car seat, my heart was primed . . . but all he could do as I got into the car was turn around and walk back into the house. He kept his eyes down, on the flagstone path, refusing to even glance at the cherry tree. I drove away. In the rearview mirror I could see his chest rising and falling.

He was weeping. I was weeping.

He shut the door.

I turned the corner off our street and began the long day's journey from our home in Lexington, Kentucky, to my sister's house in the Berkshire Mountains of Massachusetts.

It was five o'clock when I carried my restless baby off the plane at Albany International Airport. I changed her diaper in the ladies' room, brushed my hair and refreshed my pale pink lipstick (usually the only makeup I wore, an irrational yet effective source of confidence; the putting-on-of-lipstick in a mirror was something we had often watched our mother do: the stretched lips, the steady eye, the smooth stroke of color). Then I gathered our bags and sat for twenty minutes to nurse her. My cell phone service had no network this far east, so I had to find a working pay phone to let Julie know we'd landed on time.

"Expect us by seven. And Julie, don't hold dinner."

"I never eat before seven, anyway."

Having grown accustomed to late-afternoon dinners (Bobby and I were in bed by eight thirty to be up at five, day care at six thirty, work by seven), I had forgotten how skewed my hours had become. Before Kentucky and Bobby and Lexy and the good ol' Public Health Service, I too used to eat dinner at seven, eight, even nine o'clock.

"I'll have to nurse Lexy as soon as I get there and throw her into bed, so just eat when you're hungry. Did you get the—"

"Crib's all set up. I got the cutest sheets. You'll see."

I had asked her to rent a crib for the summer, but Julie being Julie (she was a successful independent marketing consultant, apparently some kind of sought-after guru), she had gone out and bought one.

"Did you—"

"*Yes*, Annie, I washed the sheets first. Just get in the car and *be* here, okay?"

By the time we picked up the rental car, Lexy had had enough of traveling and she didn't want to get into the car seat. She wanted to roll around the floor and practice grabbing for toys.

"Just a little longer, sweet baby. Promise."

I ran my hand over her peachy wisps of hair and kissed her forehead, both cheeks, her dimpled chin, her button nose. She laughed, then immediately cried. Her little face screwing up so suddenly brought me to tears. I had felt like crying for hours but hadn't wanted to attract attention to myself on the plane. All day I had felt that everyone could see me for what I really was: a wife who had left her husband, a mother who had taken a child from a father, a woman who had lost hope in a man. Did it show? I knew that from now on, when people mentioned the Goodmans, it would be with the tagline "that broken family." I was Anais (Annie) Milliken-Goodman. (*Anna-ees*, the French pronunciation. Naming us Anais and Juliet had been a flight of fancy in the romantic early years of our parents' marriage.) Would I drop *Goodman* from my name? Slice off the dangling hyphen? Go back to square one? If I did, then Lexy and I would officially be Alexis Goodman and Anais Milliken. But I had always wanted to share a last name with my child. Maybe we could drop our last names all together; she could be just Lexy and I could be just Annie. We could start a band. A sob ratcheted up my throat and escaped as a shout. I felt like such a fool. What had I done?

A headache blossomed as the little blue car's engine leapt into gear. The jolt quieted Lexy and I felt guiltily indebted to the sudden, unnerving grind of noise. Poor baby. What did she make of all this? Did she know something momentous was happening today? That the day was a knife carving a groove in our lives between before and after? Maybe I was wrong, but I sensed she felt the cut, the separation, as deeply as I did.

Why had Bobby done it? Why hadn't I been enough for him? There was a time I would have bet my soul that he and I were made for each other. With him, I had felt almost as right as I did with my identical twin: one person, joined in separate bodies.

I switched on the radio and we listened to classical music as we drove out of Albany toward the New

York–Massachusetts border. When Lexy sighed, deep and long, I felt myself relax a notch. In the rearview mirror I saw she had fallen asleep and I whispered "thank you" to the windshield. Humming along the highway, we consumed the miles to Great Barrington. To Julie's. I had never been to her new house, but I felt I was going *home*. I was as eager to arrive as I had ever been to get anywhere. Home after work. Bed after a tiring day. Birth after labor. Love after loneliness. Resolution after doubt.

After weeks of agony, I had a made a decision. I couldn't just stay there, living with Bobby, sleeping with him, working side by side, wondering who *she* was. I couldn't agree that black was white or white was black when all I saw was shades of gray. I would *not* repeat my mother's mistake, accepting my father's lies for years until finally it turned out her suspicions had been correct: he was cheating. It was terrible watching her struggle to recover from her own self-deceptions, her willingness to believe his lies. In the end, she never *did* recover—cancer got her first. We were only ten when our mother died, leaving me with the conviction that a woman should never compromise on the truth. At twelve, when our father died suddenly in a car accident, I learned that nothing was permanent or real except what you felt in your heart. You had to create your own reality, believe in it and it would make you strong. The old maxim *time is too precious to waste* became a vivid reminder to always take action when I was sure of something.

Until Bobby could tell me the truth, there was no going back.

Driving, I thought of something Julie had once said to me, about how she and I were as close as any two people could possibly be. Closer. How even marriage could not compare. It was my wedding day, a cool May afternoon in Kentucky, and I was two months pregnant. (Almost exactly one year ago—Bobby and I had not even made it to our first anniversary.) The night before, she had tried on my wedding dress and it was loose on her; I was already plumping up but not showing yet. For the first time ever, we were not exactly the same size. Standing there in my dress, waiting for my music cue to walk the aisle, she put her hand on my belly and repeated, "Closer."

My wedding day. Our first. Julie's engagement had broken up two years ago, dropping her back into a dating scene that felt more ruthlessly competitive the older you got. When I became pregnant and Bobby and I decided to marry, Julie shared our happiness. She *knew*, in the deep unspoken way of twins, how in love with Bobby I was. In the end, only motherhood could compare to the absolute connection Julie and I shared. Romantic love was intoxicating. Toxic. I felt sorry for people who didn't have a twin with whom to entwine when life weakened you, on whose fibers of love and shared memory you could always strengthen yourself. I decided I was not eligible for self-pity, not even today, because I had a daughter *and* a twin sister. Julie and I had clung together through every twist and turn of our lives, ultimately raising each other—at the shoddy Long Island boarding school where our misguided guardian, Aunt Pru, had placed us immediately after our father's funeral, in the sleepaway camps where she had sent us for two months every summer, and during the single dull week we spent with her annually in California. We had survived all that. I would survive this.

When we finally crossed the border between New York and Massachusetts, we had been on the road for over two hours, not the fifty-seven minutes predicted by the global positioning system suction-cupped to the windshield. Somehow, despite the GPS, I had managed to get lost twice. And a detour to nurse Lexy and change her diaper had inflated into a dinner stop when I realized how hungry I was. By the time we turned the car onto Division Street, Julie's street, a gentle country twilight had eased into the deep purple that comes just before the sky goes black. It was almost eight p.m. My body was screaming for sleep—and Lexy was just screaming.

Julie had explained to me that the barn she had bought last year and renovated through the winter was at the crossroads of Division Street and Alford Road. She said it was painted red and would be impossible to miss. Division Street was long and winding and dark, just what you would expect of a country road at night. But then gradually the darkness began to fade. It was like someone had spilled light all over the street, light that spread toward me. Washed over me like a wave, even filled the car. Like the car's starting jolt back at the airport, the brightness of this light quieted Lexy. Her wailing voice simply stopped as we pulled into the flashing arcs of white and blue and red lights.

Police lights.

I felt a sinking inside me, a terrible dread, as I pulled up behind the last of three squad cars parked in front of a big red barn. There was an ambulance. A series of disembodied camera flashes. A stout man wearing a Red Sox baseball cap and wrapping yellow police tape around the trunk of a tree, trailing it in search of another anchor. This close, the rotating police lights blinded us each time they swept over our car.

Chapter 2

Sweet country air seemed to pour into the car when I opened the door—air and the weird low chatter of people talking and crickets cricketing and my mind whirring like a broken disk drive. What was happening here?

Lexy twisted to the side and squeezed her eyes shut against the brightness. I had one foot on the ground and one hand on the steering wheel. I didn't want to leave my baby alone in the car, nor did I want to carry her into an unknown situation that looked very bad. There was a clump of people at the side of the road, some standing, some crouching. They all seemed to be focused on the same thing.

"Mommy will be right back," I whispered to Lexy. "Sit tight."

I walked toward what appeared to be the center of activity. Hovering together in an area defined by taut strands of yellow police tape were officers in uniform and others in regular clothes who looked official. It was their expressions: serious, focused, at work. Outside the barrier was a collection of people I decided must be neighbors; they seemed excited in a way the police were not.

I stepped to the side where I could see what was happening inside the tape. After a moment, someone left the group that was clustered together and someone else moved forward. And then I saw what they saw: a woman lay on the ground. She looked frozen. Her eyes were open, pupils large and fixed, and one of her legs was bent at a strange angle. Her head was hinged dramatically backward and her neck seemed covered by a shadow. Or maybe . . . maybe it wasn't a shadow . . . maybe it was . . . it was her neck, sliced open with clean precision, and this cleavage of her flesh was filled with dark, glistening blood. There was so much of it! A pool of blood spread steadily around her.

I felt a terrible sense of familiarity, almost a déjà vu, except I was sure I had never experienced this moment before. It felt completely foreign and completely wrong. And then I understood my strange reaction: the woman—she was *us*. Her name leapt out of me: "Julie! *Julie!*"

The murmur of voices quieted as every face turned to look at me. I couldn't tell if I was walking or standing still; it was a heaviness I can't explain. Then as the shock wore thinner I began to see differences between the woman, the *body*, on the ground and us. Her legs were heavier than ours, her body rounder, her hair thicker, though it was our same shade of reddish brown.

One of the uniformed officers stood up and walked toward me. "You okay, Ms. Milliken?"

"I'm her twin sister."

"Oh." His was the same measuring stare I'd encountered a thousand times, when someone's surprised mind doubted you.

"Who is that?" I asked.

"Local woman, cleaned houses for some of the folks along this road."

"What happened?"

"She was killed."

"Killed" was almost putting it nicely. The woman's throat had been slit, her blood was emptying out on the road and the way she was lying, like she'd fallen backward, looked like someone had come up behind her, depriving her not just of her life but of the knowledge of who took it. It was the worst thing I had ever seen with my own eyes.

"When?"

"Don't know. Pretty recently. Listen, ma'am, you'd better step back. There's your sister, over there." He pointed behind me, to my car. I turned around and there was Julie, reaching into the backseat, scooping up her niece.

My heart pulsed at the sight of Julie, and hungered at the sight of Lexy, who was crying again. I had no idea how much time had just gone by—probably just a minute or two, but it felt like much longer. My poor baby was exhausted and probably afraid. Julie was bouncing her in the air, trying to cheer her up, but Lexy was wiggling, uncomfortable. I wondered if she thought Julie was *me*, a mommy who looked like Mommy but who *wasn't* Mommy, a mommy who smelled just a little bit different and sounded just a little bit different and was a little bit thinner but otherwise *was* Mommy. A mommy who *wasn't* Mommy and who *was* Mommy. It must have felt like an insult after the long, difficult day. She was too young to know about identical twins. I hurried over to take her in my arms and comfort her.

I kissed Julie's cheek as Lexy dove at me. Never in my life had anyone been so certain of the difference between me and Julie when we were standing next to each other. Lexy's complete lack of hesitation was gratifying, but even so, I said to Julie, "She really thought you were me." I said it because she couldn't have children of her own and I could, and so we would have to share.

"No, she didn't," Julie said. "But thanks for saying so." She smiled at Lexy, who glanced back and forth between us, looking baffled. Then Julie circled me with a warm arm and I became aware of her unique and familiar smell, part perfume and part *her*: a rich musk that was more affection than fragrance, that meant I was *home*.

"Julie, what happened here?" I asked. "It's *terrible*."

"I still can't believe it. That poor woman. Can you imagine?"

"Who is she?"

"Zara Moklas," Julie said. "She's a Hungarian immigrant—I mean, *was*. She worked as a part-time secretary in town and she also cleaned houses. I was thinking of hiring her myself. One of my neighbors told me she lived with her brother and *he's* into all kinds of shady construction deals, maybe even tied to the Mob."

"Around *here*?"

"You'd be surprised."

"And the sister, Zara, she paid the price for that?"

"Who knows?"

"Well, it's awful," I said.

And Julie echoed: *"Awful."*

We paused to watch the emergency workers place Zara's body on a stretcher, cover her with a sheet and load her into the back of the ambulance. Julie reached over to smooth a finger along Lexy's soft, soft cheek. And then she looked at me. "I guess you don't know who found her."

"Was it you?"

"Nope. *Bobby.*"

"Bobby's *here*?"

Julie nodded, pinching in one side of her mouth. I knew what *that* meant: unbelievable but true.

"What's he doing here?" I asked.

"What do you think?"

"But how did he get here so fast?"

"He caught a flight right after yours," she said. "He rented a car and drove straight here, got here half an hour ago. Why did it take *you* so long? Did you stop?"

It was a rhetorical question and I didn't answer. I always stopped on the road; she knew that.

"Did he think I would just turn around and go back with him if he showed up?"

"Would you?"

My heart answered *yes*, my mind *no*. "Where is he?"

"In the house. I poured him a drink. He's in bad shape."

"So *he* found the woman? Was she—?"

Julie nodded. "But only just. Listen, Annie, before you see him, you should know that he kind of freaked out on the lawn. That's what got the neighbors out in the first place. Bobby just lost it, you know?"

"What do you mean?"

"He thought what you thought."

"He thought it was you?"

"No, he thought it was *you*."

Half an hour ago, it would have been just starting to get dark. Twilight. The least visibility of any time of the day or night, that mysterious lilac moment of near blindness. Bobby must have arrived here just in time for the half-light to trick him when he saw the woman on the ground. I could feel him *seeing* me lying there, his inner freeze, just like when I *saw* Julie lying in that pool of blood.

The ambulance drove off. Neighbors started to go home. The police ambled around finishing their work. The night air became sharply cold.

Holding Lexy, I crossed the lawn to the house. Julie was right there with me and I knew what she was thinking, that I didn't even know where the front door was (she was right), this being a renovated barn and not a traditional house. She led us around the corner to a two-step stoop and a screen door through which I caught a gauzy glimpse of just the kind of high-tech kitchen Julie would build. She went in first, holding the door open for us. We stepped into a large room of mahogany cabinets, granite counters and stainless-steel appliances, all shiny and new. A small flat-screen television, perched on the counter, was angled toward a wooden table beneath a window filled with darkness. That would be where Julie ate her lonely meals, with the TV for company. The sight of her fancy, under-used kitchen troubled me. Moving here had been a leap of faith—buying the barn on impulse during a leaf-peeping weekend meant to distract a broken heart, gutting it, uprooting herself from a lifetime in Connecticut and installing herself, alone, in this large house. She had not been here long enough to make a new social life and I knew from our conversations that all she had these days was work, occasional contact with old friends, cyber-dating that had yet to go off-line—and me.

Julie walked through a doorway leading out of the kitchen and I followed. Even in our haste I could see it was a lovely house. We passed through an antique dining room, then a small sitting room with a perfectly square curtainless window, and finally into a large comfortable living room with a cushy mocha-colored L-shaped sectional couch, a big square coffee table littered with newspapers, books and magazines, a fireplace and above it a large flat-screen television hanging on the wall. There were chairs and side tables and lamps. A big bouquet of spring flowers.

Off in the corner, at a small round table where two windows met at the joint of two walls, Bobby sat face-to-face with another man. Bobby was talking and the man was listening, writing things down.

Lexy at this point was trying to get to my breast and I had to hold her pretty tightly. I felt terrible making her wait, but I had to greet Bobby first. He stood up. He was wearing jeans and the red sweatshirt with an illustrated fish that we'd bought last summer on vacation in Cape Cod. He came over to us and took Lexy into his arms. The man seemed to watch his every move. Lexy curved herself into Bobby's chest as he caressed her little back and then she twisted around and reached for me.

"I guess you better nurse her now," he said. The soft grittiness of his voice evoked a longing in me. I had left him. We were *separated*.

"You okay?" I asked him.

Bobby looked at me—his face was so sad—and didn't answer. I heard him exhale as I turned around and settled into the couch, next to Julie, unbuttoning the bright sweater and angling myself so she could help me slide out of it. She folded it on her lap and I let Lexy into my shirt. My darling baby sucked ferociously, her chubby hands pressing on my swollen breasts; I could feel the warm milk pass through my ducts, from my body into hers, relieving me and sating her. Julie watched closely as Lexy nursed. I could hear the man stand up and walk around the couch until he was facing me.

He was small, on the thin side. His hair was pitch-black and tousled, obviously dyed, and the contrast with his pale skin made him look older than he probably was. I put him at fifty-five, give or take. His gray eyes looked tired, but he had a friendly mouth. He half smiled at me and it seemed as if he wanted to speak but wasn't sure what the rules were when a woman's naked breast was showing. He avoided looking at it. Lexy must have sensed he was there because she smacked off my nipple to face him, then nuzzled her face against my exposed nipple and latched back on. The man's face reddened as he introduced himself. "Detective Gabe Lazare, Great Barrington Police."

Ah, of course: a detective.

"I'm Annie," I said.

"Figured as much." His hand inched forward, then pulled back when he realized I wouldn't be able to shake, as my arms were full of Lexy.

Behind me, Bobby paced the room. Detective Lazare sat down on the opposite branch of the couch, away from Julie and me. He was calm, deeply calm. I felt it immediately, how the mood in the room shifted from edgy to oddly tranquil. Something about this man made me feel he must be a good detective, the way he altered the tone just by sitting down with us, just *being there* and waiting. What were we waiting for? I supposed we were waiting for the woman's killer to waltz in and introduce himself: *Here I am! Sorry for the inconvenience.* But that wasn't going to happen. Already whole minutes were sliding by with no one speaking. This could be a long wait. And the more I thought about it, the more I wondered what it had to do with us. She had been killed on my sister's lawn—no, on the road in front of her lawn. Not, officially, her property. It was a terrible, *terrible* thing. That poor woman! But for us, realistically, it would probably be over by morning.

Lexy's nursing became more relaxed, she sighed and her body grew supple and sleepy in my arms. As she relaxed so did I, at least a little. In the turmoil of arriving everything had seemed to blend into the darkness, but now details came into focus. I noticed that

Julie had on her typical outfit of designer jeans and fitted T-shirt, along with brown cowboy boots that looked weathered but must have been new; I had never seen them before. Next to my trim sister I felt big and sloppy and realized in one bad flash of a moment how out of shape I'd become since Lexy's birth. I was a fish out of water, a Kentucky mama in a posh living room on a fashionable mountain with a sexy woman who used to be me. But then I thought of Zara, *poor Zara*, who was dead, and sitting here with my family I felt acutely alive, even lucky. With a shiver of revulsion I recalled the sight of Zara's body: heavily inert, violently disordered. *Had* she been murdered? Or had it been arbitrary—the dumb luck of *wrong place, wrong time*? (What if I had arrived earlier or Julie had gone outside? It could have been *our* blood that now stained the road.) I ran my hand along Lexy's soft skin and just as I thought she felt cold, Julie picked up the sweater and draped it over her.

"Nice sweater. Very colorful," Detective Lazare said, but my sense was that he didn't like it so much as notice it because it was so bright. "I don't imagine any of you knew the victim very well."

"We didn't know her at all." Julie angled forward, legs pressed together, hands clasped on knees. "I mean, not really. I talked to her on the phone once; she sounded nice. I wanted to hire her to clean my house. She was supposed to call me to set a time to come over so I could show her the job."

"Did she?"

"No."

"Any chance she was dropping by tonight?"

"I don't think so. I mean, that would have been kind of strange; she was supposed to call first. Maybe she worked at one of the neighbors' today and was on her way home. I don't think she drives."

"You see her pass by?"

"No," Julie said. "I was upstairs working. I didn't come out until I heard Bobby screaming."

"Notice anything unusual today, before that?"

"Nothing. I was at my computer most of the day. I didn't go out at all."

"Shame—you missed a nice spring day."

"I know." Julie sighed. Missing spring days and other niceties had long been a cost of her success. "I'd really like to know who could do such a thing. I haven't lived here very long, but I had the impression things like this don't happen here."

"They usually don't," Lazare said.

"I really am sorry I wasn't more alert today. I *wish* I could help."

The detective revealed crooked teeth when he smiled, saying, "No worries."

I thought it was a funny thing to say given the circumstances, but still, it was kind of him to let Julie off the hook for being too plugged in to notice what was happening around her. She had always been a bit of a computer geek, long before it was cool. It was part of the reason she didn't meet more people off-line, in the flesh.

Lazare walked around the room, handing each of us his business card. "You can always call me if something comes to mind." He stopped in front of Bobby, who finally stood still, fastened in the detective's gaze.

"How about you come with me? We can finish our talk right now." It wasn't a question and he wasn't inviting Bobby to sit back down at the table in the cozy corner of the room. He was *telling* him to come to the police station, *tonight*.

As soon as Julie and I were left alone in the house, we burst into talk.

"It all happened so fast," Julie said. "It was so quiet, like it always is, and then all of a sudden Bobby was outside screaming."

I could *hear* his harrowing cries, thinking he had found me dead. And the thought of him now, taken to some strange police station in a town where he'd never been, being questioned by a detective, was appalling.

"Why couldn't Detective Lazare talk to Bobby tomorrow?" I asked. "He's exhausted, he's *upset*, and it's so late."

"I guess because he found the . . ."

"Right, he found the . . ."

Body. We couldn't bring ourselves to say it.

"I just can't believe this is happening," Julie said. "I wish I'd looked out the window, or gone outside, or *something*. Maybe if the guy had seen someone watching he wouldn't have done it."

A shadow of distress seemed to darken her pale oval face, *our* face, and in the strange way you notice irrelevant details during times of stress, I saw that she had plucked her left eyebrow too thin, that her auburn hair (*our* hair: it was wavy and thick and on good days, depending on an alchemy of weather, shampoo and possibly even mood, it had a striking red-gold polish) had

fallen half out of its ponytail, and that her bare arms
were rough with goose pimples. All these elements
conspired in my heart to make me want to fix her the
way she had always fixed me when we were kids and
I tumbled first and deepest into vulnerability. Tonight,
trouble had visited *her* house and it was *my* turn to be
strong for her. I wanted so badly to reach over and rub
my hands on her skin to warm her, but Lexy was heavy
in my arms.

"Jules, it's not your fault," I said. "It was just a fluke
that it happened right here. And maybe it's just as well
you didn't see him—then he might have seen *you*." I
recalled, and pushed away, that awful moment when I
was sure it was Julie lying there, bleeding on the road.
And now, my mind conflating two separate events,
Bobby's cries echoed through that memory.

"I guess you're right," she said. "It was blind chance
that he caught up with her in front of my house. Five
minutes later, it would have been someone else's
house." Her attempt at a stoic smile failed to distill the
unease from her dark brown eyes. I looked back with
my own set of those same eyes and drank in her remorse, sharing it.

"What I keep thinking, Jules, if you want to know
the truth, is that if only I hadn't left Bobby this morning, he never would have been the one to find her. He
could have lived his life without that image burned into
his mind."

"That poor woman," Julie said. "I can't stop *seeing*
her."

I rested my weight against her shoulder and we sank
into a few minutes of quiet. Then she reached over to

gently touch Lexy's forehead and whispered, "She's sleeping."

"Let's put her to bed."

Julie lifted the sweater off Lexy and put it on herself. Carefully and quietly we crossed the room.

The house had two staircases. Julie took me up the closer one, right off the living room. It led directly into a loft with a low double mattress covered by a Mexican blanket, a small desk with a computer and a bare window. It was the kind of space a teenager would be happy living in, the kind of space an adult could tolerate for maybe one night. From the loft, a short hallway took us into a pretty bedroom, fawn and white with dashes of pale blue and matching furniture that looked like it had been bought as a set out of a Pottery Barn catalog. I had always wanted to do that, call the toll-free number and order "everything on page four," but I'd never had that kind of money. As Julie led me through this section of her big new house I felt a vicarious satisfaction in her independence. *My* sister, who was *single*, had accomplished all this.

"This is the guest bedroom." She saw me looking for the crib. "Annie, *you're* not a guest. You have your own room. Come."

As we passed into another hall, Julie pointed out some of the doors. "Bathroom, linen closet, storage, another guest room."

The second guest room door was partly open, so I paused to peek inside. Even in the relative darkness I could see it was a smallish room, painted pale green, with twin brass beds covered in quilts. Two windows were framed by darker green curtains hanging off rods

with wrought-iron leaf finials. Between the windows
was a gold-framed poster of a giant pinecone, between
the beds was an oval hooked rug, and across from them
was a single tall dresser in dark wood. I was struck by
how symmetrical the room was, and then it hit me that
it looked like a room for twins, but twin boys.

"Your room's at the end," she said. "I assumed
you'd rather share with Lexy."

The Yellow Room. It was lovely! A double bed with
a heavy white jacquard bedspread was pressed into the
far corner of the room and there were five windows,
two on the east wall and three on the south wall. In
each window hung a gossamer curtain of the palest
yellow behind which pull-cord tassels dangled off the
ends of heavy shades that were all half raised. Yellow
wallpaper was covered in a tangle of tiny red rosebuds.
The buffed honey-wood floor was bare except for a
chenille rug at the side of the bed. The headboard, end
table, reading lamp, dresser and even the straight-
backed chair against the wall were all of a set (page
seven, please). All yellows, off-whites, brasses and
bronzes. Even the white crib and changing table
matched each other. Free-floating in the middle of the
room, the crib was positioned so you could reach it
from any direction, while the changing table was in the
corner, almost behind the door. Julie had stocked it
with the perfect brand and size of diapers, wipes, lo-
tions, powders—all the right accessories. I decided
against changing Lexy's diaper to avoid the chance of
waking her.

The side of the crib was already lowered and the
blanket was pulled down. I laid her gently on the

sheets, soft pink with scribbles of creamy prancing sheep. The side slid up easily and clicked into place. I picked up a stuffed animal, a cute yellow bunny Julie had set in the corner of the crib, and leaned it against the crook of Lexy's chubby elbow. She rolled over onto it and sighed.

I turned to give my sister a hug. "It's a beautiful room. Thank you."

"You can change things to the way you want them."

"No. It's perfect."

"What's in this pocket?"

She pulled away and patted her sweater pocket, where I had stashed the glass cats hours ago. Reaching in, I extracted the folded tissue and unwrapped it. One by one I laid the cats and kittens in Julie's palm.

She smiled. "I still have mine."

"I'm saving these for Lexy," I said.

"I'll probably give her mine, too, since I won't be having my own kids."

"You can *adopt*." I had reminded her of this a thousand times since her engagement had broken up, but her response was always the same:

"Alone?"

"You can afford it easily, Jules. And really, you *don't* have to wait for a man. Not anymore."

But the truth was, it was more complicated than that. Julie couldn't have children of her own, a single bout of chlamydia in college having left her infertile. She had basically been told by the school doctor *Tough luck, kid. There's nothing you can do about it now* with an insensitivity that showed he'd *had it* with promiscuous kids. She accepted it stoically and we re-dealt the cards between us, agreeing that I would provide our genetic children. Because presumably our DNA was as identical as our faces, Julie counted as Lexy's genetic mother. She would never have to suffer the anxiety of being unable to procreate because I could do that for both of us. As for raising her own children, she could adopt. It would be okay. Then a couple of years ago, during her engagement to Paul, just before the printed invitations were to be sent out, he broke down and told her how much he wanted his "own" children and how it was eating away at him to think that in marrying her he would never have the chance. So she released him and he left. Last year he got a woman pregnant, married her and now they were expecting their second.

"Well"—she glanced again at Lexy—"we'll see. So, are you hungry? Or do you want to go right to bed?"

"I ate on the road and I'm exhausted, but to be honest I don't think I could sleep."

"I know what you mean."

"Let's wait up for Bobby."

She closed her hand (those long fingers of ours) over the heap of glass cats and said, "Then come see my room."

I left the door open (I would plug in the baby monitor as soon as I got the suitcases up) and followed Julie back into the hall. She opened a door I hadn't noticed near the Pinecone Room. Off a small landing hinged two narrow staircases, one up and one down.

"Down goes directly into the kitchen," Julie said. "Up goes to me."

The stairs to her room bent twice to reach their destination and I was reminded again of Italy (maybe it was the handblown cats), climbing behind my parents up a coil of ancient stone stairs with a pole of empty space running from top to bottom. I hadn't liked being able to see all the way down, the transparency of height frightened me, and walking up I had to resist an urge to freeze in place. But I didn't; I was a good girl and I soldiered on. Then, at the top of that twisted ribbon of stairs was . . . nothing. That was the strangest thing: the stairs just ended, as if the architect had run out of ideas. We went back down and that was that. The memory made me think of Zara Moklas and how tonight, outside this very house, her life had ended as abruptly as the stone stairs in an ancient Italian ruin that was never identified (or not that I could remember).

"Jules? Who *do* you think killed her?"

Julie was a few steps ahead of me and she turned around. It was dark in the staircase and I could hardly see her face, but her hand on the thin wooden banister was lit up. I couldn't see where the light was coming from.

"I was just thinking the same thing," she said. "I can't *stop* thinking about it."

"I wonder if it was personal, something against her brother, or something else."

"There are some nasty old rednecks around here. Or maybe it was someone just passing through. Random. Do you think?"

Random murders scared me more than anything. "Personal, I hope. Right? Someone killed *her*, specifically."

Julie hesitated. "The thing is, A—"

I knew what she was going to say, that Zara Moklas looked like *us*.

"I know," I said. "I keep thinking it, too."

She opened the door at the top of the staircase and suddenly we were in the huge open space that was her bedroom. It had a high ceiling shaped like the top half of an octagon (it was the old barn roof) with long beams crisscrossing in midair. Strips of lights illuminated the bottom part of the room and seemed to press back the darkness and shadows into the circumscribed space above. From the beams on down, everything was painted white, but the furniture, in stark contrast, was black. Instead of paintings or drawings or anything prettily decorative on Julie's walls, there were mirrors of varying shapes. The bright lights bouncing off the mirrors gave the space a kind of sparkle.

Her loftlike room in the country sky had two more surprises: an enormous bathroom, the kind you could fit a couch into, and an office that was even higher-tech than the kitchen. It was spacious, with four large windows facing the back and side of the house, and I imagined that in the daytime it was bright. A long countertop desk against a red wall was covered with her characteristically neat piles of work along with a desktop computer whose 3-D ball-shaped screen saver pinged across the sleeping screen. A wide bookcase against the opposite wall was full of marketing books, collated industry magazines, the biographies she loved to read, and even a few professional awards. There was one I hadn't seen before, a gold figure with raised arms holding aloft a clear glass triangle.

"Is this your Stevie?" I asked. But my question was

answered when I saw her name etched in the small gold plaque on the base. The Stevie Award was one of the industry biggies, given annually to a woman who had excelled as a marketing entrepreneur.

"Congratulations, Jules." I hugged her. "I'm so proud of you."

"Thanks." She tried to hold a poker face but soon unleashed a grin.

Across the room was a small desk that looked unused except for a laptop that was closed and unplugged. Julie read my mind.

"That was for an assistant," she said, "but I never got around to hiring one."

"How do you manage?" In her old office in Connecticut, she had employed someone full-time.

"I don't like distractions. And I've discovered Pete and Sue in India."

"Pete and Sue? In *India*?"

"Those aren't their real names; they take pseudonyms to make it easier for us. They're called 'outsourced online assistants.' It's the new thing. They do most of what a real assistant does but in about half the time, plus they're cheaper and you don't have to ask them how their weekend was."

"Sounds ruthless."

"It's *efficient*. Did you know you can even hire an outsourced personal assistant for gift buying and stuff like that?"

"You're joking. So, did you hire one?"

"What for? My whole personal life is pretty much you guys, and I enjoy choosing your gifts."

"I know." I took her arm and led her out of her office, where the culprit *work* had consumed so much of her. I would make it my business, this visit, to distract her from work as much as possible, to fill her up emotionally. Lexy would definitely help with that.

I steered her to the corner of her bedroom next to a window where she had made a sitting area with two plush black armchairs and a small steel and glass table. Up close, I saw it was a curio table with a removable top. Inside the display were Julie's own glass cats along with some of her other memorabilia and miscellany: our mother's wedding ring (I had Dad's), a tiny enamel box containing our mingled baby teeth and identical locks of our baby hair, an opal ring whose provenance was a mystery to me, three antique miniature toy cars from an abandoned urge to collect, a few hair elastics, and a small glass dish of earrings, mingled among which I saw her pair of diamonds that matched my own. Zircons, actually, *fake* diamonds, but no less twinkly when we turned our heads in the light. They had been a new-baby gift, from her to both of us, a few months after Lexy was born.

"Isn't it inconvenient keeping your jewelry in there?" I asked.

"Sometimes at night I sit here and read and, you know . . ."

I *did* know. We had always shared a habit of removing our accessories, and sometimes elements of our clothing, when we wanted to relax.

Julie set my glass cats on top of the table so they seemed to hover in space above hers. "Want to mix them?" she asked. "Like when we were kids?"

I smiled. "Good idea."

She lifted the top of the table and together we arranged my cats with hers. Then she sat back in one of the black chairs, kicking off one of her cowboy boots and then the other, revealing hot pink socks. I sat in the matching chair and pried off my shoes, peeled off my socks, and splayed my toes to feel the cool air on my skin. Reaching into the open table, I picked up a blue elastic and put my hair into a high ponytail; then I took off my zircons and impulsively placed them in Julie's earring dish. She seemed to stiffen a little when I did that.

"What?" I said. "They're exactly the same, like the cats."

"I had an infection in one of my ears recently. Didn't I tell you?"

"No."

"I never got around to sterilizing my earrings."

"Well, then, I'll sterilize them all tomorrow. How's that?" I smiled, coaxing her agreement.

"Fine." She leaned back and sighed. "But next time, ask first."

I let her have that last word. Why not? We weren't little girls anymore; we were grown-ups and she had a point: boundaries mattered. Which made me regret mixing the glass cats, having earmarked *mine* for Lexy.

"Do you remember our old game?" I asked her. *"I wish on you flood—"*

"Witch's Wishes. I haven't thought of that in years."

It was a game we'd invented during our mother's losing fight against cancer. "I wish on you fire!" "I wish on you starvation!" "I wish on you plague!" We wished every horrible possible thing on each other, and the more we played it, the stronger and braver we grew. "I wish on you destruction!" "I wish on you decay!" But never death; death was what we were steeling ourselves against. Even at ten, watching our mother waste away, we knew death was our mortal enemy. When she finally died, we began to wish death on each other, too, to strengthen ourselves against it.

"It never worked, Jules, did it? To ward off anything."

"No, but it got us through some tough days."

She was right; it *had* provided a kind of shield, even if imaginary. I was so glad to be here with Julie. She was the only person with whom I could discuss our past in shorthand without our parents' deaths throwing a vast, tragic shadow over everything. Their deaths *were* tragic, but before that we had been a family with somewhat regular problems; and before the divorce, long before, if I remembered correctly, we may have even been happy. Our parents had certainly loved us, even doted on us. They read to us every night, greeted us with cocoa after building snow forts in our Connecticut yard, applauded at all our school plays, took us to museums and restaurants in New York. When we were little our mother had dressed us identically, but later, around the age of nine, we began to assert some individuality and in our final year with her she not only let us be ourselves but encouraged it, allowing separate traits and even insisting on them. Julie was calm, I was easily agitated. Julie was steady, I was impulsive. Julie dressed practically, I wore costumes (or what our mother perceived as costumes; to me they were gor-

geous outfits someone ought to have photographed).
Julie was the smart one, I was the pretty one.

That was the distinction that affected us most—
smart/pretty—before we matured enough to understand that as identical twins we were more or less
exactly the same. Our mother was offering us the possibility of individuality. I understood that now, but
since she died before she had a chance to explain herself we spent a good amount of our growing-up energy
trying to negate our presumed deficiencies. Before
Julie went to graduate school in marketing, she spent a
year living (with me) in the New York apartment we
had inherited from our father, wearing flowing skirts
and writing bad poetry, trying hard to be pretty inside
and out. Broke and bored, she finally packed it in, got
her advanced degree with honors, bought some nice
suits and began her quick professional ascent.

And me? I had aspired to be a photographer. But instead of following my heart and photographing people
on the street wearing their own concocted fashions,
which was what really intrigued me, I turned to buildings, proving that I was serious and *smart*, and slowly
and painfully failed over six lean years to establish myself as a freelance architectural photograper before
enrolling in graduate school to become a physical therapist. I had realized I needed to work with people in a
way that had some impact; as a PT, I could literally
touch them and *see* the effect of my work. The job at
the prison had been my entry-level launch pad to a new
career.

Once Julie and I grew up, the *idea* of a smart/pretty
discrepancy lost its poignancy. We both came to real-

ize that we were about as smart and as pretty as each other—we were identical twins, after all. Our differences were cultivated. External trappings and divergent choices might have differentiated us, but they had never defined us and they never would. Julie's eyes were my eyes and mine were hers. When I found her looking at me now, I knew what she was thinking.

"If Mom and Dad were here tonight," I said, "they'd be giving us milk and cookies and telling us everything would be all right. They would have liked Bobby, don't you think? *They* would have known he had nothing to do with that woman's murder."

Julie dropped her foot from her knee to the floor and shifted forward in her seat. "*I* know he didn't, A."

"That detective. He seems okay, basically. But I really think he's wasting his time on Bobby. Don't you?"

"Totally."

"I mean, infidelity is one thing, Jules. But murder? No way." I shuddered at the recollection of Zara's opened neck. "How much do you know about her?"

"Nothing, really. She was around our age, I think, maybe a little younger. All my neighbors who used her liked her. She worked hard. Everyone said she was honest. I'd never heard about the shady brother until tonight."

"Wouldn't it be crazy if—no, that's a ridiculous thought."

"If what?" she asked.

My eyes landed on one of Julie's empty boots, where at the ankle a brass ring united straps of leather.

Then I looked at her: "I was going to say, if *she* was the woman Bobby was sleeping with."

"You're right. That *is* ridiculous."

"I don't know why I thought that."

"Because you're upset," she said. "It's been a really bad day."

"I wonder how a brother and sister from Hungary ended up in Great Barrington."

"I guess they liked the country. Maybe they had a friend around here."

"The detective will find out, I suppose."

"The more I learn about people," Julie said, "the more I think they're incredibly unpredictable, you know?" Her forehead gathered, producing a slight crease. A sign of age. Were we getting older without having figured everything out? But maybe that was the trick: maybe you *didn't*.

"I know I left him, but Bobby was never unpredictable. He isn't most people."

"Not Bobby," Julie corrected me. "I meant Zara."

But for me, Zara Moklas was completely predictable. She would always exist in my mind the only way I had ever seen her: splayed on a dark country road in mottled hues of arcing lights and her own red blood. My only expectation for Zara, ever, could be death.

"All the neighbors said she was such a nice person," Julie said. "Maybe she was. But maybe she *wasn't*. That's all I'm saying."

"Because we don't really know. I do get your point."

"Exactly. We don't know. Maybe under her nice-

nice facade she was a drug dealer and she got it for a bad debt or something."

"I hope so," I said, "because that would mean the killer was specifically after *her*. But honestly, why would she work as a secretary and clean houses if she was making money selling drugs?"

Julie smiled wickedly. "Good point. Okay. Then maybe cleaning houses was a front and she was a madame and one of her girls went postal."

I pictured a cartoon-sleazy hooker with a knife on the bucolic road in front of Julie's house. We laughed. And then suddenly I was crying.

Julie crossed over to my chair and we held each other and soon she was crying, too. Her hands found my face and began to smear away tears.

"It isn't funny." Julie.

"It's horrible." Me.

"We *shouldn't*, should we?" She didn't ask it as a question because it wasn't a question. We were making light of something dark. Laughing at someone else's catastrophe. Digging a moat around the *us* that had always offered protection. As children we had practiced this art of separation without remorse, but as adults we had learned better. Now, when we slipped into defensive isolation against the world at large, we felt guilty and stopped. At least we tried to stop. But we both knew that I had come to Julie to escape to her, into her, with her. It was a deep and irresistible impulse of our twinhood.

"Can we bring up my suitcases now?" I asked.

"Come on. We'll get you settled and put you to bed."

"I think I'll check on Bobby first."

I called the police station and was put on hold for five minutes, only to be told that the detective said not to bother waiting up. I wondered if those were his exact words: "Don't bother waiting up." Even from our brief contact it didn't seem like something Detective Lazare would say. He seemed subtler than that. "Get some sleep and he'll be back with you soon," seemed more like it. And then I wondered where Bobby would sleep when he did return. Would he find me in the Yellow Room? Slip between my yellow sheets? Find my body? Would our mile of distance reduce itself to the plain fact that we loved each other? Would he finally either tell me the truth or find a convincing way to unbraid my suspicions? Or would he default to my decision to leave him and find his way to a guest room? I didn't even know where I wanted him to sleep. It would be a comfort to feel him next to me in the dark but a source of confusion if I woke to him in the morning. I had never known how perplexing it could be to deeply love someone not-Julie yet find it necessary to leave, but of the many things my parents' deaths had taught me, one was that severing the artery of love was ultimately survivable.

Once Julie and I had lugged in all my stuff, we stood together in the silvery darkness of my quiet room and watched Lexy sleep.

"She's beautiful," Julie whispered.

And I reminded her: "She's *ours*, Jules." I one-armhugged her against me as we stood there staring at my beloved daughter.

After a while she went upstairs and I went to bed,

sure I wouldn't sleep—but within minutes, I did. I slept a solid six hours, until the ringing phone interrupted a dream I lost as soon as I opened my eyes. Through the diaphanous yellow curtains I saw the gentle hues of early dawn. The phone rang again and, afraid it would wake Lexy, I picked up my extension. I heard Julie's scratchy morning voice talking to a woman; we must have answered the phone simultaneously.

"Slow down, Carla. What van?" Carla, I remembered from last night, was one of Julie's nearest neighbors. She was at least in her seventies and obviously a very early riser.

"A white van, parked down the street from your house. I saw it twice yesterday, oh, about two hours apart."

"I didn't notice it. I was in my house all day, in my office, working."

"It was a white van, just sitting there, with a man inside. It gave me the willies—when I got home I wrote down what I recalled of the license plate. It's crazy, I know, but I didn't think of it until just now. I was making my tea and, well, that's how it goes at my age sometimes. I remembered."

"Did you call the detective?"

"Yes, I did. He thanked me. I just can't believe it, Julie. Right here, on this street, a *murder*."

Chapter 3

Seated in our circle of canvas folding chairs in Julie's backyard, beneath a bruised morning sky that promised rain, Detective Gabe Lazare put down his tall blue glass of iced tea so it sat lopsided on an uneven piece of slate. I'd noticed he didn't skip pleasantries before getting down to business and I was grateful for the gentle transition from a harsh awakening. Julie and I had been up for hours, battening down the hatches, after Carla's call about the mysterious lurking van. I'd learned how the windows locked (we agreed to keep ourselves sealed up tight every night), where flashlights and candles were stowed in case of a power outage (deliberate or otherwise), and Julie was just explaining how the alarm system worked when Detective Lazare called and asked to come over. *Asking* was his polite method of telling us he was on his way.

"Delicious iced tea." Lazare nodded in Julie's direction.

"You can thank my sister. She's the chef, not me."

"Tea isn't cooking," I said, "but I'm glad you like it."

The baby monitor was in my lap and I jumped at every fizz of sound. I kept expecting Lexy to wake up; her morning nap had gone nearly two hours now. Instead what I heard was sounds of Bobby, finally awake, his footsteps echoing down the hall, presumably to the bathroom. He had been released sometime in the night and was deeply asleep in the Pinecone Room when *we* woke up at dawn to the ringing phone.

"Your neighbor's partial license plate turned out to be pretty useful." Lazare leaned over to reach into his leather briefcase for a piece of paper, which he handed to Julie first. When she in turn gave it to me, I saw that it was a grainy fax of a photograph—a mug shot—of a fiftyish man with a buzz cut and skin weathered beyond his years. He was squinting as if he normally wore glasses. "His name's Thomas Soiffer. Owner of a white van, Massachusetts plates, resides outside Springfield. E-Z Pass had him driving west on I-90 across Massachusetts yesterday morning."

"And?" Julie.

"Why was he here?" Me.

"What we know about Mr. Soiffer is mostly on paper. He's a plumber by trade, but he has a criminal record. Not what you'd call the finest of citizens. Did some time for assaulting his girlfriend—nearly killed her."

"And he used his E-Z Pass to drive here and sit outside my house before killing someone?" Julie said. "Not the brightest bulb."

Lazare's eyes paused a moment on Julie and I could

just see his detective mind calculating a diplomatic bridge between our layman's comfort zone, where the most obvious assumptions ruled the borders like trigger-happy armed guards, and his professional instincts to carefully navigate the unknown.

"Well, Forensics found some other blood along with Zara's, but we don't know if it belonged to Soiffer or someone else," he said. "If we had a murder weapon or a DNA sample on file for him, it would make this a lot simpler. But we don't. So now it's all about legwork. We're trying to find him."

Just then Lexy issued a fairly dramatic sigh and I sat forward, ready to get up and go to her. But the sigh melted back into the monitor's static silence; she had gone back to sleep.

"Does that name—Thomas Soiffer—ring any bells with either of you?" Detective Lazare asked.

Julie and I agreed that neither of us had ever seen the man in the picture nor had we heard his name. It was a stranger's name, though one we would now never forget. A stranger with a criminal record, a *dangerous* man, hanging around outside Julie's house yesterday morning, only hours before a murder.

"So far none of the local plumbers and electricians and so forth recognize the name either," Lazare said. "We've put the word out and we'll see if we hear anything in the next few days."

"Detective," I said, deciding to risk a theoretical leap, "do you think someone might have thought Zara was one of *us*? Since she resembled us, I mean."

"Anything's possible." Lazare sort of smiled. "Why? You wouldn't know that name from the prison back in Kentucky, would you? He didn't do time there, but sometimes these guys know each other. They talk."

"I've never heard the name," I said. "Not that I can remember. But I saw a lot of the prisoners. I saw *hundreds* of people. And Bobby's been working in that one prison for over ten years—he's seen *thousands*."

It was a medical prison. Some of the prisoners had a real need for physical therapy, but some used it as a way to break their routines. You could tell, mostly, who was in pain and who was just bored. It was the restless ones I most hated working on, pressing my hands into their muscled flesh, the intimacy of that, while their eyes darted around the office, looking for something—what? A way out? A weapon? All the prisoners there were white-collar criminals, but incarceration had a way of transforming some people, creating a taste for violence. And the detective was right: *talk* they did, sometimes endlessly and often with an absurd amount of self-righteous indignation.

"We'll check it out with the prison," Lazare said. "We'll also find out if any prisoners released recently had anything against you." He pulled a notepad from his pocket and jotted a reminder. "Julie, you renovated this house last year. Am I right?"

"Yes, I did." She had gutted the barn and rebuilt the interior from scratch. "My contractor's name was Hal Cox. He brought in a lot of people. I didn't know their names—I was still living in Connecticut."

"Could you e-mail me the particulars of your contractor? And anyone else involved in the project."

"Sure," Julie said. "The contractor handled everything with the architect. I can put you in touch with her, too."

"Much obliged."

Julie nodded. "So, Bobby's not a suspect anymore?"

That was a sticky word, *suspect*, and it caught in my mind.

"Bobby and I had a good, long talk," Lazare said, "but at this point, no one is officially a suspect."

"Not even Thomas Soiffer?" I asked.

"Yes and no. We'd like to speak with him." He pulled his mouth into a thin, evasive smile.

"What about Zara's brother?" Julie asked. "I heard he works in construction. I heard he's a not-so-nice guy."

"I heard that, too," Lazare said. "And I checked it out. All her relatives are in Hungary—the bad brother's just a rumor. Not unusual in these cases. Violent death kind of uncaps people's imaginations. Makes our job a little harder, but it's human nature, can't be helped."

"What now?" Julie asked.

"Sit tight. There's no real reason for the two of you to worry. Chances are this was a random incident. But just to reassure you, I'm putting a security detail on your house. Unmarked car, maroon sedan. He'll be parked outside. Best thing is to leave him alone—don't visit him, no coffee and such. It'll just draw attention."

I was a little surprised to be offered the extra support from what I assumed was a small local police force. But he himself had said that they rarely saw this kind of crime and I guessed they felt more comfortable erring on the side of caution. So did I.

Julie and I simultaneously thanked him and this time he smiled in full. The *matched set* effect; we were used to it.

"How long?" Julie asked.

"As long as you need him. We'll see how this thing plays out." Lazare bent down to pick up his empty glass. And then he hesitated, sat back and looked at me.

"Annie, I hope you don't mind my asking, but why did you leave home yesterday?"

That phrase, *leave home*, threw me off. It sounded so final.

"I guess you already know, since you've been talking to Bobby," I said.

"In your own words." He clicked his pen twice, drawing the ballpoint in and out, and waited for an answer.

"Bobby's been unfaithful."

"And you can substantiate that," he said, not phrasing it as a question, but I answered anyway.

"Yes." One clear word, no ambivalence, so he wouldn't ask again.

"That's good," he said, "because someday you may need to fall back on that to comfort yourself."

"What exactly did Bobby tell you?" My tone had sharpened. I didn't care.

Detective Lazare slipped his pen into his shirt pocket and closed his notebook. The gestures seemed contrived to reassure me that he was *just curious* or this was *off the record* or some other ineffectual apology meant to gloss over the intrusive line of questioning. "Annie, I'm not taking sides in this. I'm just a detective doing his job, wondering why so much happened in one family in one day. Wouldn't you?"

Of course I would. I *did* wonder that. But we had started this meeting in the spirit of shared information and now I felt, well, *guilty*. I didn't understand why. Or why he would want me to. I didn't answer his part-rhetorical, part-combative question and after an awkward moment he offered an olive branch of sorts.

"Well, anytime you feel like talking," he said, "my door is open."

Julie glanced at me and I *knew* she was thinking the same thing I was: that if I needed a therapist, I'd find one. She stood and reached for his glass, which he handed her without a word. He used the armrests to push himself up from the canvas chair.

By way of good-bye, he said, "Cases like this, they're tough. Woman like that. Comes from a nice family over in Hungary. Her people were poor; she was helping support them, sending money home. From what I hear she was a political activist in her town until things got a little too hot and she lost her job. Came here on a short visa and stayed. Immigrants like her, well, they've all got their story, don't they?"

It came at us like her eulogy—brief, helpless—and we listened. Softened. He was a master at saying two things at once: *remember, Zara is the victim here* and *I'm just a guy doing my job.*

Julie walked him through the house to the kitchen door.

Sitting alone in the yard, I realized the detective had left behind the fax of Thomas Soiffer. I suspected he had left it on purpose; he wanted us emotionally involved in this, to open us, in case our proximity to the murder held some special secret. Had he rattled me on purpose, just to test my reaction? I studied Soiffer's photo and the longer I looked at it, the more that grizzly face seemed to gain dimensions of cynicism and rage. I could *see* him with a knife in his hand, slipping through the twilight, behind Zara, one sinewy hand grabbing her hair to yank back her head, the other drawing the blade across her neck like a violin bow. Had anyone heard her scream? Or was her death silent, her final sound muted by the violent severance of her vocal cords?

I was startled by a shuffle emanating from the monitor, which soon began to issue the cranky sobs of Lexy waking. Creak of a hallway door opening, thud of footsteps, clank of the crib's side lowering.

"Shh, honey." Bobby's disembodied voice floated from the monitor. "Daddy's here."

I folded the fax into eighths, slipped it into my pants pocket and went through glass-paned French doors that led directly into the big living room, which I had come to think of as Sundance East. Through a front window I saw Detective Lazare drive away in a silver car. The maroon car sat parked to the left of the house under a leafy tree with an enormous bark-striated trunk that seemed to twist out of the earth. There was a man in the driver's seat, but I couldn't see his face or any detail. He was very still.

Halfway up the living room staircase on my way to find Bobby, I met him on his way down, holding Lexy. He was wearing jeans and a burnt-orange T-shirt; he must have packed himself a bag before leaving home yesterday. His hair was wet—he had showered—but he was unshaven. When Lexy saw me she dove in my direction and I had to reposition myself on the stairs to simultaneously catch her and keep my balance. She immediately rooted for my chest. Bobby followed us down the stairs and stood in front of the couch while I settled in to nurse our baby.

"Detective Lazare's a real piece of work," I said, once Lexy was latched on. I was still smarting from our conversation, the therapist bit. *If I ever wanted to talk.* I *always* wanted to talk—but to him?

"Yup." Bobby nodded. "That he is."

"But I don't think he really suspects you of anything, Bobby. I think he's maybe, well, a little misguided."

"There never did seem to be a question of arresting me." Bobby's hand nestled in a pants pocket, fiddling with something. "He's trying to figure things out, I guess. There was just a lot of talking. Though he did take a sample of my saliva."

"Saliva?" But even as I said it, I knew why: that was one way the police now chronicled DNA.

"I don't think it meant that much. It seemed pretty routine, actually, like they do it all the time. It would be stranger if he didn't take all this seriously."

"That's true," I agreed. But *a DNA sample*? "By the way, he's got a cop sitting outside in his car, keeping watch, and I admit it's a relief."

Bobby crossed the room to look out the window, then came over to sit with me on the couch.

"I heard you got pretty upset last night when you

found Zara out front," I said. "It must have been awful."

"I rushed to get here. I needed to talk to you, Annie. I should have known you'd make a few stops and probably get—"

"Lost." He knew me. "Plus I took a dinner break."

"But I'm glad you didn't get here first," he said, "because if you'd seen what I saw when I pulled up and found her lying there . . ." He shook his head. Ocean eyes dulled by a very bad night.

"What did you need to talk to me about?" Say it: *Lovyluv.* Or better yet, give her a real name.

"I was hoping something would come to me, some way to convince you to come home. I jumped on the first plane out."

"And?" Meaning: Tell. Me. The. Truth. Now. And. I. Will. Come. Home. With. You. How plain could I make it? I had already practically drawn him a road map. The old frustration welled up inside me and I turned away from him and looked down at our baby. She must have sensed my attention because she snapped her mouth off my nipple and blazed me with her best smile. I smiled back.

"When I saw you dead, Annie, I freaked. I mean *freaked.*"

Hearing him say that sent a chill up my spine. "But it wasn't me."

"The time it took me to realize that was the longest minute of my life."

The longest minute of my life: a cliché. I wanted more from my husband. I wanted him to peel back the surface of what was happening between us, to *dig.*

"But why would someone kill *me*?"

"That's what I spent half the night explaining to the detective," Bobby said. "No one would, especially not me. I wasn't angry at you when you left. I was upset. I was frustrated—but not angry."

He spoke with such intensity that I was drawn into his emotions, wave by wave. He seemed helpless, marooned on an island of misapprehension—helpless and very hurt. I had hurt him. I had brought all this on by storming out of our life and coming here. I wanted to touch him, but it would send the wrong message. I hadn't changed my mind about what had propelled me here in the first place.

"Just so you know, Bobby, I *did* see what you saw last night. I knew something was wrong because of all the police, but I still saw what you saw and thought what you thought. I *felt* that horror you felt when I saw her lying there. Except I thought I was looking at Julie."

He leaned into me on the couch, his left side warm against my right. My body wanted to melt into his, find comfort and healing the easy way. But we had already tried that at home, using sex to settle the argument, and it had never worked for more than a few hours. By morning, my brain would wake up, my eyes would open.

"Here," I said, handing Lexy to him. "Could you please burp her?" He got up and paced the floor with Lexy over his shoulder, gently patting *the spot* on her little back. He was a good father; you had to give him that.

"What did Lazare want this morning?" he asked, kissing the side of Lexy's head.

I pulled the fax out of my pocket and unfolded it. "Did you ever hear anyone at the prison mention Thomas Soiffer?"

Bobby took the crushed paper and looked it over. "Who is he?"

"A neighbor saw him lurking around outside the house yesterday," I said. "Well, not lurking. Sitting in his van—but for hours."

He dropped the fax on the coffee table, on top of yesterday's newspaper, and kept moving, patting and bouncing Lexy. "If they knew about this guy, why did he put so much time into me? He kept me for *hours.*"

"The neighbor didn't remember the van until this morning. That's when the detective found out, too."

"So last night I was the best thing they had?"

"He said they never get cases like this. They probably don't know what they're doing. So what kind of questions did he ask you?"

"We went over every minute of yesterday, every *second*, over and over and over." He chanted those last words "over and over and over" as he bounced Lexy in the air in front of him, the way she liked. He angled her side to side, eliciting happy squeals. Then he sang a stanza from Dylan's "Just Like a Woman," which his parents had sung to him as a lullaby when he was small. Bobby's parents had been hippies, and though he had rebelled early against their peripatetic, under-funded lifestyle (rebellion by bank account), their bohemianism had peppered his inner life. His social consciousness may have come from them—he was a strong advocate of prisoners' rights, as liberal a liberal as you're likely to find—but his stalwart, conservative sense of stability came from himself.

Lexy burped, and I said, "Why don't you put her down now? She hasn't had any floor time since yesterday morning."

He set her on her stomach on the carpet. I picked up her favorite teether—a sticky red rubbery duck—from the coffee table and put it in front of her. She grabbed it and stuck it in her mouth. Bobby sat down next to me again and reached for my hand, which I pulled away. He smelled so good; I *missed* him. But it was too soon.

Julie walked into the living room and stopped when she saw us. She seemed a little startled, realizing she had interrupted our awkward reunion.

"Jules," I said, "would you mind watching Lexy for a few minutes?"

"I'd love to." Julie picked Lexy up from the floor and held her high, earning smiles and a cackling little laugh.

Bobby followed me through the French doors into the backyard. The overcast morning cast a muted, tentative light over the sweep of lawn, dulling the green grass and darkening the bank of forest at the edge of Julie's property. Without agreeing on a direction we walked around the side of the barn-house to the front, where a bright seam of orange marigolds defied the shadowy imminence of rain. Spring, glorious spring, and my heart was aching. I knew I was going to send Bobby home alone.

In the daylight I could see how isolated Julie's house was; none of her neighbors was visible from her property. The barn sat looming on a plot of landscaped green that extended back from the intersection of two roads, gray ribbons of asphalt that crossed each other at an uneven angle, with one becoming a hill and the other curving into a turn. We were alone here (except for the maroon car and the man inside it, who I could now see had short brown hair and a double chin—and *really*, I thought, what would be the difference if we brought him coffee? Stationed in his car, on this lonely road where *everyone* knew there had been a murder, he stuck out like a sore thumb), and I immediately saw the appeal: the rolling hills, the woven greens, the candy-sweet air. I breathed deeply, and again.

On the road almost directly in front of the house was a white outline of Zara's body. I was shocked to see this because I hadn't noticed it last night, though they must have drawn it while she was still lying there. I had been aware of the unnatural angles of her limbs, the deep bloody slice in her throat and the presence of all the people, but not this painted-on caricature of the last action of a woman's life. *Here she lies.* The yellow police tape surrounding the *crime scene* (I hated that phrase for her, for us) had drooped on one side and detached on another. The disengaged end floated up on a breeze and then settled back onto the ground. That morning a local reporter had been poking around (we had declined to come out of the house to be interviewed; we were still too upset) and I wondered if *he* had detached the yellow tape to get a closer look at the ground. I wondered how much the reporter knew about what had happened last night, how much anyone knew. I wondered what would become of Zara's body.

"Listen, Bobby—"

Before I could say it—*I'm not going home with you*—he put his hand on my shoulder and said, "I would never try to stop you from doing what you need to do."

He had jumped halfway through the discussion, but he was right: there was no point repeating the same talk, talk, talk that had gotten us nowhere these past weeks.

"It's not what I *need*."

"I know how much you hate living in Lexington."

So true.

"And the prison isn't for you."

Correct.

"And now you've got this new job lined up for yourself in Manhattan. You've been wanting to live in the city."

Yes. Yes. "But, Bobby, it isn't about all that. I wouldn't break up our family for any of *that*."

"Wait, Annie. Please hear me out."

"Credit card bills don't lie." The familiar chorus of my recent song.

"No, they don't. I don't understand it either—"

"And love letters, Bobby!"

"It's my turn to talk."

He was right. By now I had hogged most of the talk for myself and it *was* his turn to contribute something substantial.

"I'm going to walk the path you walked to get here," he said, "so I can see exactly what you mean."

"Good. Finally."

"I guess I didn't realize how serious this was until yesterday, when you left."

That floored me. I had been very specific, very clear. I had even given him a file of collated bills and printouts, evidence to examine.

"You mean you haven't looked through the file?" I asked.

"Of course I did. I even called the credit card companies and entered disputes for those charges. But now I'm going to go over them again, differently, and really think about what you've been saying. Because I did not make those charges, Annie. I've told you a million times."

"What about the e-mails? All those personal details?"

He sighed. I felt the familiar clamp of frustration. Here we were again.

"I didn't write them and I didn't receive them. I never even *saw* them until you pointed them out to me."

"That's *ridiculous*."

"I do not use the computer." He hammered out each word. True, he didn't use computers much, he wasn't any good at them; but that didn't mean he didn't know how. "I'm going to take a much closer look at everything, okay?"

"It's all on the desk at home," I said. "And in the computer." *Good.* When he saw what I saw the way I saw it, we would be on the same page and could *finally* begin the same conversation.

"Okay," he said.

We walked slowly, away from Zara's outline, toward the side of the house where lawn had been carved into a thick edge of woods. His fingers brushed mine and then tentatively, almost shyly, he took my hand and I let him.

"Annie, I have to go back today. It'll give us some time. And if I miss any more work—well, *you* know how happy it would make Kent if he could fire me right before my pension matures."

One year. Bobby had only one year left before he could retire. And it was true: our boss, Kent, was a petty bastard. He had made a pass at me when I was first on staff and when I rebuffed him he made my life miserable. Then, when I got together with Bobby, he extended his spite to us both with a heartlessness that he blamed on the military culture. Kent would have loved to find a way to dismiss Bobby at the eleventh hour of a career he'd stuck with this far mostly so he could enjoy the second half of his adulthood. With me and Lexy (and hopefully more children; we'd had our plans).

"I can't let this go now," Bobby said. "My benefits are going to take care of us for the rest of our lives. We'll have health care and money and we'll be able to put Lexy through college."

"We?"

"Do you really think we should pack it all in right now, *everything*, without any hope at all? Without even trying?" He stared at me. My Bobby. Of course he was right.

"No, I'm not saying that. I *never* said that."

"Can't we take this as a trial separation? Nothing definite?"

"I guess so."

He smiled, revealing the slight gap between his front teeth. That sexy smile. I felt a blossoming of heat in my center.

"I thought I'd visit next weekend," he said. "Or do you need more time apart than that?"

"I don't know," I said, wanting him, *resisting* wanting him. "Can we play that by ear?"

"Whatever you say."

It seemed a tepid response. Why wouldn't he fight harder for me? *I* had no idea how much time we needed. Would a week be enough time for *him* to reassess the evidence? Would he open the Infidelity File, as I had come to think of it, as soon as he walked in the door of our house? Or would he settle back into disbelief and revert to hoping I would change my mind? What I *did* know was that regardless of what happened to our marriage, I would not return to work in the prison or move back to Lexington. He was right in a big way: it wasn't for me. If our marriage somehow survived this, we would have to figure out the logistics. In a week there was a job orientation for all new employees at the Manhattan hospital that had hired me conditionally, based on a meeting with an off-site interviewer, and I planned to go. Once the higher-ups had met me face-to-face, finalized the paperwork and approved my employment, I could start looking for a suitable apartment.

Bobby reached out and touched my cheek. It was a good-bye touch, a see-you-soon touch that left a cold spot on my skin as soon as his finger retreated. Then he leaned in and kissed my lips. I couldn't help it: I grabbed him. We held each other for a few minutes before I pushed him away and ran into the house.

I went straight upstairs to my room, feeling soaked through with sorrow and confusion and regret and determination. Peeking through the yellow curtains, I saw him standing on the front lawn, hesitating. The man in the maroon car was watching him. I knew Bobby was thinking of Lexy, whether or not he should go in and say good-bye to her or just leave. She was little enough that she wouldn't know the difference, but *he* would. And I would. He had almost nothing to pack and could have turned around, gotten into his rental car and driven straight to the airport. Instead he walked across the lawn and entered the house through the kitchen door. Ten minutes later I heard his car drive away.

The feeling of loneliness was overwhelming. Bobby was gone. Lexy was downstairs with Julie, beginning a process of bonding I didn't want to interrupt. I finished unpacking, then stood at one of my bedroom windows and looked out. Stillness. Quiet, except for the low buzz of a lawn mower somewhere in the distance. The overcast sky had developed threatening rain clouds. I moved to another window, took in another tranquil view, then went from window to window, realizing I couldn't see the crime scene from anywhere in the Yellow Room.

As soon as I thought of Zara's outline, her final mark in the world, I knew the imminent rain would wash it away. I couldn't let that happen unrecorded, so I got my digital camera and went outside to take pictures.

I took shots from every angle, and the more I took, the more her shape abstracted. She had gone from three-dimensional woman to two-dimensional contour, a memory, in a matter of minutes; that was death. After a few minutes a cloud moved and the sun blasted. Suddenly my shadow filled Zara's outline, wavering over the fading white edges. I managed two shots of the strange, disturbing image before the sun vanished again. In seconds, the sky darkened and it started to rain. I took one more picture before running into the house.

Ten minutes later, that last blurred image, downloaded into the loft computer, piqued something in me. Yearning—to fill Zara's outline with more than shadow. Curiosity—to see how filled shapes might change, how the lens might alter assumptions. Inside the house, with the rain coming down and no agenda whatsoever, I decided it was a good day for portraits. Lexy was the only one I had ever photographed endlessly and with a sense of fascination. Now I turned my lens on Julie.

She protested at first, but I insisted she let me; projects, quests, were a great diversion from worry and she knew that photography was my lost love. Like a true big sister (she was three minutes older), she humored me. She hammed it up, posing and voguing, but after a while she stopped noticing the camera and that was when my lens really found her. She sat primly at her office computer without trying to seem relaxed; jumped at Lexy's cries when she woke from her nap; hunched over the turkey-and-pesto sandwiches I made for our lunch; stared hungrily when I nursed my baby;

sprawled on the couch with the newspaper without trying to contain her limbs. And I photographed my sister and daughter together, wondering if they would look like *us*, like me and Lexy, *convincingly*, the way Julie and I could pass for one another.

Before I had a chance to download the newest images, the rain suddenly stopped, the sun reappeared in force, and Julie and I looked at each other.

"Let's get out of here." Julie.

"Good thinking." Me.

"There's a playground in Stockbridge with baby swings. Want to make it our destination?"

"Why not?"

We got dressed for *out*, swapping clothes as we always had. I wore Julie's cowboy boots with my swishy velvet skirt, one of her expensive white T-shirts, my old jean jacket and my fake diamond earrings. (As promised, I had sterilized both pairs that morning.) Julie wore loafers with her jeans, my striped blouse, *her* fake diamonds and a new corduroy blazer I decided to lay claim to in due time. Just for fun, we traded lipsticks: she wore my pale pink, I wore her brick red. Outside, the asphalt driveway had partially dried after the rain. We settled into her car, a new Audi I hadn't paid much attention to until now, without discussing its obvious luxuries. Before we were halfway down the road to town, our conversation had covered Bobby, Zara and Detective Lazare, specifically his offer to "talk" whenever I felt like it.

"Sometimes we run focus groups that way," Julie said, driving carefully along Division Street. We drove

with the windows open and a lovely soft wind filled
the car. The spring air was sweet and the surrounding
greenery—trees and bushes and fields—was verdant
after the nourishing rain. "It's based on the talk therapy
model: just see what comes out and take your cues
from that."

"Are you saying marketers use the same psychology
as the police?" I asked.

"I guess so. In some ways—yes."

"Don't you think that's a little creepy?"

"Not really. I mean, it all boils down to the same
thing, right? You're looking to tap into those quiet
pockets of desire just kind of festering in people's
minds."

"Desire?" I almost laughed. But she had a point: desire for self-expression, desire for acknowledgment.
Didn't we all suffer from the desire to be understood?

We entered town on Maple Street, where the police
station sat at the intersection of Main, just beyond a
traffic light. The one-story brick building, trimmed in
white with a small cupola on its roof, was fronted by a
blue sign with fat, cartoony lettering: GREAT BARRING-
TON POLICE. So this was where Detective Lazare
worked, in an innocuous little building that was like a
welcome mat for a country town. But there were cops
in there, and guns, and criminals. Much like the man
himself: easy on the outside, barbed on the inside.
Well, I should never have assumed otherwise. Appear-
ances were famously misleading. As an identical twin,
I understood *that* well enough.

Main Street was busy with shops, boutiques, gal-
leries and restaurants, a town center more polished and

inviting than I'd expected. Unlike the strip malls I had grown used to down south, with their utilitarian chain stores, this was the kind of place where you might like to walk and browse. I was an unabashed shopaholic—prime feed for marketers like my twin, advertisers, telephone solicitors, the whole bunch of them—and in light of our conversation on the way into town I began to feel supremely stupid sitting in my sister's leather passenger seat. Her keen awareness of the workings of the world, her mastery of it, afforded her leather, while our car back in Lexington was upholstered in stained cloth. I wondered if it was possible that everything I did, half of what I thought, was influenced by someone else and I didn't even know it. After all, in recent years the *marketing* of stuff had grown more ubiquitous and even sexier than the stuff itself. Were we offered what we wanted before we knew we wanted it? Were our own lurking desires being used to formulate and *transform* our wants into needs? I considered this as we drove ten more minutes along Route 7, the lush, hilly road that led into Stockbridge.

Stockbridge was another jewel of a New England town in a prosperous area. It had its own Main Street, similar to Great Barrington's, but it felt different in a way I couldn't put my finger on at first. Then, when we passed a sign pointing in the direction of the Norman Rockwell Museum, I knew what it was. I remembered Rockwell's classic midcentury painting of this very street: a lineup of brick and whitewashed storefronts on a cold winter night at Christmastime, a serene and pastoral small-town moment that anyone could recognize in his or her own way. His painting had become an

American icon, reminding us of the simplicity and
peacefulness of our national soul back when existence
was organic—not just the food but people's daily lives.

But the town *I* saw didn't look or feel like the painting. Around the linchpin of a huge Victorian hotel
were all the signs of a tourist trap gone to seed: a can-
dle shoppe, a candy shoppe, a store featuring sweatshirts advertising the names of local towns and
attractions, a crowded eatery. It looked to me like the
painting's fame had driven the town around the bend,
devouring the innocence that had brought it acclaim in
the first place.

Was this—this sweet but faded town—what marketing left you with after the sale? A vague memory that
you had once valued something but you could no
longer recall precisely what it was because you had, almost inadvertently, replaced it with something else? It
was cynical—I knew that—but there was something
about this place, these scenic, almost staged towns and
roads and flower beds and skies, that made me want to
scratch their pretty surfaces to see what really was beneath. I liked it here, but none of it felt precisely *real*.

I sighed, lay my head back against the headrest and
pressed my fingertips into my temples. What I needed
was to stop thinking. It had been an *awful* twenty-four
hours.

"What's wrong?" Julie asked. We had reached the
playground and she pulled up to the curb alongside it.

"A little headache coming on," I said.

"It's been that kind of day." She smiled, trying to
cheer me, and popped the locks automatically from her
side. "Come on. Let's show our baby a good time."

Julie carried Lexy, while I pushed open the playground gate with my foot; there was a fuzzy brown caterpillar inching along the top of the gate and I *hated* worms of any kind. It was a large and generous playground and we had it all to ourselves—swings, monkey bars, a sprawling modern jungle gym linked by gliders, tunnels, bridges, slides and ladders. Julie went straight to the baby swings, put Lexy into one and pushed. I had never put her in a swing before and was thrilled to see how much she loved it. I imagined how happily she would be to play here when she was older, on visits from the city to Aunt Julie: exploring the tunnels, scaling the ladders, rocketing down the slides. I stood in front of the swing, cooing and opening my arms each time Lexy swayed toward me. She would give me one of her big toothless smiles before swinging backward for another gentle push from Julie.

Another caterpillar crawled onto the toe of my boot and I kicked it off into the grass. And then I saw more. There were so *many* of them. They were dark brown with tiny yellow balls—eggs?—dotting their backs. I looked around and realized they were everywhere: crawling along the picnic table, climbing up a leg of the swing set, inching along the jungle gym, swarming through the grass, hanging from the canopy of branches.

"What's with all the caterpillars?" I asked Julie.

"What caterpillars?" She pushed Lexy, who laughed in delight.

"There are hundreds of them. It's *disgusting*."

"It's the country, is what it is. We've got bugs."

"*That's* why there's no one else here," I said. "Let's go."

"But she's having so much fun. And honestly, A, do you really want to go back to *the house* already?" *The house*. The way she said it, I knew what she meant. Going back to the house meant going back to Zara's murder, going back to Bobby-not-being-there.

"Not really," I answered. But just then a caterpillar landed on my shoulder and I whacked it off with my bare hand, feeling the recoil of its furry body. Without thinking, I grabbed Lexy when her swing hurtled toward me, stopping her in midflight. She protested with an angry squeal, twisting to look back at Julie, but I pulled her out of the swing, letting it fall backward through the air.

Julie followed me as I walked toward the gate through a web of sticky caterpillar threads, previously invisible and *revolting* now that I was aware of them. On the sidewalk outside the park I saw caterpillars creeping in every direction.

"You're overreacting," Julie said.

"No, I'm not. *Look* at this." I stood impatiently next to her car. "Open it, Julie, *please*."

She opened the doors remotely and we got in.

"You're silly," she said, starting the engine.

"What *is* that?"

"Gypsy moths, probably. They come in cycles."

"It's horrible. Didn't you notice?"

"You're really sensitive, Annie. Do you know that? It's been a crappy couple of days, but that doesn't mean there's a dark side to *everything*."

We drove in silence for a few minutes until I realized we weren't heading back to Great Barrington. I looked at her, wondering where she was taking us; she glanced back at me, grinned and said, "Lemons into lemonade?" It was what our mother used to say to convince us to turn around a bad situation.

"Okay," I said, "but please admit that was gross."

"It was gross."

"Thank you."

"Good," Julie said. "Now I'm taking you out to dinner."

I twisted toward her, about to protest—*In what we're wearing? With a baby? When we're too tired to enjoy it?*—but she stopped me before I could utter a word.

"We're not cooking tonight. They're great with kids. And it's casual."

A few minutes later we pulled into the tiny village of West Stockbridge and parked across the street from a gray clapboard house that had been turned into a restaurant called Rouge. A waitress seated us in a small front room that was both cheerful and elegant, with sponge-painted yellow walls, purple tulips lilting out of glass vases suspended on the wall and strands of colorful glass discs that hung in a large bay window overlooking the quiet street. Before long, we were laughing over "the caterpillar incident." I had to admit it *was* a little silly. We ordered delicate organic salads, which we ate with warm bread, trout and asparagus. Julie had a glass of wine. Lexy nursed on my lap. Outside it was a bright spring late afternoon in a world filled with caterpillar infestations and marketing infiltrations and police interrogations, but inside, in *here*, we relaxed in a moment of unexpected ease. She had brought me to the perfect place to get my "sensitive" mind off *stuff.*

Over a plate of pistachio biscotti and dime-sized chocolate cookies, we decided things. I would buy a short-term membership at the local gym to help shed stress and a few leftover maternity pounds, and Julie would babysit, getting Lexy used to being without me in the house. We figured that with planning we could manage the transition to my two-night absence next week, when I went to New York for the job orientation, so as to cause everyone the least inconvenience and distress. Leaving your baby, for however brief a time, felt like arranging a trip to the moon; there was no end to the potential complications. We would have to find a local pediatrician, but Julie assured me there were plenty.

"I guess we should start getting her in the habit of taking bottles from you," I said. "I brought my pump and all the bottle gear."

"I thought you hated pumping."

She was right: I did. During our phone calls between Lexington and Great Barrington, I had frequently moaned about the discomforts of pumping breast milk while at work in the prison so that Lexy could drink the real thing at day care.

"It's just that I want her to stick with breast milk for a while longer," I said. "It's so much better for her and she's still so young."

"What about supplementing with formula? Wouldn't that free you up a bit?"

Dreaded formula, full of artificial additives. Julie,

not being a mother herself, couldn't have realized what she was asking of me, how every bit of mommy-baby attachment I relinquished would be a loss. And yet maybe she had a point. Lexy had been fed on mama's milk (pure gold) for nearly half a year. Was it time for more flexibility? It would be a matter of training my milk ducts not to produce milk every day at a certain time. The idea of formula saddened me a little, but things were changing now. I had to be strong.

"Okay," I said. "Let's do it, but gradually."

"And maybe we should start her on solid food, too. She seems kind of hungry."

Hungry? I resented that a little. "Maybe it would be easier if I just took her with me."

"Right. And bring her to the orientation at the hospital? Not exactly professional."

"You could come with me to New York, Jules. It could be fun."

"I have some work things coming up—nothing I can't do with Lexy around, but I have to be here. Anyway, we'd be pretty cramped in Dad's old apartment, don't you think? Just leave Lexy at home with me—"

"But you have so much work—"

"Not *that* much. Don't worry! I *want* to take care of her. It'll be *fine*."

So it was settled. I mean really settled: I was going, alone; and Lexy would gradually be weaned to bottles and solids. I thought it seemed like a lot to ask of my baby all at once, especially after being separated from her daddy and her home, but Julie seemed so confident.

On the way home, passing through Great Barrington, we caught the local cell phone store before it closed at seven. Julie bought herself a new phone— slender and pink—and signed me on to her service, getting me a lesser phone that was still a considerable upgrade from what I was used to. After, she pulled the car up to Brooks Pharmacy so I could run in and buy four new plastic bottles, silicone nipples and a can of formula. Then, as the sun set along a spectrum of vibrant, dying color, and the green mountains grew dark and shadowy around us, we headed back to the house.

The days passed in a modest kind of peacefulness, a respite from upheavals and traumatic events. The street out front washed clean with two more rains. Thomas Soiffer seemed to vanish like a puff of smoke, and with it the murder investigation, news of which appeared in the papers with less and less frequency. We went on with our lives; what else could we do?

Julie and I fell into routines. I would sit alone in the Yellow Room at appointed times, pumping milk from my breasts and freezing it in plastic bags, every few days omitting a pumping, retraining and literally downsizing my breasts (though they still managed to reach near-explosive proportions if I didn't get to the pump on time). Lexy was started first on a mix of breast milk and formula once a day, then one full bottle of formula a day, then two. Julie worked at odd hours, making and taking phone calls, hammering information out of and into her computer, but as always she directed her energies with admirable focus and seemed to have plenty of time to spend with Lexy. Which was good: our plan, for my baby's comfort and happiness when I was away in New York, seemed to be working. Lexy was adjusting beautifully to the bottle-breast trade-off between look-alike mommies.

Sometimes, when Julie fed and napped Lexy, I skedaddled, haunting the house and grounds with my camera, capturing the final traces of Zara Moklas's evaporation and documenting my family's daily life. Sometimes I went to the gym, where I grunted and groaned myself in the direction of something close to my previous and Julie's current form. Sometimes I ran errands. I was getting to know the town, shopping for groceries at Price Chopper, gathering fresh fruits and vegetables at Taft Farms and joining the local fashion aficionados to troll the designer racks at Gatsby's—where, on Thursday, I broke down and bought matching tie-dyed hoodie sweatshirts, silkscreened on the front with a seated Buddha, for we three Milliken females. It was an indulgence, but we deserved it; our little tribe had come a long way together through a strange week.

That evening, as the day waned through shades of lilac, burgundy and brown into a black country night outside, we all wore our matching psychedelic sweatshirts and danced to Tina Turner belting out a ballad about love-and-what's-it-got-to-do-with-anything. A pot of rosemary beef stew simmering on the stove filled the kitchen with its rich fragrance. We were happy. After dinner I nursed Lexy in a rocking chair Julie had moved from the loft into the Yellow Room. Put my baby to bed, put myself to bed, and slept . . .

Until my sleep-self was pulled unwillingly and in total confusion out of a deep well. That was how my dream-mind transformed itself from sleep to abrupt, panicky wakefulness. I was in a well attached to a rope that pulled me up up up up up and I did not *want* to go up, I wanted to stay asleep. But it was out of my control.

Gradually as I awoke I became aware of a tremendous, awful, deafening sound. The alarm system: it had been triggered.

Someone was in the house.

Chapter 4

Lexy was screaming, though her screams had little impact against the shriek of the alarm. I had never heard anything like it. The sound was large and overwhelming and so shocking that I couldn't think of what to do. I picked Lexy up and tried to mute her hearing by pressing her head between my chest and one hand. Holding her, I darted into the hallway; then, terrified, I went back into our room and locked the door. The panic and hysteria of the moment made it impossible to *think*. To know what to *do*. I threw open window after window, looking for a way out. *Where was the maroon car?* Either it was too dark out to see it or it was gone. Chilly air streamed into the room. The fourth window opened onto an abutment that Julie had earlier explained was original to the barn, tacked-on grain storage or something like that. I couldn't remember. Looking down at the lower section of tar roof I could hardly see its edges in the country darkness. How would I know where to step? How could I take a *baby* out there?

But I had to. *Someone was in the house.*

I swung one leg out the window, straddling half in and half out, and was about to lift my other leg over— holding on to Lexy for dear life—when the alarm went off as suddenly as it had blasted on.

The abrupt silence froze me. *What did it mean?* Outside my door, footsteps grew louder. I raised my other leg to swing it out the window so I'd be sitting, ready to jump down.

My doorknob jiggled.

I inched myself forward, *ready*. I felt turned on in a way I never had before, not in a *good* way but like a machine. I didn't like it, being animated for pure action. And yet the urge to survive was irresistible.

"Annie?" It was Julie's voice. "Open up. It's okay."

Movement, fear, urgency gelled. Coolness spread over my skin. The phone started ringing, just as Julie had said it would; if it was a false alarm you gave your password and the alarm company called off the police. Was that what this was: *a false alarm*?

Coming back inside, I felt sick at what I had almost done. If I had made the small leap down, I might have dropped Lexy. Anything could have gone wrong.

I opened the door and there was Julie in black-and-white cow-print pajamas, ear pressed to phone, telling someone the password: "Peanut Butter Jealous." (A stuffed monkey we'd both loved and claimed and fought over as young girls; *she* had funnily mala-propped the name.) I bounced Lexy, calming her, while Julie recited information about herself and her house to prove that she was who she said she was. After the call she looked at me apologetically. "Sorry,

A. I turned it off from the control pad in my bedroom. It flashed something about a battery in one of the kitchen windows."

"A battery?" Impossible! The epic battle I had just waged against fright could *not* have been caused by a *battery*—faulty, expired, whatever.

I followed her downstairs into the dark kitchen. She flicked on the light and the room glowed, quiet and still, just as we had left it after dinner. The door and windows were closed. Nothing looked out of place. Julie inspected the window nearest the door and pronounced, "There's no sensor magnet. It must have fallen off and triggered the alarm."

"Why would that happen?"

"Beats me. I watched while they installed the system. The magnet's about an inch long, stuck on with glue. It makes contact with the battery."

Just then a face appeared outside the window: a man. We both screamed and Lexy began to wail again. The man looked frustrated, pressing something flat against the glass: his open wallet. He was showing us his police identification. I noticed his short brown hair, but he had a beard and no double chin—this was not the man I'd seen earlier in the maroon car.

"Call Detective Lazare," I told Julie. "Find out if it's a different guy."

She called—it *was* a different guy; the shift had changed at midnight. So we let him in. He introduced himself as Mack and went directly to the window to inspect it himself, reaching the same conclusion: the magnet was gone.

"Do me a favor, ladies, and sit tight while I have a

look around." Mack reached under his fleece sweater and pulled out a gun. I *hated* guns, for everything they represented. I'd had to endure mandatory target practice at the prison, and just seeing one now brought back the bitter smell of singed metal and the sound of a bullet piercing the air, smashing into a distant cardboard figure. But I said nothing. What if someone *had* slipped into the house and Mack confronted him? I was *glad* Mack had the gun.

Julie and I sat at the table while I nursed Lexy, which was the only way to calm her at this point since she was so agitated. Finally she fell asleep in my arms. After a while Mack reappeared to reassure us. "Everything looks okay," he said. "No one's here except us chickens." We thanked him but didn't laugh; we were exhausted, on edge. "You might want to look around, though. See if anything's missing."

Julie got up and took a quick glance around the kitchen. The TV she kept on the counter was still there, as were our purses, hanging off the same hook right by the front door. In the adjacent dining room I heard her opening drawers before calling out, "Silver's all here." Mack and I stayed together in the kitchen, he standing by the door with his hands in his pants pockets, trying not to eye the high-end appliances, and I at the table, holding sleeping Lexy. Julie moved through the house, inspecting for the obvious things a thief might take: electronics, jewelry, hidden cash. Everything was there.

When my arms began to lose circulation I went upstairs and put Lexy in her crib. I closed and locked the windows, checked the closets and under the bed, then carried the listening end of the monitor with me back to the kitchen. I set it on a counter, raised the volume to high, put water on to boil for tea and then reached into my purse for one of the packets of artificial sweetener I'd borrowed from a diner in town.

I found one easily in the mess of stuff at the bottom of my purse. *Too* easily. My wallet—the bulkiest item I carried and inevitably the obstacle in my searches for lipstick, pens, tissues, cell phone, keys—was not there. But how could that be possible? I dumped the contents of my purse onto the counter and saw that it was true: no wallet.

"Oh, jeez," Julie said, watching me. "But nothing was taken from the house. Why would anyone break in here and steal just your wallet? Annie, maybe you lost it again."

I was a little famous for that, having mislaid my wallet three times in the past two years, leaving it behind at stores, on my dresser, in my desk at work. Each time it became less a catastrophe and more a tired farce.

"Check *your* purse," I told Julie.

She did. Everything of hers, including her wallet, was accounted for.

"I lost my wallet once," Mack offered. "Badge and everything, gone." He cringed at the memory of whatever he had suffered as a result.

"Gatsby's," I said, leaning my elbows on the counter, sinking my face into my hands. "I probably left it behind when I bought the sweatshirts."

"Probably," Julie said. "You'll call them first thing in the morning."

"I wonder why they didn't call me."

"Because you don't have any local ID." Julie squeezed my shoulders with both her hands, simultaneously relaxing and forgiving me. "You've got to put my address and phone number in your wallet. When you get it back, I'll give you one of my business cards."

"Right." I felt like such an idiot. "I wonder if Bobby got a call."

"He would have let you know, A, don't you think?"

I nodded. "I guess the store just figured I'd be back."

Mack stayed until Detective Lazare arrived, looking freshly dragged from sleep, his cheek bearing the indentation of a wrinkled bedsheet. He listened as Mack said there was no sign of breaking and entering, as Julie told him she had searched the house and nothing was missing, and as I explained about my wallet. Lazare then had his own look at the rogue window and, apparently satisfied with Mack's assessment, opened his pad and made a few brief notes.

"You should have the alarm company come in and check out the system," he told Julie. "Do it tomorrow. You don't want to lose another night of sleep."

"I will," she said.

"I'll send someone over first thing in the morning to dust the window for fingerprints, just to be sure." He peered sleepy-eyed into the blackness beyond the window, then slipped his notepad into the pocket of his nylon jacket. "If someone was out there, Mack would have seen him. Well, I'll give you a call tomorrow, let you know what Forensics has to say about the window."

Julie saw him out. I went upstairs, back to my room,

where Lexy's deep, rhythmic breathing seemed to warm the air. And yet, when I got into bed between the chilly sheets, I felt *cold*. The glowing red face of the digital clock showed 2:16 A.M. At the sound of Julie's footsteps in the hallway, I got up and popped my head out to say good night.

"Think you'll sleep now?" I asked.

"Probably not. Damned *malarm*." She didn't have to explain; I knew she meant *malfunctioned alarm*.

I smiled. "Sweet dreams, if you can."

"You too."

But I tossed and turned, wired from the excitement of the malarm. I felt a sickening awareness that I had never been so afraid, *controlled* by fear in a way I didn't like. Being severed so abruptly from deep sleep had triggered a Pavlovian dread of the alarm's ever going off again, even in the case of an actual intruder or a fire or some other reason we would need to be alerted to real danger. If the mere *thought* of it going off made me so tense, how had it registered in Lexy's brain? They said that children had no memory until generally the age of three, but clearly some things were programmed during those early years. I remembered reading about a woman who had grown up in Israel saying that years later, living in America, every time she heard a car backfire she hunkered down, taking cover. To her, every explosive sound was a bomb. Would Lexy associate sudden noises with falling out of windows? Would her mind catalog the experience as having almost been *thrown* out of a window? Not that I was ever going to throw her, but what had her baby eyes seen from our angle at that height? Would our moments in the window later translate into an amorphous mistrust of me?

As my mind ground over the possibilities, something else occurred to me. *Why* had the magnet slipped? I could understand it if the glue holding it in place had grown old and dried out, but the alarm system had only recently been installed. Could something have shifted it, like a movement of the window? *Had* someone tried to open it from outside?

Definitely a paranoid thought. The magnet had simply slipped. But now I knew it would be impossible to sleep, so I got out of bed, checked Lexy (sound asleep; an angel), double-checked that all my bedroom windows were locked, picked up the receiving end of the monitor and walked quietly through the hall, thinking I'd go downstairs and read a while. The house was so *still.* Nothing creaked; floorboards and hinges were still too new to have acquired the complaints of an experienced house. Standing on the split staircase I wondered if Julie was awake and on impulse, instead of going down, I went up.

She was sleeping, a long lump under her white blanket in her big king-size bed. The high-contrast room in the depth of night was neither black nor white but *silver.* A soothing, peaceful space. I put the monitor on the floor and got in beside her. Her bed was very comfortable and I immediately felt calmer and warmer, reassured, and without thought I fell into a dreamless sleep.

In the morning I woke up with Julie swiveled in my direction, propped on her elbow, watching me. When I opened my eyes, she smiled.

"Couldn't sleep?"

I stretched my arms. "This mattress is supercomfortable."

"It's some kind of space-age foam," she said, "supposedly developed by NASA. It holds the shape of your body."

"How much?"

"Don't ask."

Then I thought of Lexy and turned to look at the monitor. The sound and motion sensor was unlit, reassuring me that all was well.

"Not a peep," Julie said. "You can relax."

"Easier said than done. I haven't felt really rested in weeks."

"Well, that's no surprise, considering everything you've been through."

"We," I told her. "You're going through it with me."

"The Zara thing, yes. But not your separation. I'm not losing anything; I'm gaining."

I couldn't bring myself to remind her that her gain of me and Lexy would be temporary, just for the spring and part of the summer.

Julie went downstairs to make breakfast while I set up my breast pump in the downstairs bathroom (so as not to wake Lexy with the loud motor) and expressed a bottle of milk. It relieved my swollen breasts, which by this time of the morning had usually fed Lexy once. When I was finished I stowed the bottle in the fridge and joined Julie at the small table by the *good* kitchen window—the one whose alarm had not gone off last night. She had prepared a delicious breakfast of scrambled eggs and thick slices of toast slathered with strawberry jam from a local farmers market. Outside, flickers of light showed the sun's struggle to break through the clouds. I hoped we wouldn't have more rain.

We ate our breakfast and, as Lexy slept in to compensate for last night's rude awakening, Julie and I discussed the day, which largely involved reviewing last night. Detective Lazare had promised an official, forensic analysis of the window. The alarm company was sending someone over. And my wallet was missing, presenting a host of inconveniences, since I was leaving for New York (on the bus, I guessed, now that I was without a license) on Sunday night, just two days away, and there were preparations to be made. Simple but difficult preparations, for in many ways I was a reluctant participant in my own plan. Meanwhile, it was still up in the air if Bobby was coming this weekend—and now on top of everything else, if my wallet *wasn't* at Gatsby's, I would have to tell him that I was canceling our joint credit cards once again. Because it was a long trip from Kentucky, I knew he wouldn't come until tomorrow if he came at all, so I would have a little time to straighten out as much as possible before delivering the news, if necessary.

No one answered at Gatsby's and a quick Googling on the Web told me that they didn't open until eleven o'clock. So I would wait. Meanwhile, Ray the Forensic Specialist arrived at just past nine a.m. and introduced himself to us before hunkering outside the kitchen window to dust and brush and photograph surfaces for telltale fingerprints. He then dusted the inside window frame, thanked us and left. It took all of fifteen minutes, and another ten to clean up the chalky white residue he'd left behind inside and out. No one seemed particularly worried about the malarm; in fact, I was getting the feeling from all the law enforcement guys—Mack and Gabe Lazare and Ray—that they dealt with misfired alarm systems on a regular basis.

By the time we had scrubbed all traces of Ray from the window, Lexy was awake. Julie got dressed and I left them alone in the kitchen so aunt could give niece her bottle of expressed breast milk. I showered and dressed and from the Yellow Room heard another car pull up and stop outside the house. Looking out the window, I saw a van from the alarm company. Another guy carried another toolbox up the flagstone path and rang the kitchen doorbell. Then it was quiet; Julie must have let him in. The thought that she could navigate feeding a baby cradled in her arms while getting up to open the door encouraged me that my brief trip away would go smoothly. Julie was nothing if not competent and responsible and she *loved* Lexy.

Later, while Julie played with Lexy in the living room, I headed outside with my camera, stopping to say hello to the malarm man. He was wearing a blue uniform, pacing the grass, staring at the ground.

"Searching for a needle in a haystack?" I asked.

He looked at me. Moss green eyes. A nice smile. "I just can't figure out where that magnet went. Not inside, not outside. The new one's going to stay in place, though. I made sure of *that*."

I realized he thought I was Julie and that we were continuing a conversation they had started earlier in the house—Julie with her hair now in a ponytail, wearing different clothes and pounds heavier. It was funny how often people failed to notice the details. But I went with it, stepping closer to take a look. On the inside of the window a new half-inch strip of magnet had been stuck into a prodigious bed of glue. Now, tonight, the alarm system could go to bed happy.

He produced a clipboard with a form for my signature. I signed Julie's name and he gave me the bottom half of the carbon, which I folded and stuck in my pocket. I'd give it to her later, after she was finished with Lexy.

"Baby down to sleep?" He must have met Lexy, too; Julie must have said something about feeding Lexy before her morning nap, not bothering to explain that today's nap would come later than usual.

"Just about."

"You can call us twenty-four/seven if there are any more problems with the alarm."

"Thank you," I said, and watched him get into his car and drive away. And then I walked to the curb and into the road, where day by day I had made a habit of photographing Zara's gradual evaporation.

Though her outline had washed away, there was still some visual evidence of her blood. It was as if the asphalt had absorbed it, leaving shadowy splotches that were more or less pronounced, depending on the time of day and the weather. I didn't know what I would eventually do with the photographs—maybe superimpose them and see what emerged, maybe just keep them as they were, to speak for themselves. For now I was collecting them, counting days forward, building Zara a passageway, in my mind, between the time zones of life and death. Or maybe my little project was just plain voyeurism. I didn't know, but I felt more compelled to lift my camera to this moment than I had to anything else—except Lexy—in years.

At exactly eleven o'clock, I called Gatsby's. I recognized the voice of the clerk, an older woman who had sold me the sweatshirts.

"No, dear," she said. "We didn't find a wallet here. There were two of us working yesterday and we closed up together. Give me your number and if it turns up we'll call you."

I gave her Julie's house number and my cell number, thanked her and hung up. I had *counted* on my wallet being there; it was the last place I'd paid for anything. Now I had no idea where it could be. Someone must have picked it up in the store, not said anything and kept it.

So that was that. My wallet was nowhere. I left Bobby a voice mail saying that I was going to have to cancel all our credit and bank cards. Then I sat down at the kitchen table and began the arduous task of listing everything that was in my wallet, calling 800 numbers and making my way through labyrinthine automated customer service systems. The day passed. Darkness fell. Julie gave Lexy some rice cereal and her evening bottle, then bathed her. By dinner I was on my second glass of wine—the milk I would pump later tonight would be useless.

After dinner I lulled Lexy to sleep in the rocking chair in the Yellow Room. I had discovered, with the overhead light dimmed just so, that at night the room acquired the richness of glazed apricots. This mutability of shades reminded me of the bloodied asphalt, how it revealed differences depending on elemental shifts. I thought about the unreliability of perceptions as Lexy fell asleep in my arms. I thought about love. I thought about Bobby on our wedding day and how scrubbed and handsome he'd looked in his tuxedo, beaming as I joined him in my white gown. How I dropped my bouquet of ivory roses and he picked it up and handed it back to me.

I set Lexy down in her crib and went downstairs, where I sank into the bend in the living room couch and closed my eyes. I was *tired*. When the phone rang, Julie shouted from the kitchen, "It's Bobby!"

"What happened exactly?" he asked.

I told him the whole story—the middle of the story, that is, since I still didn't know its beginning: how I had managed to lose my wallet in the first place.

"You canceled all the credit cards?"

"I think so. I wanted to go over it with you to make sure I didn't miss any."

"So neither of us has any credit cards now. Or bank cards. *Wow.* How are we supposed to get money?"

"The old-fashioned way: You walk into a bank before it closes, talk to a human being and make a withdrawal."

"It's *Friday night* and I've got no money."

It sounded like a song with an inevitable (to my burned-out brain) next chorus: *And I got a date with my Lovyluv honey.* As quickly as the lyric popped to mind, I banished it. Imagining *her* was driving me crazy.

I took a deep breath and plunged into comforting, mundane detail. "Our bank keeps Saturday-morning hours, nine to noon. Just get there before eleven forty-five because sometimes they lock the door early." I read him the confirmation number the bank had given me to verify that new cards had been issued and were snail-mailing their way in our directions. "Visa and MasterCard said we should have our new cards by Monday. A couple others said Tuesday, but now I can't remember which ones." All told, we had about seven credit cards—way too many, but neither of us had gotten around to paring them down.

"Okay, we'll just have to cope with this," he said.

"We have no choice."

"I just wish you'd been a little more careful, Annie. I mean, this isn't the first time you've lost your wallet."

I said nothing, just stretched out long on the couch and listened to our phone static. The living room had six windows, all of which were pure black rectangles. A complete lack of ambient light, the totality of the night's darkness, seemed to erase the outside world. For a moment, before Bobby spoke again, I thought of this living room and this house as a spaceship that was carrying me away from trouble.

"Listen, I cleared the weekend off with Kent. If it's okay with you, I'd like to come see you guys tomorrow." The softened tone of his voice told me that he had already, just now in that minute of silence, forgiven me for the wallet. And I felt my body relax. There had been much good in our marital give-and-take. I hadn't forgotten that. How had we gotten to this distant spot in so short a time?

"Okay. It'll be good for Lexy to see you. But how did you get Kent to agree?" I knew that Kent had threatened to make Bobby work Saturdays in retaliation for my bailing out of what he actually, upon occasion, called "the Evil Fortress" (always with a sinister little chuckle).

"I had to pull out my employment contract," Bobby said. "He couldn't argue with that."

"I think I really hate that man."

"Yeah, me too. But I'm not giving in to him."

"I guess you'll have to buy your ticket in cash."

"Well, actually, I went online yesterday and booked it—flight and rental car—so I'm set." We both knew that if I'd asked him *not* to come he could have used the air ticket later. "But I can only stay one night. I'll have to leave Sunday afternoon."

"I'm leaving Sunday night for Manhattan," I said, "so that's perfect."

We spent a few minutes going through our credit cards to make sure I'd called everyone. I could picture him sitting on our green velvet couch with the Infidelity File. I had worked hard collecting our financial data in one place and it contained the most current list we had of all our credit sources.

"Bobby? Bring the file, why don't you? I can't take much more of this in-between-ness. We have to really face this now."

Pause. I could *see* him freeze, sitting on the couch, the file in his lap.

"Okay, I'll bring it."

So this would be it. Finally, we would go over the file together and in the face of so much hard evidence he would *have* to confess. Unless . . . unless I was wrong. I had to admit I was beginning to wonder if there was a chance I had made a terrible mistake. I doubted I had, but if I didn't allow for that slim possibility I never would have let him come. Bottom line: I really missed him. And if he *did* confess, finally, and if he promised to give her up and stay faithful, couldn't I forgive him—just this once?

The next day Bobby's flight arrived on time, just before eleven o'clock, but the rental car agency refused to honor his reservation without a valid credit card on hand. A taxi for the long drive would cost far more cash than he had with him and he had no way to access an ATM. And the next bus didn't leave for four hours. So he called me and somewhat sheepishly asked for a ride. I told him where to wait and promised I'd be there in about an hour.

The problem was, I had no driver's license. The Lexington DMV was sending a replacement, but it wouldn't arrive until Monday. I would have to ask Julie if I could borrow a credit card and call it in to one of the taxi companies that serviced the airport.

I found her at her desk, hooked up to a headset and talking a mile a minute. She had told me she made all her international calls through her computer because it was much cheaper—and now that I thought of it she had also told me that today she had an important conference call with a client in a country where our today (Saturday) was their yesterday (Friday), a workday, and thus her availability was unquestioned. I stood in the doorway separating her bedroom from her office, feeling dense to have forgotten about this call. There was a lot of money involved, she'd told me, and many people were to be included in the meeting.

I shut the door as quietly as I could and stretched out on Julie's neat white bed, getting comfortable, as I waited for her to finish her call. Sinking into her spot, I wondered if her mattress's space-foam memory would mistake my body's impression for hers, the way people in town had lately been mistaking us for each other. I shut my eyes and tried to rest.

"What is it?" Julie was standing in front of me, still wearing the headset with its male end dangling.

"Finished?"

"No, they put me on hold. I have, like, one minute, so what is it?"

"It's fine. Go back to your call."

But I knew Julie. She was an epic multitasker and if anyone could handle an international conference call on a Saturday-that-was-still-Friday and at the same time solve someone else's trivial problem, it was my sister.

"Just *tell* me. Quick."

I spit it out as fast as I could. "I have to pick Bobby up at the airport, but I don't have a license so can I borrow a credit card so he can pay for a taxi?"

"A cab from the airport's going to cost a fortune."

"I know, but he's waiting—"

"Use my license and borrow my car. And take a credit card until yours comes."

"Are you sure?"

"*Yes.* Annie, you look exactly like me. No one will know and I'm giving you permission."

"Julie—"

"Just do it, okay?"

"Thanks. Should I wake Lexy from her nap so you can work?"

"Bring the monitor up here; I'll keep my ears open. I'll be done with this soon."

She hustled away, back to her call. Downstairs in the kitchen I opened her wallet and saw what she meant. No one would know the difference if I borrowed her ID for a few hours. Trading identities was a skill we'd practiced, for fun, as teenagers. We had even mastered each other's signatures. I slid out her driver's license, her car registration, her insurance card and one credit card just in case. Her keys were on a hook by the kitchen door. And her car, well, it drove like a dream.

I found Bobby waiting calmly on an airport bench, reading the well-thumbed copy of *The Stone Diaries* I had recommended to him. It had been sitting on his bedside table for months; he must have started it after I left him. I loved novels that ambled and leapt and created drama purely from character, but Bobby was more a history buff, so I knew he was reading the Shields novel as a way of holding on to me. Because he missed me. His legs were stretched out long and crossed at the ankle beside his carry-on suitcase. When he saw me coming he stood up so abruptly the suitcase fell over and he lost his place in the book.

"I'm sorry I'm late," I said.

"No problem."

I hugged him. He smelled delicious, like an accidental whiff of a wood fire on a chilly day. I took another breath and was transported to last autumn, before

Lexy was born, cuddling on the couch in front of our fireplace at home.

He zipped the book into an outside pocket of the suitcase and rolled it behind us through the parking lot to the car.

"You drove Julie's car?" he asked.

"I *am* Julie today."

He couldn't resist taking the wheel of this beautiful car and I didn't mind letting him (*his* driver's license being one of the few things I had not had to cancel). Steering with one hand, he operated the sound system with the other and still got us to Great Barrington in under an hour. Bobby made things seem so easy. I loved being encapsulated with him in the car with the road humming beneath us, pretending everything was okay. I assumed he had the Infidelity File in his suitcase. Neither of us mentioned it.

When we got back to the house Julie had lunch waiting. She had closed up shop (the other side of the world having finally tipped into Saturday) and there was an air of celebration; our days had grown so quiet that Bobby's arrival was an event. Julie welcomed him with hugs and hellos, seating him at one end of the dining room table. We sat on either side of him and he held Lexy in his lap. In the center of the table Julie had arranged a bouquet of flowers from the garden. We ate the tarragon chicken sandwiches she had prepared; the chicken salad, one of those dishes that improved with age, was even more delicious than yesterday when I'd made it. I was impressed by how Julie had freshened the leftover loaf of ciabatta as I'd shown her by dampening it and setting it briefly in a low oven. She had extended the iced tea and made a fresh fruit salad with lemon juice and a sprig of the wild spearmint that grew abundantly outside.

"I read in the *Eagle* that Zara Moklas's body is being flown back to Hungary on Monday," Julie said. "Her uncle came to get her."

"I haven't seen anything else about it in the paper for a few days," I said. "I get the feeling the investigation isn't going much of anywhere. I don't think they'll ever find out who did it."

"They never located that guy?" Bobby asked. "Thomas . . ."

"Soiffer." The name was ground into my brain; whenever I heard it or even *thought* it I saw blood and heard malarms.

"Nope, never found him," Julie said.

In the window behind Bobby the afternoon dramatically brightened as a cloud moved along. The lawn outside Julie's house turned Technicolor green. Two birds landed simultaneously to peck at the ground.

"Well," Julie said, standing up to clear the table, "anyone for coffee? Bobby? I think I'll have some."

"I'll pass, but thanks." He lifted Lexy up and sniffed her diaper. "Time for a change."

I helped Julie clear while Bobby took Lexy upstairs. In the kitchen, where the baby monitor now sat by the phone, we listened to him change her diaper and fiddle with something in the room. I pictured her becoming restless as his voice murmured, "Do you want Mommy? Is it Mommy time?" and right on cue my milk dropped.

"Want me to give her a bottle?" Julie asked.

"I think I'll nurse her."

"Leave the dishes. I'll take care of it."

I peeled off the rubber gloves and headed upstairs, intercepting my family, all two of them, in the hall on their way to find me. Bobby and Lexy had the very same smile, only hers was all pink gums and so, so very sweet. When we were all together my love for them felt not so much *equal* as completely *merged*; love for one was love for the other, like nested cups or echoes. Separating Bobby out of this feeling was a brutal emotional surgery and at this moment, encircling them both in my arms, it felt completely impossible.

I nursed Lexy on the rocking chair in the Yellow Room. Bobby stretched sidelong on the bed and watched us. He had put his suitcase at the foot of the bed (reflexively, I assumed, as sleeping arrangements were undetermined and I for one had assumed he would again sleep in the Pinecone Room). I felt a need to smash the coziness of the moment because we were drifting together without having resolved a single thing.

"Did you bring the file?" I asked.

He exhaled. "I brought it."

"This is probably as good a time as any to talk."

He opened his suitcase. The manila file was on top of his folded clothes. Sitting cross-legged on the bed, he opened the file and rested his handsome, squarish hand on the top page. The hand that knew ligament from bone, that expertly probed muscle and had healed the pains of countless inmates.

"The credit reports are practically in another language," he began. "I must have gone through these reports twenty times and I really can't find anything, well, interesting."

It was true: the voluminous credit reports, with their lists and codes and keys, were almost impossible to read. I could imagine how frustrated Bobby felt trying to pry information from the long, impenetrable documents. He hated bureaucracy in any form, which was frankly absurd since he had made his career in government service. But I didn't feel an iota of guilt; I had suffered through the mind-numbing papers, so why shouldn't he? In the two months since I'd bought our reports from the three major credit reporting bureaus, my searching fingers—and now Bobby's—had softened their edges to tattered curls. And still, *interesting* was not the word I'd use to describe them.

"The credit reports don't show much of anything," I said. "It's the credit card bills, mostly. And the e-mails. *That's* where you need to concentrate."

"I realize that. I've been studying the bills. I've called every retailer and vendor that posted every one of these charges we can't account for."

Retailer. Vendor. Posted. He *had* been on the phone. In our time together Bobby had never dealt with a bill or any of our various service accounts. I had often wondered how he survived before I came along. Basically I think he just paid his bills on time and never sought any discrepancies to balk at. The ignorance-is-bliss approach had served him well enough—until now.

He moved aside the clipped reports and got the stack of credit card bills, which I'd marked up with yellow highlighter and red pen. There was now blue pen, too, I saw—Bobby's contribution. Seeing his markings made me hopeful. In a strange way those blue lines, their earnestness, increased my willingness to accept the possibility of his innocence, because if he *wasn't* innocent then his notes were just more documented lies, which would promote him from faithless to fraud.

"I put in a dispute for every one of those charges, but it's going to be weeks before we hear anything back," he said.

"Well, one of us bought that stuff, Bobby, and it wasn't me."

"It wasn't me either." He stared at me as if trying to drive home a point I didn't quite get. "Something's really wrong here, Annie."

I felt like laughing—no, not laughing, *crying.* We were back at the same old dead end: something was wrong but we couldn't name it and he wouldn't admit any responsibility.

"Just say it, Bobby."

"I won't lie just to end this stalemate."

"She wrote you *love letters.*"

"Annie, those e-mails aren't real."

Oh, that was a good one! He didn't think they were *real.* They looked real to me with their *Bobbybobs* and *Lovyluvs* and their accurate descriptions of his body when he made love. I felt like such an idiot sitting here listening to this nonsense.

"You know what, Bobby? Just forget it. It's over. We can't keep going through this."

"Annie . . ."

That one tired word, my name, seemed to suck all

the air out of the room. Suddenly we were ten thousand feet above the clouds in a world without atmosphere.

"I'm hiring an investigator," Bobby said. He was sitting on the edge of the bed now, his body alert, refusing to let me give up what I'd started. "He's coming to the house Monday night. He's some kind of computer specialist. He's going to go over our files, our whole system, with a fine-tooth comb. If you need answers before you'll come back home, Annie, I'm going to find them for you."

He crossed the room, stroked Lexy's hair and then took my hand. His palm felt dry, familiar. "Please, Annie, sweetheart, don't give up on me. I'm going to do whatever it takes to solve this."

I had to do it, give him another one-more-chance— but slowly and carefully. He slept in the Pinecone Room that night while I lay alone in my pretty bed in the Yellow Room, comforted by the soft rhythm of Lexy's breathing, until eventually I fell asleep.

I stayed in bed later than usual the next morning, taking my time nursing Lexy. When I went downstairs there were already breakfast dishes in the sink. I set about giving Lexy her "morning mush," as we had come to call it, preparing the area surrounding her high chair for an onslaught of mucky mess. Halfway through her bowl of rice cereal—some of which assumedly made it into her stomach on its way onto her face, her bib, the high chair tray and the floor—I glanced out the window and saw Bobby and Julie appear together in the distance. They were nearing the house, returning, it seemed, from a walk down the road. I wondered how long they'd been out and what they were discussing. Lexy, of course. Zara, I imagined. Me.

Julie was wearing my pale green capris, rubber flip-flops that I suspected were also mine because they just weren't her style and her tie-dyed Buddha sweatshirt. She was dressed more like *me* than like her usual tidy self. There was something so weirdly familiar about seeing her with my husband because I was seeing *us*, Bobby and me, and yet it wasn't us because it was *them*. Definitely them. To the naked eye they might have looked like "Annie and Bobby," but they were not. *I* could see the difference. There was a solid two feet of space separating them, whereas when Bobby and I walked together our bodies always veered sloppily toward each other, invading each other's spaces, preventing solitude. Bobby and I shared something they lacked; invisible yet emotionally palpable, it was what made us a couple . . . or what used to make us a couple.

I thought of Lovyluv, the interloper, and how she had invaded and eroded our couplehood. I thought of Bobby, who had allowed a stranger to come between us and was so focused on the wrong version of events, the easy version in which supposedly nothing had happened, that he was failing to grasp what was most important as it slipped away. I thought of Julie, my beloved, amazing twin, and how much impact she had on me just by being alive and reflecting me back to myself in a way that intensified every experience. I thought of my mother, who had been gone so long it was hard to believe she had ever actually been alive or

that I had once existed inside her body. I thought of my
father, who had been ruthless enough to leave his family twice—once with divorce, once with death. I thought
of my own daughter and how I felt her absorbed into
every iota of my being. And then I thought about my
self and realized that I had never been alone long
enough to know what that really was.

Watching Julie and Bobby for those brief moments
before they vanished beyond the scope of the window,
I had the strangest thought that if I'd had a gun I could
shoot directly through the empty space between them.
It was an alarming image; I didn't know why I thought
it. I scraped some mush off Lexy's tray and spooned it
into her mouth.

Then I remembered last fall when I was heavily
pregnant with my baby and out on the prison's shooting range with Bobby and a few others for our required
annual training. We were all wearing protective ear-
phones and goggles, emptying nine-millimeters at a
black-and-white silhouette that was chewed up, full of
holes from practice. Suddenly I imagined *my* silhouette, pregnant, and realized what a big target I would
make. I looked at Bobby, wondering if he could distance his emotions and fears, his *imagination*, from our
practice with guns; wondering if he kept thinking, as I
did, about how ironic and absurd it was for physical
therapists to hone our skills in the destruction of the
body. *Fix 'em up, shoot 'em dead.* But Bobby didn't
notice me watching him. His attention was sharply focused, his trigger finger squeezing, his bullets hitting
the figure with precision. He was performing a job and
doing it well, which impressed me and yet made me

feel peculiarly lonely. *Why* were we doing this? What *exactly* were our intentions for this day of rigorous practice? What were we *afraid* of? I really didn't think that I, personally, could fend off a prison riot with a single gun and a few rounds of bullets. That was the moment I knew I wanted to leave the prison. My personal contributions there were relatively useless, weren't they, if I had to learn to defend myself against my own patients? I didn't like it there. I didn't belong. I was not cut out for the job.

That was the resonant feeling now, I realized: isolation. The memory of when I knew I could leave, before I ever learned about Lovyluv. I don't know why the sight of Bobby and Julie briefly appearing together in the window so sharply recalled that feeling, but I realized I would never know what they were saying because I was separate from both of them, from my husband and from my twin. Not because there was window glass between us. We were just *separate*. I looked at Lexy's lovely mush-covered face and knew that one day in the future even *our* connection would fade. It was an intolerable thought.

I cleared her bowl and spoon, cleaned her face with a wet paper towel and sponged the high chair and surrounding area, telling myself, *Snap out of it. Don't think about stuff so much.* There was a long day ahead with all kinds of complicated good-byes: husband, sister, baby. Tonight I would travel alone to Manhattan. I would be gone two days and nights, the longest I had ever been away from Lexy. Maybe *that* was why I felt so nervous.

Upstairs, I threw on some clothes, changed Lexy's

diaper and dressed her. I grabbed my camera and, back downstairs, settled Lexy into her stroller. I hoped Julie and Bobby were still out walking; I wanted to find them.

They were and I did, though they weren't specifically walking anymore. They were sitting on a bench under a weeping willow in Julie's expansive backyard. The feathery branches ended five feet above the lawn, so I had a good view of them: Julie leaning back, her legs crossed at the knee; Bobby pivoted forward, elbows bent on spread knees, fisted hands supporting his chin. He was twisted so he could see her and they were talking intently about something. I was a hundred feet away from them and they didn't seem to notice me. I crouched down, popped off my lens cap, zoomed in and focused. I was curious to see how they would translate as a camera-captured image free of personal references, though it was a stretch to think I'd be able to look at pictures of those two, alone or together, without nuance. Still, it seemed a worthy experiment, like giving myself a Rorschach to test my first reactions.

I had taken half a dozen shots before Lexy's "Dadadadada" drew their attention. Julie waved. Bobby got up and came toward us. Standing, I quickly reviewed the pictures and felt a strange combination of disappointment and relief: there was *nothing* new for me here. Even in a photograph I could not see Julie as a reduction to physical image—to me, she did not look like *me*. And the sight of Bobby in any dimension still frizzled with unresolved feelings. The last one, though, showed me a moment that had escaped me while it was happening: as Bobby listened to Julie, an expression of displeasure had crossed his face.

Bobby pushed the stroller and I walked beside him into the house.

"What was Julie saying to you just now?" I asked him.

He shook his head and squeezed half a smile onto his face. From the dark swaths under his eyes I could tell he hadn't slept well either. "I told her about the computer guy I've got coming over and she basically gave me an earful."

"Of what?"

"I'm wasting our money. I'm wasting our time. I should either tell you 'the truth' or let you move on. Not that it surprises me that she believes everything you believe. You two really are . . ." His words trailed off. He had always been appropriately reluctant to voice any strong opinions about me and Julie; after all, no two people as close as twins or couples ever welcomed commentary from outsiders. "I'm hiring the computer guy whether or not she approves. So, my plane's in three hours; any chance I can bum another ride? Julie offered, but to be honest—"

"It's okay. I'll drive you." I'd have plenty of time to pack later. I wasn't planning to leave for New York until evening so I could spend as much time with Lexy as possible. I *hated* leaving her, even for two days.

In the end, we all went to the airport. Julie was either eager for any excuse to get out of the house or she was too annoyed with Bobby to let him drive her car, which we all knew he would, given the chance. She drove, I rode shotgun and Bobby sat in the back with

Lexy. We listened quietly to radio jazz the entire way there.

At the airport, Julie hung back with the stroller when we reached Bobby's gate. We hugged and, unable to resist the soft skin behind his ear, I kissed him. He pressed his mouth into my hair. I *loved* him. But I couldn't help whispering, "Tell me her name."

He sighed and lifted the handle of his rolling suitcase. "I'll know more tomorrow night. If the guy doesn't stay too late, I'll call you. Otherwise I'll call you Tuesday morning."

"It would just help to *know*." To know her name. He knew what I meant.

He chuckled, actually laughed, but there was no humor in it. "Good luck in New York."

Leaving Bobby always felt like having my insides vacuumed out. Last time, alone in the Yellow Room, I had allowed myself to mourn, but not here in the airport. I sucked back my feelings of ripped-away loss and went to join Julie, who had pushed the stroller into a little bookstore that greeted you with all the latest magazines and a copious assortment of gum. Before I got all the way there, a familiar voice sailed up from the other side of a stand-alone bookshelf: "Hel-lo! Fancy meeting you here! Did you ever find that wallet?"

"No, not yet, unfortunately," Julie answered.

"Too bad. What a pain. I lost my wallet once and it took months to get everything straightened out."

I recognized the voice: it was the woman from Gatsby's, the clerk who had sold me the matching sweatshirts and to whom I'd spoken on the phone about my wallet. Then the voice went high and syrupy. "Not in the mood to match with Mommy today?"

At first I felt confused, but then I got it. She had greeted Julie, who was wearing her new sweatshirt, and was now speaking directly to Lexy, who was not. And she thought Julie was *me*. I gave it a minute because it was always fun to see how people who didn't really know us reacted when the second twin appeared and they were caught in their error. "*Actually I'm not Mommy.*" "*Of course you are!*" "*No, I'm Aunt Julie. Mommy Annie is over there.*" But that was not what I heard.

Julie laughed. "My adorable daughter's sweatshirt got covered in food and it's in the wash today."

"Oh? I'd worry the colors would fade with too much washing."

"I should have thought of that, but you know how it is. Half your brain cells go out the window with childbirth."

"Oh, I *know*. I have four children—all grown now. In fact, I'm off to meet my very first grandchild and I don't want to miss my plane." The woman hurried past me on her way out of the bookstore, turning to do a double take as she rushed for her gate.

Julie and I had played many a trick on unwitting people over the years, pretending we were each other, but this was the first time I knew of that she had actually pretended to be my daughter's mother. The second time, I reminded myself: when I came upon the malarm man in the yard, he'd thought he'd already met me with Lexy in the kitchen. The difference now was that I had witnessed Julie pretending and it bothered me. Yet I couldn't begrudge her her deep love of my child; it was perfectly natural. I was leaving tonight for Manhattan and my sense of disquiet suddenly felt acute. But wasn't it normal for a mother not to want to leave her child? Especially such a young baby? I took a deep breath and stopped the coil of anxiety, disciplining myself to view this next couple of days alone with Lexy as my gift to Julie. And then it would be back to reality.

I walked around the bookshelf as if I had just that moment breezed into the store. Lexy reached for me. I bent down to unbuckle her and lifted her out of the stroller. Squeezing her close, I inhaled her luscious baby smell of powder and milk. "Yummy," I cooed into her ear. "Yummy baby, all mine."

Neither Julie nor I mentioned the woman from Gatsby's. Julie bought a magazine and we went back to the car. She drove us home. On the way we discussed my plan to catch the last evening bus to the city and she convinced me, instead, to take her car. We agreed that when my new license arrived in the mail tomorrow morning she would borrow it, along with my rental car, until I returned to Great Barrington and we could switch back.

In no rush to leave, I played with Lexy after lunch and, during her afternoon nap, pumped some milk to leave behind. I packed my bags and then, after a simple pasta dinner, nursed Lexy once more before leaving. As I changed her diaper and zipped up her feetsy pajamas, I realized there was one thing I had neglected to pack: a photo of her to bring along with me.

Once she was snuggled peacefully in her crib, al-

most asleep, I crept out of the room with my camera
and went to the spare computer in the loft. I hadn't
downloaded in days and it took a few minutes for the
nearly hundred images to scroll into the photo program. Here were the pictures from the other day when
I had taken portraits of Julie and Lexy, separately and
together, and Julie had taken a few of me and Lexy. It
was one of those I wanted to print for my trip. As a
quilt of thumbnail images began to fill the screen,
miniature photos you could only roughly discern, even
I couldn't tell who was Julie and who was me. It was a
strange, disturbing sensation. One by one I selected the
images, assuming, *hoping*, that enlargement would
show who was who.

And it did. The images startled me, *pleased* me, in
how clearly they showed Julie as *Julie* and me as *me*.
The lens had revealed our essential difference. The
photos of Julie and Lexy together were family shots,
aunt and niece, *not* mother-daughter. I was surprised at
how satisfying this was and understood instinctively
that I mustn't share the perception with Julie. *She's
jealous*, I thought, looking at a photograph of her and
Lexy smiling at each other. *Jealous that I can make
children and she can't.* This hit me harder and more
simply than ever before. I was tempted to delete the
pictures from the hard drive *and* my camera's memory
card, wipe them out of existence along with envy
(Julie's), betrayal (Bobby's) and death (Zara's . . . and
Mom's . . . and Dad's). Too many rough emotions had
settled on this pastoral road. But what was the point?
Erasing the images wouldn't expunge the thought.

I chose a photo of me holding Lexy, both of us

twisting to make eye contact with each other, and printed it. Half an hour later I was sitting in Julie's car, alone, equipped with her ID and a suitcase of clothing to last two days and nights in the city.

I sat quietly in the car, in the dark, in the cold. Inside the big red house with its warmly lit windows were my sister and baby. Lexy didn't understand yet that I was leaving for longer than usual. I could go back inside, scrap the whole thing. I didn't *want* to go, but the plan was in motion. I felt certain I was doing the right thing. Yet I didn't. Was I making a stupid mistake? After all, Bobby continued to assert his innocence. And I kept hearing Detective Lazare's voice warning me that "someday you may need to fall back on that to comfort yourself." Fall back on what? What was I so sure of, exactly? Had I left Bobby because I wanted to quit my job and leave Kentucky? Because my hormones were raging so loudly I couldn't hear basic common sense? But the credit card bills. And the love letters. And the details.

I put Julie's car into Drive and pulled away from the house.

Chapter 5

I arrived late at my father's East Fifty-sixth Street pied-à-terre; well, that's what he called it when we were girls and he was alive and we would come into the city occasionally from our Connecticut home. It was a crumbling studio apartment whose rent-controlled lease he'd taken over as an aspiring young writer, one of those gifts you just fall into. In the early eighties, when the building went co-op, he bought in at an amazing price. It was the best, and possibly only, investment he ever made. At his death, Julie and I inherited the place, and when we came of age, we kept it. Why not? It was a paid-off crash pad in the city of cities. Not suitable for my family or Julie's extravagant taste, but it was *ours*.

I lugged my suitcase and garment bag up the five flights. The studio was predictably musty, so I immediately opened both windows. Night air trickled in with its pleasant springtime bite and I felt a little bit at home. This tiny space was so familiar: four cream-colored paint-crusted walls defining a twelve-by-twelve cube of a room with an incongruously high fifteen-foot ceiling. The small, dusty chandelier no one could reach, an old Murphy bed that had been here when Dad originally got the place, a small table and two ornately carved wooden chairs. The kitchen consisted of a couple of time-worn appliances jammed in one corner; there were no counters or drawers and in lieu of a cupboard there were three dusty shelves. The place was a hovel—presumably the only apartment in this co-op building that had never been renovated—but I was glad to be here. I opened my suitcase on the table, brushed my teeth, lowered the Murphy bed, made it up with clean sheets, stripped naked, pumped some breast milk, which I stowed in the tiny freezer, and went to sleep.

I was up by six. The orientation wasn't until ten, so I pumped milk and then went out for breakfast at the same diner where Mom and Dad used to take us for lunch when we visited the studio as children. I bought a *New York Times* and sat on a ripped vinyl stool dipping toast into runny eggs and drinking decaf coffee that was remarkably delicious. It was very strange being alone here, family-less, without Lexy. I ached with missing her and tried to keep my mind off all my doubts and to force myself to go along with the program I had set for myself.

I expected the job orientation to be a breeze. It was a big corporate hospital chain that held new-employee orientations once a month. You would learn their rules and they would further process your paperwork and get a chance to eyeball you in advance in case the off-site interviewer had made some awful mistake. I had planned, after the orientation, to go apartment hunting, giving myself this afternoon and tomorrow to look, but decided on impulse that that could wait. I missed Lexy way too much to stay. As soon as I was done at the hospital, I decided, I would return to Great Barrington.

I finished my coffee and went back to Dad's to shower and change. I felt uncomfortably raw, hyper-aware that one way or another this was going to be a pivotal day—depending a lot on what Bobby would tell me after his session with his computer sleuth—that I was either beginning a new life or spinning my wheels. I dressed in the same interview suit I'd worn two years ago for the prison job—boring beige, neutral and unthreatening—and blew my hair dry. Makeup. Stockings. High heels. Once the job was sealed I would put this outfit away until the next job change. Too restless to wait in the tiny studio, I headed outside.

Because the hospital was far west, between Ninth and Tenth avenues, I started walking (regretting the heels). I had always enjoyed walking in New York and today in my business clothes I blended easily into the rush-hour montage of people flowing through the urban grid. The morning air felt crisp and exciting. I wondered how long it would take me to feel I belonged here and then, reaching Seventh Avenue and Columbus Circle, I realized how long it had been since I had set foot on this island.

The old Coliseum was gone, razed, and in its place was a huge, glittering mall. I had heard about the transformation, but this was the first time I had seen it with my own eyes. It was startling and phenomenal. My first impulse was to hate it because it was different, pulling the plug on one of my antiquated Manhattan memories that I had never really cared about but suddenly, when it was gone, I mourned. Then I felt the tug of curiosity and crossed the street. It was not yet nine o'clock, so I still had some time. I pulled open one of the big glass doors and went inside.

The space was enormous, a granite-and-steel temple to commercialism. I knew shopaholic heaven when I saw it and strolled happily through the lobby past looming metal sculptures of twenty-foot naked giants (yes, real art here: we *are* more than we buy), gleaming plate-glass windows beckoning with displays of luxury goods, stuff stuff stuff teasing you, just daring you to come inside. I rode the escalator up one flight and saw immediately that the anchor store on the second floor was a large chain bookstore, with other stores flowing off two hallways adjoining a lobbylike gallery displaying more artwork, all with weighty price tags. Another flight up took me to *another* gallery-lobby with five-figure art and a Samsung store as its anchor.

I was drawn by a display case in the lobby, the kind of horizontal vista where you might find a whole city in miniature. Upon closer inspection I saw that it was a virtual map. A wave of the hand morphed neighborhoods recognizable by their iconic symbols: a paper food container sprouting chopsticks for Chinatown, a dollar bill for Wall Street, a painted canvas for SoHo, an espresso cup for Little Italy, and so on and so forth up and down and across the city. Technology didn't particularly interest me, but *this* was fun and before you knew it I was peering into the store through a glass wall beneath a big sign announcing Samsung Experience. It was a showplace for high-tech gizmos so cutting edge you couldn't even buy some of them yet: bitsy cell phones and featherweight laptops and massive televisions with precious living rooms you could sit in and actively pretend you were relaxing at home with your *very* big big-screen TV. When I turned away from the *experience* I felt a little high, a sensation that turned to dizziness when I spotted . . . Clark Hazmat? . . . waving his hand over the virtual map in the lobby. The hair was different, but the laughing-skull tattoo on his right shoulder was definitely his.

Clark Hazmat. I couldn't believe it. He had been one of our orderlies in the prison clinic up until just a few months ago. *A nice guy,* Bobby and I had always agreed—a white-collar criminal, a computer hacker, not a *real* criminal—easy to say so long as he was behind bars. Seeing him here now, free and "on the outside" came as a considerable shock. My mind skipped like a stone over a crystal lake of political correctness beneath which darker, realer prejudices mingled like drunken harpies—*prison prisoner criminal guilty risky scary vulnerable Zara killer murderer following-me dead*—until sinking into the depths of automatic judgment. Just like that, I sized him up as a threat, even though in the PT clinic he had been a reliable helper and I had genuinely liked the guy. Everything was context: there, he was safe; here, he was dangerous. Period. And why *was* he here, anyway? My finger itched to dial Detective Lazare and find out if Clark Hazmat had been on the list of recently released inmates.

Before I had a chance to slip past him to the escalator, he saw me.

"Miss Milliken? Hey! It's me! Clark from *back home!*" Wink wink. I looked around; there was no one else there. I guessed that on the outside we were supposed to act as if we'd never done time.

Clark was a small man with a big embrace. At the prison, inmates were strictly forbidden to touch us and so I hadn't known what a tactile guy he was. He was wearing cologne, an improvement over the generalized smell of sweat that had clung to many of the prisoners regardless of how clean they were. After the hug we stood back and smiled at each other. Clark wore the shadow of a teenage acne mask, a misfortune he couldn't help, and a new hairstyle he definitely should have done something about. His inmate's regulation buzz cut had sprouted into a frizzy topiary puffed high in the front, long down the back of his neck and trimmed short in between. And he had a big, bushy mustache. I felt like asking what was up with all the hair, but I pretended I didn't notice.

"Clark! What are you *doing* here? It's *so* great to see you!"

"Yeah, yeah, that's what they all say." He smirked and nodded rapidly, but that was his special humor: dry, self-effacing, a little obtuse. "Looking for work. Busboy, shit like that. I just talked to someone at the fancy-pants restaurant upstairs, *Per Say.*" I had heard of Per Se—it was considered one of Manhattan's finest restaurants—but I hadn't realized it was right here. "That joint's a con. Guy as good as told me the prices were fixed. Menu on the way out said it all: two-ten apiece just for lunch. Thought I'd choke. Guy gave me such a friggin' attitude, even with all my experience I *know* I'll never hear from that queer again."

All my experience. Clark's criminal record detailed a range of experience from petty to grand larceny; he was what they called a nonviolent felony repeat offender. I didn't want to insult him by asking if he was showing prospective employers his real résumé—or why he was showing them his creepy tattoo. I knew that finding his place in the law-abiding layers of society would be a real endeavor, which was no doubt why he was aiming low, at busboy, when he might have sought something a little more dignified and better paying, some kind of starting position in an office somewhere.

"You can do better than busboy, Clark."

"You think?"

"I do."

"Maybe you're right. Maybe I'm selling myself short. Maybe I oughta try for something better than that restaurant shit. Problem is . . ." He trailed off. With ex-cons, it was always the same roadblock.

"Your record. But you did your time and the rules are we're supposed to give you a chance to succeed now."

"Rules." He smirked.

"Well, some people follow them."

Clark smiled. *Back in the slammer,* as he might have said, we used to have these conversations about different kinds of people. In his world you were guilty until proven innocent; in my world it was the opposite. Our debates had been friendly and sometimes fun, but we'd never convinced each other to change our views.

"So what brings you here?" he asked.

"I left the prison. I've got a new job here in the city."

"Get outta *town*."

I nodded, smiled, stayed in town.

"So what about Mr. Goodman?" Wink wink wink. "I thought he was some kind of lifer in the joint."

"He's still there."

He nodded heavily, hair bobbing all of a piece. "Too bad. I thought you guys'd last."

"It's just a temporary separation, for a year or so, until he earns his pension. We'll see each other every weekend."

Clark eyed me as if I were conning him, which of course I was. But I had my privacy to protect.

"You know what they say about long-distance romances."

"No. What?"

"They're for the birds."

I laughed out loud. "*That's* the truth!"

"So, who left who? I mean, besides you being the one who flew the coop."

"No one left anyone."

"That's such fuckin' bullshit, if I may say so myself."

I stared at him. "That was really out of line."

"It's just that I always liked both of you. You were both good to me in the clinic, and believe me, that was the only thing kept me sane. Mr. Goodman, he's the kind of guy's got his nose to the grindstone, makes a good living, stays straight. I mean, what more do you want from a guy?"

"Fidelity." It slipped out before I could stop myself and then there seemed no point in holding back. "He cheated on me, Clark. So now you know."

"Mr. G?"

I nodded.

"You caught him in flagrante, I guess."

I didn't know whether to laugh or shout or walk away. "No, I didn't actually catch him in the act, but I did find evidence." And then before I knew it, I was telling him my story. It poured out in minutes and afterward I felt naked and there was Clark Hazmat, nodding at me sympathetically with the saddest look on his face. I felt so foolish, so *exposed*, and now to make matters worse my eyes started to tear, though I was able to hold myself back from really crying.

He gave my arm a warm squeeze. "Well, I never woulda guessed it of Mr. Goodman. But proof's proof, right?"

"It's all right there on paper." I found a tissue in my purse and wiped my eyes before my mascara had a chance to run. Then I lifted my wrist to somewhat dramatically consult the time. "I really have to get going. If you ever decide to work in a physical therapy clinic, I'll be happy to give you a recommendation." I had to brace myself to avoid visibly cringing when I said that, but I *had* to find a way out of this conversation and my orientation *was* starting in half an hour.

In a flash he handed me a neon orange business card reading CLARK HAZMAT, PRIVATE CITIZEN and his phone number.

"Get it? *'Private Citizen.'* That's my personal touch."

I smiled genuinely, because in some counter-intuitive way I really *did* like Clark. Sort of. He then gave me a pen and another one of his cards, blank side facing up.

"Put your info right here for me. Now that I'm out, I told myself I was going to stay connected to good people."

What could I do? I wrote down my new cell number.

"Thanks, Miss M. Let's stay in touch. Everybody needs a few friends—am I right?"

"Absolutely."

He hugged me and I kind of hugged him back, then made my way to the down escalator. As I zigzagged my way to the first-floor lobby and back onto the street, I felt increasingly disturbed to have revealed myself to Clark. He was a *convicted felon*; he'd done *jail time* for hacking information that was none of his business. What had I been thinking? Walking west, in the direction of the hospital, I dialed Detective Lazare.

"I'm in Manhattan and I just ran into an inmate from the prison: Clark Hazmat. Is he on your list?"

"Hold on. I'll check."

In the minutes it took me to walk west on Fifty-eighth Street to Ninth Avenue, where I could see the hospital entrance down the block, the detective was back on the line.

"Yup, he's on the list and he's cleared. No connection to Zara Moklas or Thomas Soiffer. Our people talked to him, but don't worry—he doesn't know why."

"It's just that he was right there when I came out of the store—like he was waiting for me."

"We'll check him out a little more if you want."

"Thank you," I said. And then, "Detective Lazare . . . the window . . . were there fingerprints?"

"Only from the guys who installed it and the people who put in the alarm system. No Thomas Soiffer, or Clark Hazmat, if that puts your mind at rest."

My mind at rest. A contradiction in terms.

"Yes," I answered, "it does."

"So you're in Manhattan . . ."

"The orientation for my new job is today. I told you about it."

"I remember. It's just that I thought I saw you in town this morning with your baby."

As soon as he said it, Julie and Lexy appeared in my mind: walking down Main Street, Lexy with one chubby leg thrown over the side of her poppy red stroller, a plastic shopping bag hanging off one handle. It made me so happy to see them even if it was only a fantasy.

"That was Julie," I said. "She's watching Lexy while I'm here."

"So, you're going through with it."

"Are you married, Detective?"

After a pause, he answered, "Yes."

"How long?"

"Thirty years."

"Congratulations. I hope by now you've both aired all your secrets."

"Not everyone has secrets, Annie."

"I have to go."

"By the way, speaking of secrets, Clark Hazmat isn't his real name. It's Jesus-Ramon Hazamattian."

"Yikes."

"At least he didn't change it to Clark Kent. Hazmat's not so bad. Probably thought it up after a long road trip with a few bridge and tunnel crossings."

I thought of the ubiquitous highway signs declaring No HAZMATS. *Hazmat*: hazardous material. It was the perfect name for Clark.

"So will you call me if I *do* need to worry about him?" I asked.

"Yes, I'll call you."

"Any news about Thomas Soiffer?"

"Nothing. But Annie, don't worry about him either. He's a person of interest, that's all."

Aren't we all persons of interest? I wanted to say, but instead chose a simpler good-bye. "Thanks, Detective. I really have to go now."

I had walked into the hospital's bustling lobby, where a sign on the wall read: PLEASE TURN OFF ALL ELECTRONIC DEVICES. He said good-bye and I turned off my cell phone and dropped it into my purse. At the information desk a man listened to my name and reason for visiting, made a phone call, then handed me a stick-on personalized guest badge. I peeled off the backing, which I balled up and tossed into an unused ashtray in the elevator bank. Wearing my green-rimmed name tag, I rode the antiseptic-smelling elevator to the third floor, as instructed. The doors parted with a ding. I stepped into an empty foyer. To my right was a wide glass door through which I saw what had to be my fellow new employees, about ten of them, also conservatively dressed and wearing their names in bold black marker.

"Annie Milliken?"

I looked to my left. A woman with straight brown hair and rectangular glasses smiled at me pleasantly. She was wearing red slacks and very pointy shoes and stood in front of a wooden door. A laminated identification card hung like a necklace over her white silk blouse.

"We've been waiting for you," she said. "Would you mind coming with me?"

"But I'm here for the orientation. Isn't it that way?" I pointed to the glass door.

"Please." Her pleasant smile seemed frozen in a way that made my skin crawl.

"And you are . . . ?"

"Emily Leary, human resources director. *Please.*" She opened the wooden door and gestured for me to go in. "We don't want to embarrass you."

Embarrass me? What did I have to be embarrassed about, here in this hospital, where I had never before set foot? All my life's transgressions flashed through my mind as I tried to rationalize being culled from my orientation colleagues. Had my mascara run before when I started to cry, talking with Clark? Or had Kent, Lord of the Evil Fortress, been in touch with Ms. Leary to pave my way with unmerited land mines? That had to be it. The hospital had been going through my paperwork in advance of my orientation, as they'd said they would, and had had the dishonor of a conversation with Lord Kent himself. That man was even viler than

I'd thought, but I was sure it was nothing I couldn't clear up.

"Thank you." I smiled politely, following Ms. Leary through the door and along a well-lit hallway. Our leather soles smacked arrhythmically against the glossy linoleum floor. We didn't speak, just smiled and walked until we reached a door with an embossed nameplate reading DIRECTOR OF HUMAN RESOURCES. She swung open the door and stood back as I walked into a cozy blue-carpeted reception area that buffered her office beyond it. I barely heard her whisper, "I'm sorry," as she closed the door behind me. She herself stayed out in the hall.

Sorry? I turned to face the door, wondering *why.* And then from her office into the reception area with its unmanned desk came two New York City police officers. The tall one had apparently been preappointed as the talker.

"Anais Milliken?" He pronounced it *Ann-anus,* and I resisted the urge to correct him (*Anna-ees*).

I held my tongue, answering simply, "Yes."

The chubby one lifted a pair of handcuffs off his heavily laden belt. He averted his eyes from my face and lifted my right wrist, gently, like a prom date about to bestow a corsage. Then he shackled both my wrists together behind my back.

"What is this? Where's that woman? *What's going on here?*"

"Anais Milliken, you are under arrest for grand larceny. You have the right to remain silent. You have the right to counsel. Anything you do or say can be used against you in a court of law . . ."

PART TWO

Chapter 6

The big fenced-in windows of Midtown North were so grimy that hardly any light filtered through and the bright spring morning quickly darkened. Before we could get much beyond the front doors I was directed through a security checkpoint. My stocking feet felt the coldness and hardness of the floor as I walked through the portal to collect my purse and shoes.

Voices clapped and echoed through the vast lobby with its high ceilings and marble floors, leftovers from another era. The place was busy, crowded with a crazy salad of cops, office workers, criminals—and me. My arresting officers jostled me through the flux of people until we reached a baroque wooden counter etched with graffiti: *dogeetdog, 20/2/life, poppa-ratzi*. A large black woman with a gold chain around the neck of her police uniform glared at me and then smirked at my companions.

"Whadygot, boys?"

"Booking."

"Name?"

"Ann-anus Milliken."

"*Anna-ees*." And then I spelled it: "A-n-a-i-s." If she was writing it down, it had to be right. "*Please*, this is a mistake. I didn't do anything wrong."

They all three laughed as if they'd *heard it all before*. Unless it was my *please*: white woman in business duds being so polite. Though both my cops were also white, they weren't white like *me* in my beige suit, my makeup, my done hair, my nice diction. In fact there were plenty of white people around; this was about something else, some huge misunderstanding.

"I'd like to make a phone call," I said.

Ignoring me, she took a large paper envelope on which she had written my name and the date and inflated it by slapping it against the air. "Phone, keys, jewelry. Empty your pockets. Dump the purse. Put it all in here."

"What?"

"I said—"

"No, I heard you, but—"

"You heard me? Then *do it*."

I did it.

"Take her upstairs."

Officer Williams nodded (he was the tall one; since the shock of my arrest I had taken note of their name tags and removed my own) and P.O. Kiatsis (flabby, pale) tapped my shoulder. I walked between them, weaving past harried clumps of people for whom my presence here was a non-event. Didn't *anyone* realize that I didn't belong here? That this was a terrible mistake? I tried to make eye contact with a professional-looking woman in a nice blue suit, but she ignored me, as did a short man with a blond toupee and a kind face, and a young woman with a high ponytail and huge hoop earrings, lugging a stenotype machine. *No one saw me.* We rumbled up three flights in a battered elevator, they looking anywhere but at me, me searching back and forth between their blank faces. Down a long hall. Through a reinforced-glass door with DETECTIVES UNIT in black lettering so degraded it was hard to read. Into a desk-crowded, noise-addled room where again no one paused to notice me. An odor of hamburgers and French fries lingered in the air. Scattered across desks were the remnants of half-eaten early lunches—splayed paper wrappings, pried-apart plastic salad containers, water bottles, popped soda cans. I felt sick and involuntarily heaved, just slightly, but enough that one of the detectives bothered a glance: a thick-necked young man in a T-shirt with a tiny bicycle on his chest. He looked away.

Against the wall, in a corner, was a shallow cell open to view like a cage. Officer Williams swung open the cell door. Kiatsis unlocked my handcuffs. My arms fell freely to my sides and I felt a warm rush of blood to my hands, realizing only now that they had grown numb. Both officers stared at me, waiting for me to step into the cell.

"Just tell me one thing," I said. "Who is charging me with grand larceny?"

"The Feds," Williams answered.

"No, I mean *who*? What organization? Who says I stole from them?"

"Don't know." His bland tone spoke volumes: *didn't*

know, didn't care. "There's a felony warrant on you. We're just holding you until the Feds get here."

I walked into the cell and turned around to face them. Williams clanked the door shut and turned the key. I was locked in now. Alone. *A prisoner.* And as I realized that, as it really sank in, panic switched on inside my brain. The awareness that I was trapped in this cell amplified my desire to leave it, and my inability to move, to burst out of here, quickly transformed into a feeling of suffocation. I had to get *out*, talk to someone, get some help.

"Officer Williams!" I said.

His attention had swerved to a pair of nearby detectives analyzing last night's baseball game. He turned partway back to face me now. "They'll get here soon," he said. "There's a phone on the wall. You got three calls."

"Then what?"

He nodded slowly (like he knew something I didn't), sighed deeply (like I wouldn't understand even he if tried to explain), shook his head (like I was a lost cause anyway) and turned his back on me (as if I didn't exist). Kiatsis was already across the room at the coffee machine.

As soon as he walked away I began to cry, and as I wiped my tears with my hands, I saw that bracelets of red swelling had replaced the depressions left by the handcuffs. I felt massively confused about why I was here—and yet *here I was.*

I turned to face my cell. *My cell.* Hard shelf of a bed, stainless-steel toilet with no seat, tiny stainless-steel sink. Affixed to the wall was a boxy blue phone with a short curly cord and push buttons. I lifted the receiver and the dial tone, a direct link to *outside*, was to me as brilliant and miraculous as the sound of the ocean discovered improbably inside a shell. I dialed, but four numbers into it I heard the incessant bleating of a blocked connection. Dialing nine for an outside line didn't work, nor did any other number.

"They don't make it simple."

An obese man in gray slacks and a blue dime-a-dozen button-down shirt was standing on the other side of my cell bars. An accumulation of sweat made his forehead shine. He carried an unlabeled manila file folder stacked atop a yellow legal pad.

"Maybe they should," I said, "if they're going to confiscate our phones."

He laughed, actually *laughed*, and opened the file, humming as he surveyed it. In the tense silence of him reading and me watching him I recognized the theme song of *Evita*. After a minute he closed the file and smiled at me.

"Anais," he said, pronouncing it correctly. "That's what I always wanted to name a daughter."

"Who are you?"

He stepped closer. "Evan Shoemaker, FBI. Sorry about all this. Normally I would have come for you myself, but Federal Plaza's on lockdown—anthrax scare; can you believe that's still going on?—so today everyone's getting processed through the City. Anais." He repeated my name. "I've been looking forward to meeting you." He reached through the bars to shake my hand. His was sweaty, but I didn't allow myself to flinch. This might be the person who could get me out of here.

"Thanks for coming," I said, meaning it, but it came out as a flippant remark that failed in the context of my crying-puffy face. He dug into his pants pocket and handed me a crumpled tissue. "I still don't know why I'm here," I said. "The officers wouldn't really speak to me."

"They take Poker Face 101 in cop school. The point is to speed up the arrest and get you in here faster so I can get you *out* faster."

He smiled, a nice smile, and I realized that trapped inside the fat was a handsome man. He motioned for Officer Williams to unlock the cell door and joined me inside. Sitting with me on my bench bed, he opened my file and consulted it again. As he read, I saw that his nails were perfectly filed and that he wore clear nail polish. His breath, each time he breathed out, was noticeably sour.

"This is some kind of mistake," I told him. "I was going to a job orientation. I'm a physical therapist."

He looked up with light brown eyes that struck me as gentle and understanding and even safe—until he spoke. "Grand larceny, it says here: embezzlement of federal funds. That's a felony. You're looking at some serious time."

"But that's wrong. They must have me mixed up with someone else."

He read off a list of details and they were all me. *Me*: name, birth date and place, Kentucky address, marital status, number of children, even my height, hair and the color of my eyes.

How could this be happening?

"Who's bringing the charge?" I asked.

His finger trailed down a page in the file, and stopped. "Says here, Federal Bureau of Prisons, Federal Medical Center in Lexington, Kentucky."

When I heard that, my stomach turned, my face felt clammily cold, my head seemed to spin. I glanced at the toilet, preparing to make a run for it.

"Take a deep breath," he said.

I did; I took two. And then the nausea passed. "Agent Shoemaker, please listen to me."

"I'm listening."

"Until recently, I was a commissioned officer with the United States Public Health Service. I worked in that prison, but I never embezzled anything. I am not a thief. I resigned and I think my boss might be getting some kind of revenge."

"If that's the case," he said calmly, "it shouldn't be a problem."

"I need to make my calls."

He crossed the room, dialed in the code for an outside line and held the receiver in my direction. "Here you go."

I tried Julie first. She didn't answer at home or on her cell. Then I thought of Bobby. He would be at work; he could speak directly with Kent and find out what was going on. I reached Bobby right away and told him everything.

"All right, Annie," he said in his most determined voice. *I'm going to build a chair; I can prune that tree myself; I plan to retire at forty-five; we'll get married; I will get you out of jail.* "I'm going to do two things now. No, three. First I'm going to make some calls and find you a lawyer—so don't say anything else to anyone. Promise?"

"Promise."

"Second, I'm going to find Kent. I've had it with that jerk-off and this time I'm not going to be diplomatic. If he did this, he's dog meat."

"*Thank you*," I said, trying not to cry again. "And Bobby, will you call Julie? I couldn't reach her. Tell her I'm okay."

"I will. And I'll be on a plane as soon as I can. Don't worry, Annie."

Don't worry? I was beyond worry; I was insane with panic. Alone and under arrest in Manhattan, a hundred and fifty miles from my baby. When I hung up the phone I realized that leaking breast milk had bled through my blouse. I had no choice but to test Agent Shoemaker's sympathy.

"I'm a nursing mother," I said. "My baby's in Massachusetts with my sister and my breast pump is in the apartment where I'm staying on Fifty-sixth Street."

"Your what?"

"Breast pump. To get the milk out of my breasts before they explode."

He seemed appalled at the thought of my breasts exploding in this very small cell, exploding all over *him*.

"They won't literally explode," I said, "but I could get mastitis and end up with an infection. If I don't get the milk out right away, it could get very bad." When Lexy was a newborn I once ignored my swelling, hardening, reddening breasts and within half an hour was shaking with fever. I massaged out the lumps and drained the milk, solving the crisis, and later learned that engorgement could lead to a serious infection that might actually land you in the hospital.

He ripped a clean sheet off his yellow pad and handed it to me along with his pen. "Write down what you need. I'll see what I can do."

I listed the particulars. "Thank you. You can send someone to the apartment for my pump or you can buy something new—I'll pay you back."

He nodded. Clearly he was in new territory here, but at least he was being polite about it. He took the sheet of paper with my instructions and stood up with his pad and file. Then he called to Officer Williams, who unlocked the door.

"I'm taking her downtown," Shoemaker told Williams.

Officer Williams reshackled me and the chafed skin on my wrists instantly burned on contact with the metal. Shoemaker handed him my list, which he then passed off to Officer Kiatsis as we crossed the room busy with detectives doing their jobs. Anonymity had never frightened me more than during my walk through that bustling room. These were the people, or the people of the people, who had mostly ignored me when I was brought in here before. When an older man with a single earring in his left lobe glanced at me with the shadow of a smile, I felt, instead of grateful, a shiver of hypocrisy; it was a hypocrisy I recognized, having once been on his side of the divide. In my Kentucky prison the staff had been *us* and the prisoners *them*, and now I had flipped categories, becoming one of *them*, without consideration, a social pariah. I knew this well from working at the prison clinic: you had a job to do and you did it the best you could without thinking about whether the prisoners were actually guilty or innocent. All you knew was that they were locked up and you weren't, and you took it from there. I ignored the lone friendly detective; despite his presumed good intentions, he could not possibly know my predicament and his almost-smile raised the barrier between us even higher, which made me feel even worse. My last view as I passed through the glass door—with a half-flaked-off TINU SEVITCETED confusing me for a moment before I realized it was DETECTIVES UNIT backward—was of Kiatsis reading my list and eyeing me with suspicion. And I felt overcome by helplessness. Would he bother to get the breast pump? Would I have to ask again? Would anyone listen?

After signing me out and picking up my envelope of belongings, Williams led me into the bright May noontime. Outside: warm springtime air; gas fumes and honking horns from cars jammed at the intersection; a young woman in a red dress and black sandals; a man in jeans and a leather jacket rushing into the precinct; a wiry messenger on a gold bike, weaving through traffic. I was steered toward a waiting squad car, which I'd been told would take us to Central Booking.

Shoemaker sat up front, separated from me by a scratched bulletproof barrier, and I sat alone in the cigarette- and sweat-reeking backseat where perps and prisoners rode to judgment. We drove downtown in a blur of swiftly passing blocks until, between hulking ornate buildings, I caught a glimpse of the Brooklyn Bridge. Its spun-sugar supports arced and dipped over the glistening slate blue river and I thought fleetingly of the sea, its endless acreage and horizons so distant they appeared unreachable. And then suddenly a building blocked the view and we pulled up in front of a ziggurat of a courthouse, tiered like a wedding cake. Officer Williams parallel-parked in a row of other authorized cars. Shoemaker stepped out onto the curb and opened the back door for me. Three abreast, we walked up the broad steps flanked by giant granite columns into another high-ceilinged nineteenth-century lobby that greeted you with twenty-first-century security checkpoints.

Central Booking was in the basement of the criminal courthouse. We rode down in a too bright elevator that delivered us into a cinder-block hallway with black stenciled-on arrows pointing us to Processing. There, in full view of everyone, I was fingerprinted, each fingertip rolled individually onto a pad of purplish ink and pressed onto a square on a white form labeled specifically for that finger. I had gone through this once before, when I joined the Public Health Service, and so the residual ink staining my fingers came as no surprise. What *did* surprise me, what in fact shocked me more than I would have imagined, was being photographed. A small board was hung around my neck, identifying me by place of arrest, booking number and today's date. When the flash went off I could feel from within the stunned expression, captured in digital memory, which would forever mark me as Accused. They had my mug shot. I was *processed*. As I was ushered along another cinder-block hallway,

Agent Shoemaker explained that the next step would be my arraignment.

"When?" I asked.

"Soon," he said. "The law says arraignment can't be more than twenty-four hours after arrest. In reality, though if it's crowded sometimes it takes longer."

We reached the women's holding cells. After consultation with the guard, Shoemaker assured me the courts were on schedule today. The guard was a hefty woman whose hair had been transformed into a mat of shiny, springy Jerri curls. She unlocked the least-crowded cell, where four other women sat or crouched or stood and a clogged toilet putrefied the air. When I stepped inside, the women looked at me and I looked at them, but none of us said hello. One of my cellmates, a skinny black woman in a plaid flannel shirt, slumped asleep or unconscious on the floor. Two plump Hispanic teenagers in hot pants and matching American flag tube tops watched me closely when I came in and then returned to their high-speed chattering. One girl had a cantaloupe-size bruise on her upper thigh. The fourth woman, a stout Chinese granny with gray hair in an ironed bandanna, stared angrily at the wall.

When I turned around, Officer Williams was gone. Shoemaker waited until I was locked in and then bid me good-bye with the promise that my lawyer would be along "soon." *Soon.* What did that mean? There were no clocks on the walls, no windows; the dim light that leaked from an overhead bulb kept you stationary in time. Waiting. The girls chatted. The skinny woman slept. The Chinese woman fumed. I paced, mind grinding, heart throbbing. From time to time I paused to gulp air, forcing deep inhales when I realized I'd stopped breathing.

Eventually someone delivered a brown paper bag containing a breast pump. Facing the corner of the cell, pumping milk from my engorged breasts (with an apparatus that was neither mine nor new; it had been offered with no explanation of its origins), I could feel the girls' eyes on my back. By their whispers I gathered that they were both curious and disgusted by the mysterious collaboration between suctioning machine and woman's breast; and just as I thought that, I wondered if, despite their age, either had ever known motherhood—motherhood truncated, perhaps, at some point in the process.

Finally the Chinese woman's voice rang out: "Okay, that enough. Show over!" She had a strong accent and an unmistakable tone of authority. When I turned to look at her, her gaze was back on the wall. Still, I was grateful. On the floor I collected two uncapped baby bottles of milk that Lexy would never drink. My cellmates all kept clear of the bottles, respecting them, it seemed, and it struck me as an unexpected respite to be here among women.

I didn't know what time it was when my attorney arrived, but it felt like the end of the day. There had been a change of guard and the soupy light seemed to have grown dimmer. The new guard, a middle-aged Puerto Rican with manicured fire red claws, unlocked the door and waved me over. I was taken to an interview booth—two counters facing each other in a tiny cubicle halved by foggy Plexiglas—where a woman in a turquoise blouse introduced herself.

"I'm Elizabeth Mann. You can call me Liz," she said in a confident, professional voice. Her bleached blond hair fell stiffly to her shoulder blades and was parted in the middle, dead center. "I've been working on your case all afternoon, Anais—or do I call you Annie?"

"Everyone does."

"Anais is just so beautiful." Her teeth were perfectly straight but yellowed from caffeine and that was when I started to trust her: despite the easy prophylactic of blonding her hair, the rest of her showed the real stripes of her age. She had a superbly weathered face and enough bloodshot in her pretty blue eyes to suggest she worked hard. I knew that Bobby would spare no expense in getting me a good lawyer. *Liz Mann.* Yes: welcome to my world.

"Annie's easier," I said, "and I'm used to it."

We talked. She took notes. I explained everything I knew, which wasn't much. She and Bobby had spoken at length and she knew about our marital problems and she also knew about Zara Moklas's murder. She knew *all* about Kent, who had sworn on a Bible, personally, to her on the telephone, that he had nothing to do with this. What she didn't know was that I'd lost my wallet.

"When?" she asked.

"Thursday."

"Where?"

"Great Barrington," I said. "Probably somewhere in town—I'm not sure."

"How much was in it?"

"Not much, maybe twenty dollars."

"Credit cards? Other kinds of identification?"

"Lots, I guess. Credit cards, driver's license, car registration, my Social Security card, some store cards, stuff like that."

"*Very* good," she said.

"It didn't seem like it at the time."

"Have you ever heard of identity theft?"

"Of course." And then it hit me: my lost wallet. Why hadn't I thought of it before? The shock of being arrested and held and *processed* had sent my thoughts reeling in all the wrong directions. "But I canceled all my cards."

"How soon?"

"The next day."

"One night is plenty of time for an identity thief. The damage they can do in minutes is mind-boggling." She leaned forward, so close I could see details of her skin through the thick plastic partition, how her face makeup was a little too dark and how it filled enlarged pores. "Arrest warrants don't take that long to process through the system. As soon as they're issued, they're out there and the police respond to them. I'm not saying this is what happened, but it's possible that whoever has your wallet got right to work and committed a crime using your identity."

"That fast—it's hard to believe."

"I know it is," she said, "but time the way we think of *time* doesn't exist in cyberspace. With enough information, someone can nab your identity in minutes on the Internet, sitting at home in their bathrobe. Believe me, *anything* is possible."

"So how do we prove that?"

"We don't. We start by demonstrating to a judge that it's a *possibility* and showing that you have no criminal record. We ask the judge to set reasonable bail. We get you out and then we start searching for the proof."

"But *how*?"

"I'm going to explain everything to you as we go, but first things first." She stood up and tucked her files and pad under her arm. "I'm going to see if I can get us on tonight's docket. I'll see if we can get you an ROR. Otherwise I'll ask the judge to set bail."

I must have looked as bewildered as I felt.

"Release on recognizance, without having to post bail," she explained. "The charge would still stand, but you could move freely within the state."

It sounded more hopeful than anything else I'd heard in the last eight hours, and I thanked her.

A few minutes later, back in the cell for more waiting, I was surprised to find only the Chinese woman there, alone, still staring at the wall. I felt a little disappointed that the Hispanic girls were gone; I was sure they would have wanted to know what had happened and I wanted to *talk*.

"I have a lawyer," I told my lone remaining cellmate. "I'm getting arraigned soon."

She looked at me now. In her small, dark eyes I saw that it wasn't anger I'd perceived in her face before. It was longing.

"Good," she said.

"And you?" I asked her.

She said only, "I finished," and then her eyes again found the wall.

Liz eventually returned. When the guard unlocked

the cell I said good-bye to the Chinese woman, but she didn't respond. I felt terrible for her, worse than for the other women. I had the sense that something unexpected had shattered this woman's life, that she may have reacted badly to some grave surprise and she already knew that her reaction would cost her everything. *Did she have family who would help her now?* I wondered, following Liz down the hall.

We walked quickly through a maze of underground corridors until a different elevator took us up two flights to the courtrooms. "We've got a decent judge," Liz said. "He was willing to squeeze us onto his docket. And your husband's waiting."

"Bobby's here?"

Liz nodded. "You'll only have a minute to talk before we go in."

We found Bobby pacing in the broad hallway outside the courtroom. The marble floor was glassily polished, making his every step squeak, and under the high ceiling he seemed very small. His work clothes—blue slacks and white shirt—looked wilted after the long flight. He was wearing his brown corduroy jacket, the one he kept in our downstairs hall closet, which told me he had stopped at home on his way to the airport. I wondered why he had taken the time. That he had changed from shoes to sneakers said he was planning on testing his endurance. His face looked a little haggard, as if he had already been up all night.

I stood in front of him, all rumpled beige suit and torn stockings and scrambled hair and mascara-darkened eyes, hands manacled behind me, lawyer and guard on either side.

"Oh, Annie." It was that luscious voice of his, soft and a little coarse when he felt moved.

I stepped toward him and he put his arms around me. He kissed my cheek twice and the tears just seemed to heave out of me. "It's okay. Shh, shh. We'll work this out."

"Did you reach Julie?"

He shook his head. "I left her a few messages. I gave her your cell number since mine won't work here."

"They took my cell phone," I said. "She won't be able to reach me."

Liz, who stood off to the side, interjected, "You'll get that back when this is over."

"But what if something happens to Lexy?" I asked her. "What if Lexy or Julie *needs* us?"

"I know it's frustrating," Liz said. "Just be patient."

Easier said than done, but what choice did I have?

"What about Kent?" I asked Bobby. "Did you talk to him?"

"He doesn't know anything about it," he said. "He seemed pretty upset, actually. He said he was sorry we were going through this and he wanted to be supportive."

"*Kent* said that?"

"Believe it or not, he did."

Liz glanced at her watch. "All right, guys, let's have a word before we go in." Her voice fell to a whisper: "I think we'll do fine with this judge, but he's famous for not giving RORs. We should expect bail, so, Bobby, why don't you save your wife some time by getting the ball rolling?" She handed him a business card. I managed to read the larger print: BAD SEED BAIL BONDS.

"It's across the street and left one block. They're open twenty-four hours. Ask for Vinnie and tell him I sent you. Tell him to start the paperwork; I'll call you at Vinnie's number with the amount. You brought it, right?"

"Yes." He touched the outside of his jacket and I remembered that it had a deep inner pocket.

"Brought what?" I asked.

"Don't worry, Annie," Bobby said.

"Don't *worry*?"

"He's right," Liz said. "All you should be thinking about right now is getting out. Your house should have enough value to cover a bond. We'll get you out, we'll clear up the charge, and you'll buy back the bail bond."

Was *that* what he had in his jacket pocket? The deed to our *house*?

"No, Bobby!"

"Annie," he said, "we have no choice."

He turned around and left us, and the nightmare continued. I could hardly believe how quickly things could fall apart. Liz took my arm and guided me through a smaller-scale security checkpoint and into the belly of the courtroom.

Chapter 7

My bail was set at two hundred fifty thousand dollars, less than the value of our house if you counted equity. That house amounted to most of what I had, since I'd failed to vest my pension by the time I resigned my commission. I was glad that Bobby had his own well-funded pension, because if this nightmare continued to implode, if we couldn't find the proof Liz was so certain of, I wanted him to have more of me than just my share of the house. He would have Lexy if I landed in jail for this crime I didn't commit; he would have Lexy and his pension and the house; he could sell it and move. He could find a new wife. He could start over.

"What are you thinking?" Bobby sat beside me in the back of a yellow cab. It was nearly midnight and Liz had taken her own taxi home. He had turned his attention from the cascade of urban images to look at me, but I couldn't look at him; I had my purse, my watch and my cell phone back—with only one unlistened-to voice mail, from Clark Hazmat, of all people; Julie still hadn't returned Bobby's calls—but my dignity had stayed behind in that paper envelope.

"Nothing." How could I tell him what I was thinking? Despite my innocence I felt ashamed for having been arrested. I even felt ashamed for having ever left him. I was glad Lexy would be too young to remember this episode in our lives and I vowed that if we came through this whole I would never let my imagination stray from what was important: each other, our family, our home. "I want to see Lexy. Can't we go straight back to Julie's?"

"We have to do what Liz said. Get some sleep, find out why this happened, work with her to get it cleared up."

"Could you actually go to sleep?" I asked.

"No. Could you?"

"No way."

"Listen, Annie. On the plane I started reading a book about identity theft that I picked up at the airport. It said everything shows up on credit reports, even arrest warrants."

"Liz said there's no such thing as time in cyberspace and that if this is all because of my wallet getting lost—"

"That's right. She told me the same thing. That's why I bought the book."

"But it's just so hard to believe a thief could accomplish so much in four days!"

"According to the book," he said, "it can happen that fast. Those reports are updated daily. So if whoever has your wallet also bought stuff before the accounts were canceled, if he committed a crime, it'll all show up."

"Embezzlement? In four days? That's impossible!"

"I don't understand this either. The computer guy who was coming tonight was going to help me pull our current credit reports, but obviously that didn't happen. So let's do it right now. We'll start there, see how far the damage goes. Is there a computer at the apartment?"

"No," I said. Bobby had never seen the studio; we had often discussed coming for a New York weekend but had never gotten around to it.

"There must be a cybercafe open somewhere." He leaned toward the front seat, presumably to ask the driver where we could rent computer time, but I stopped him.

"I need about fifteen minutes with my pump. We have to go back to the apartment." As always, biology trumped all, and we continued to East Fifty-sixth Street.

When we arrived, the street was illuminated by the generalized ambient glow that spread over the city at night. It was never completely dark here. Bobby paid the driver and we hurried into the building, winding up the five flights of stairs.

I switched on a few lights in the apartment and stood at the dish drainer piecing together my breast pump with such haste that parts of it fell to the floor. I didn't bother rewashing them; I wasn't going to take the time to save the milk tonight, breast relief being my only goal. Bobby sat at the table leafing through the Yellow Pages while I pumped on the couch. When I was through I washed up and changed my clothes. Twenty minutes later we were out the door and in another taxi on our way to Twelfth Night, an Internet cafe on Twelfth Street and Seventh Avenue—the third one Bobby had called and the first one that was open all night.

The street outside was so quiet, it was a surprise to find the cafe as full as it was. About twenty men and women sat alone at tables with their laptop screens glowing in the barely lit space. Some typed furiously, others pecked, and a few sat staring at their screens. Everyone here was alone, busily absorbed in their personal space, surrounded by crushed newspapers, open books and chunky white mugs dripping coffee, tea, cocoa down their sides. Except for the two young men behind the counter—one skinny and spike-haired, the other shaved bald with a massive beard gathered in a frontal ponytail—Bobby and I were the only two people who were in any way together.

Most had brought their own laptops, but there were also five computers bolted down on a shelf against one wall. Three of these were available. We went to the counter to rent one.

"How much time?" Spike-head smiled and all the implied toughness of his hairdo melted away; he was just a kid, probably barely legal. His tight-fitting T-shirt read JOEY where a breast pocket might have been.

Bobby opened his wallet and produced a twenty-dollar bill. "I'm not sure. Can we just pay by the half hour?"

"We don't do cash after midnight. Credit cards only." The man-boy pointed to the brick wall behind him, where a handwritten sign repeated his words verbatim. "We got robbed like three times after midnight this year alone."

Bobby and I looked at each other. Between us we had no plastic: zero credit cards, zero debit cards, not even a check (though they probably didn't do checks either, especially from out of state). Then I remembered that I still had Julie's credit card and driver's license. I pulled them out of my purse's interior pocket and handed them over. "Here you go, Joey. And will you put two coffees on that, please?"

"Name's not Joey." He looked at me like I was insane to have thought so.

Bobby forced back a smile and I saw us fifteen years later, agreeing with whatever illogic our teenage daughter insisted on. Then I saw other children pop up around us. We *had* to get through this so we could reach that time.

Not-Joey swiped the credit card through the machine and while we waited he compared Julie's driver's license photo to my face. When I signed the chit he checked the signatures against each other. Then he handed back the cards along with my receipt.

"Thanks." I zipped the cards back into my purse.

He checked a notebook, then wrote something on a slip of paper, which he handed to Bobby. "You're on Number Five. This is your password. The computer will time you, but when you're done you gotta log out or you'll keep on paying. I've seen it happen."

"That would be bad," Bobby politely agreed, sliding me a cynical glance. The kid had no idea.

"You gonna print?"

"Don't know."

"Printing costs extra. It's by the page." He pointed behind him to another sign reading PRINTING CHARGED BY THE PAGE. "If you print, we'll add it on after."

"Thanks," Bobby said.

We carried our coffees to the far end of the counter closest to the window overlooking a semidark middle-of-the-night Greenwich Village street. All around us our sleepless noncompanions clicked away and ignored each other. I logged us on and our flat screen sprang to life. Bobby and I were alone in that cafe, in our own little bubble, as we set about searching for answers.

"Here we go," he whispered.

"I love you, Bobby, for all of this."

He smiled tentatively, as if he wasn't sure I'd really said that, then pulled a paperback copy of *Identity Theft in a New World* out of his jacket pocket and thumbed to a glossary in the back. After a moment of looking he typed the address for Equifax into the browser's window. The Equifax home page appeared. One of their products was a "3-in-1" combination of reports from all three of the major credit-rating agencies: Equifax, Trans-Union and Experian.

"That's what we want." Bobby clicked on it and a new menu appeared.

He was a little slow navigating the cursor through all the steps, so I took over. We used Julie's credit card to order a report that promised to show activity on all of Bobby's and my accounts as recently as yesterday. In less than a minute our receipt informed us that the report would arrive via e-mail within half an hour.

While we waited I Googled my name to see if anything incriminating popped up in relation to my new life as an embezzler. I was listed in only three places: on a federal prison staff directory and on two sites related to photography. Then we Googled Bobby's name and learned that he was even more nonexistent in cyberspace than I was, appearing only on the staff directory. Lexy's name brought up nothing (a relief). But Julie—Julie was famous. Her name brought up over ten thousand hits, ranging from her Web site to professional articles to marketing blogs to cyber-dating links. Seeing the repetition of her name made me sharply miss her and by association Lexy (*always* Lexy) and if it hadn't been so late I would have tried calling them again. I clicked on a few of Julie's links, but we were far too anxious about seeing our credit report to really check them out. Every few minutes we maximized my Web-mail page to run e-mail. The usual junk just kept coming in, flying to me like I was a cyber-magnet, everything except the one thing I really wanted.

And then, there it was. Our credit reports came in two separate files: Anais Faith Milliken and Robert Bowie Goodman. We opened mine first.

After my name was my Lexington address (calling our road a lane and with the zip code completely wrong) and my job history (showing me as a therapist, not a *physical* therapist, at the prison and completely omitting my underrealized career as a photographer, which made it look as if I hadn't been gainfully employed for most of my adulthood, whereas in one way or another I actually had been). Below those blocks of misinformation blared the words FELONY WARRANT.

"Look at the date." Bobby's outstretched finger touched the screen.

"That's last week."

"*Before* you lost your wallet."

As we paged through the voluminous report it got stranger and stranger. There were Visa and MasterCard accounts with store and company associations I had never heard of, all opened in the recent past. I had never shopped at Neiman Marcus or Harry Winston or bought myself *anything* at Bergdorf Goodman. I had *never* had that kind of money. There were also loans— loans *I* had never taken. I did *not* own a Jaguar purchased from a dealer in Santa Monica!

The more I read, the more my blood boiled. I started pounding the keyboard so hard as I scrolled through screen after screen of me-getting-ripped-off that a couple of the great American novelists in the cafe turned around to notice me, annoyed. I ignored them. Bobby put his hand on the back of my neck and the warmth of his touch automatically slowed my pulse. I heard his deep, deep sigh. My fingers stopped typing and I turned to him.

"Why haven't we gotten any of these bills?" I asked.

"I don't know."

"I've been going over our credit reports with a fine-tooth comb, Bobby. *None* of this was there. This doesn't make any sense."

"Those printouts are two months old."

"I didn't realize they'd be wrong so fast."

"Neither did I." He shook his head. "If one of us had thought to look this up before you walked out—"

"You were having an affair!" My voice, I realized,

sounded hysterical. From the corner of my eye I saw a writer arise and whisper to the bearded man behind the counter. They both glanced our way. I shrugged and pressed an extended finger to my lips in a promise of future quiet.

Bobby leaned in close and whispered as adamantly as a whisper could be: "But I wasn't! *That* was all part of *this*. Don't you see it?"

I reared back on my stool. Yes, I saw it. All of a sudden it was very clear: the amorous-looking credit card charges had been signs of betrayal, but not the kind I had assumed. They had been a mere foreshadowing of something far worse. Some thief had not been stealing Bobby—he had been stealing *me*. In secret. He had established credit accounts in our name and made sure the bills never reached us—but why had he put those Lovyluv charges on the cards we regularly used? Had he wanted me to *think* Bobby was having an affair? But what was his reasoning, knowing we would ultimately learn about the rest?

"What about those e-mails from Lovyluv?" I asked. "I know I've said it a million times, but how did she know so much about you?"

"I don't know. I'm as baffled by this as you are, Annie. That's what I've been telling you all along."

He was right. The first suspicious charges made more sense than they ever had and the e-mails made as little sense, but somehow they were part of this.

"There are 800 numbers listed with some of the credit cards," Bobby said. "Let's start calling them."

He recited a MasterCard customer service number and I dialed. Three a.m. not being peak business hours, there was no wait for the "customer care specialist," who turned out to be a young Indian man introducing himself as Don. My call had clearly been routed over-seas and normally I might have coaxed him a little, asked him for his real name (Sanjay? Rajeev?) but not now. I told him I had never received a bill for this ac-count and he confirmed that it had been open for nearly two months, generating two monthly bills, both of which had been sent to my home address in Lexington and both of which had been answered with the mini-mum payment.

"But that's not possible," I said. "I didn't make those charges and I didn't pay those bills."

"But, ma'am, they have been paid."

"Can you find out who paid them?"

"Yes, ma'am." Far off in some other country, his fin-gers clicked away. "Here it is. You paid them."

"But it wasn't me!"

"Do you feel these bills may have been intercepted, ma'am?"

And then I got it. The accounts had been opened in my name, but someone had intercepted the bills before they reached me, which was why we never knew about them.

"I *know* they have been."

"We can put a fraud alert on your account, if you wish."

"I wish."

I listened as he typed some more.

"All right, ma'am. It is done."

"Thank you. Now can you do something else for me? Can you please read me the bills?"

"Every item?"

"Are there *that* many?"

"I will read them." And he did. And there were. Dozens and dozens of outrageous charges had been made to this one credit card, things I would never buy in a million years. High-end electronics. Car supplies for the Jaguar. Home furnishings. Expensive hair salons in three different states. Top-of-the-line skin-care products. Men's clothing. Women's clothing. When he read off an eight-thousand-dollar charge to a jeweler, I nearly choked.

"Where?"

"Jewelry.com, ma'am. Would you like their 800 number?"

I wrote it down. He read off a few more items, but his voice had become a drone in my buzzing brain. Eight thousand dollars on jewelry? I had never owned a decent piece of jewelry in my life! I watched Bobby watch me hearing Don list the financial degradation of my (formerly) good name. The concern in my husband's expression was painful. Bobby Goodman was a practical man; he wouldn't waste eight thousand dollars on jewelry for me or Lovyluv or anyone else. When Don got to the end of the list, his voice trailed off as if he were ashamed. I felt it too; there was something almost obscene about such brazen spending.

"Thank you, Don."

"My pleasure, ma'am. What I mean is—"

"That's okay. You didn't buy all that stuff . . . did you?"

There was silence.

"I'm *kidding*."

"Oh, I see." And he forced a laugh. "Ma'am? If I may make a suggestion? You might contact a credit agency and ask them also to post a fraud alert. It doesn't matter which one, they will share the information."

"I'll do it right away."

"Is there anything else I can help you with today, ma'am?"

Night, I wanted to cry. *It's night, not day, and this isn't happening to me.*

"Thank you, no."

Bobby went online to find out how to post a fraud alert with Equifax while I dialed the 800 number for Jewelry.com. Being an Internet retailer, it employed a twenty-four-hour customer service center to handle their calls. Again I was routed to India, this time greeted by a young woman whose real name undoubtedly was not Mary. I asked her to look up the purchase and gave her the date and amount.

"Yes, here it is. Earrings, ma'am. Diamonds. They must be very beautiful. I hope you are enjoying them."

"I'm *not* enjoying them. I don't *have* them."

"Did you purchase the optional insurance?"

"I didn't purchase anything." I tried to explain, but she continued to think the earrings themselves had been stolen.

"The credit card may offer insurance, ma'am. You may wish to call the credit card company."

"I just did." *Frustration.* But it wasn't Mary's fault. "Just one more question. Do your records show a description of the earrings?"

"White diamonds," she said. "One carat, round studs in a platinum setting."

"What address were they delivered to?"

"Let me see." Fast, clicking fingers thousands of miles away. "It was a UPS store in Lexington, Kentucky, 838 High Street, Ashland Plaza."

I knew the place, I'd passed it, but I'd never gone in.

"Is that the same address as on the credit card?" I asked.

"No, it was not. I am not authorized to release that information. For that, you must call the credit card company."

"Can you *please* just tell me where the card was issued? What state?"

"I am very sorry."

I took a deep breath and managed a polite good-bye, reminding myself that this was not Mary's fault, that eight thousand dollars could probably feed her entire extended family for a year and she should be commended for managing to keep her disdain to herself.

Bobby swiveled to face me. "Done. Equifax has the fraud alert and they'll share it."

"Good." Then I repeated my conversation with Mary. As I spoke, whispering, Bobby seemed to search my face. Then his gaze settled on my right ear; he was staring at my earring. He lifted a finger and gently touched it.

"These are round," he said, "and isn't this platinum? I wonder how many carats they are."

"*Zero* carats, Bobby. And it's silver, not platinum. They're *fakes*."

His hand fell to his lap and he stared at me, thinking

something over, weighing the decision to speak his mind. Bobby was not the kind of person who made idle accusations and yet as soon as he started talking I knew what he was thinking. When Mary had described the earrings, I'd thought it too—she was describing *my* earrings—except for one crucial difference: mine were fakes and they didn't cost eight thousand dollars. They were a gift from Julie and obviously she had nothing to do with this. Why would she? And anyway, Julie had bought *two* pair, one for each of us, and this charge was for only one pair. It took all my strength not to tell Bobby to save his breath. He had been very patient with me, forgiving in the extreme, and the least I could do was hear him out.

"Those accounts and those charges start appearing about two months ago, *before* your wallet was stolen, right?" he asked.

"Right."

"About the time of the other charges, the ones on our real accounts."

"The Lovyluv charges," I said.

His jaw ground a little at that.

"Okay, the bogus charges I *thought* were gifts for Lovyluv."

"Exactly. Which were made around the time of the e-mails that we both agree were fake," he said. "Right, Annie?"

"Right, though I don't get how such personal e-mails *can* be faked, you know? That's what I can't figure out—"

"Annie!"

"But it doesn't make *sense*."

"It doesn't make sense to me either, but they're obviously connected to all this. Don't you agree with that?"

"Yes. Yes, I do, Bobby. It's just . . ."

I could see how frustrated he was getting with me, but my mind was stuck on the e-mails. I agreed that they were connected to the bogus charges; I believed that because it was logical. But *why* was this evil e-mailer of Bobby's trying to ruin *me*? My attempted replies to Lovyluv had bounced back, but surely they could be traced to a real person, and maybe this person (who knew so much about Bobby's body) had sown this havoc in revenge. Maybe he had broken up with her when he realized I might really leave him; *that* was logical, too. Bobby had spurned his lover and she had gone berserk.

"It's just that . . . the description of your birthmark on your lower back, Bobby . . . the nickname . . . the description of you making love—"

"I think Julie wrote those e-mails!" He blurted it out just like that.

"That's *ridiculous*!"

"I confronted her about it last weekend—"

"Are you saying Julie was your lover?" Even as I said it, I couldn't believe it would be true.

"No."

"Then *why* would she send the e-mails?"

His neck had thickened and his face was red; he looked like he was tamping down an explosion. And then it just burst out: "Because she *wanted* to sleep with me. She tried to seduce me and I turned her down."

"What?"

"It's the truth." He shook his head slowly as if he himself could hardly believe it. "I didn't want to tell you. I knew you wouldn't believe me, I know how close you two are, and things were hard enough between us, so I kept it to myself."

He was right; I *didn't* believe him. "If you make that kind of accusation, Bobby, you better be able to back it up. Because it is way way *way* out of line. You're talking about Julie, my twin sister—"

"I realize that, Annie. She's like a part of you."

"No. She *is* part of me. We are *one* person. What you're saying cannot possibly be true."

He tried to take my hand, but I pulled it away. *No.* Our voices had risen again and now everyone in the cafe seemed to be watching us, but I didn't care and evidently neither did Bobby. His tone was firm as he persisted in trying to convince me of something I found unbelievable.

"It was last Thanksgiving," he said. "When you were pregnant. She wasn't subtle about it."

"I don't believe you."

"It's true."

"I *hate* you."

"It's still true. *Think* about it, Annie."

But thinking was impossible. I was engulfed by blustery hot feeling that told me Julie would never seduce my husband and that if she had (which she wouldn't!) I would have known about it. Somehow I would have sensed it.

"It's a lie," I said.

"I think she sent the e-mails. I've thought so all

along. I mean, she's seen me in a bathing suit; she knows what I look like enough to fake these descriptions."

"Then why didn't you say something to me?"

"For this very reason. Because of *this*—your reaction. I was afraid of exactly what's happening right now. I mean, my God, if I criticize her hairstyle you take it personally."

Even as he spoke, even as I hated him for what he was saying, I knew he was right about the predictability of my reactions when it came to Julie. Bobby had never been allowed to critique so much as a hair on her head; I had made that perfectly clear from the beginning.

"And when you confronted her over the weekend?" I could see them sitting together beneath the weeping willow, the look on his face caught by my camera: vexation. "She denied it, didn't she?"

"Of course she did," he said.

"Then why did you bother asking her?"

"I don't know. I guess I was hoping she'd admit it and tell you and we could put an end to all of this. I wanted you to come home with me."

"So you thought if Julie came to me and said, 'Oh, don't worry. I sent those e-mails,' I would have just said, 'Oh, okay, that solves that,' and then I would have just packed in all my plans and gone back to Lexington? You actually thought it would be that simple?"

He didn't answer.

"And you honestly think Julie made all those charges to our accounts and took out all those new credit cards and bought a *car* on our dime? You really believe that? Julie, who earns more money in one year than either of *us* will ever see in a lifetime?"

"Yes," he said.

"Well, I *don't* believe it."

"But it could be true."

"Then prove it."

"We'll have your earrings appraised and then—"

"No way, Bobby!"

"What could you lose by getting them appraised? It's cold, hard information."

"Cold and hard. That's right." I stood up. "I'm going to get my stuff and I'm heading back to Great Barrington."

"Annie, you have a bond that says you can't leave the state."

"Well, I *am* leaving the state. I'm going back to see my daughter."

I grabbed my purse and stalked out of the cafe with all those introverted eyes watching me. Well, now they really had something to write about! Outside, I hailed a cab and told the driver to take me to Fifty-sixth Street. All the way back to the studio, I fumed. What had I been thinking? How had I imagined it would be so simple for me and Bobby to get back together? And why would I want to? The suggestion that Julie could have had anything to do with the nightmare that had swallowed me today—had been swallowing me, it turned out, for *two months*—was outrageous, insulting, ludicrous, unbelievable, *so* off the wall that I didn't think I could ever talk to Bobby again. I stormed around the studio, packing, then went downstairs to walk the two blocks to the garage where I had stowed

Julie's car (*an Audi*, I wanted to tell Bobby, *that she bought with her own money*).

It was dark out and chilly. The city was eerily quiet at almost five in the morning. My heart raced when a taxi revved around the corner. I felt safer when I passed an all-night deli in which the counterman was deep in conversation with a woman dressed like a hooker—no, it was a man dressed like a woman dressed like a hooker. I kept walking, grateful for the constant shafts of artificial light against which darkness failed to assert itself. Almost inevitably as I walked, pulling my suitcase, I thought about Zara Moklas. How she had looked like me and Julie; how easy it would have been for anyone to mistake her for us in the dark. And then something really disturbing occurred to me: Could Bobby have gone that far in his delusion about Julie? *Could* he have tried to kill her, coming upon Zara instead? Had he thought that if Julie was gone everything would just stop and I would come home? That I would be heartbroken and run back to him?

Could he possibly be guilty of Zara's murder after all?

I walked faster now. The red-and-white PARKING GARAGE sign was visible down the block. My suitcase's wheels made a racket when I broke into a jog. The streets felt unsafe to me now and I wanted to be inside the garage's office, in the warmth, paying (with Julie's card) and making my way back to safety . . . to my sister . . . to my baby girl.

When I turned into the garage the smell of gas fumes was familiar and even a little reassuring and I felt a warm rush of relief. But then my insides jumped. There was Julie's car, engine running, and there, standing next to it, was Bobby.

"Get in, Annie."

I looked around. I didn't see an attendant anywhere.

"Please get into the car."

"I can't. You said so yourself: the bond says I can't leave the state."

"I spoke with Liz about Lexy and how we can't reach Julie, and she made a call. The judge agreed to modify your bond so you can travel to Massachusetts; he'll have the modification filed first thing in the morning. You just have to check in with the Great Barrington police when we get there. Come on, *get in*. We're wasting time."

His tone was clear: he wanted to get to Lexy (and so did I! *So did I!*) because she was alone with my sister, whom he now openly distrusted. I knew he was overreacting; Lexy was safe and sound with Julie, who loved my little baby almost as much as I did. It was Bobby I was worried about now. I hadn't realized his thinking about Julie had grown so extreme. The gas fumes inside the garage were strong and I felt a little queasy. My body wanted to get into the car, to hurry back to Lexy, but only because I missed her. I just wasn't sure about going with *him*. I had to say what I was thinking, to find out.

"*Did* you kill Zara?" I asked.

"Are you serious?"

"I've never actually asked you, so will you just tell me?"

"No," he said.

"This is really it, Bobby. Everything's getting said tonight, so just *tell* me."

"I said *no*."

And then I realized he had never refused to answer the question; he had answered it now twice.

He reached into the car to pop the trunk, then took my suitcase and put it in. Without deciding anything, I got into the passenger side, pulled the door shut and buckled up. Bobby got in next to me and drove us out of the garage and through the city streets to the West Side Highway. He was a fast, able driver and soon we were in the outer fringe of suburbia where it mingled with the last brick high-rises of the Bronx. We settled into the dark, the green, the quiet and the hum of the car on the road.

We didn't speak. The things we had said to each other tonight still burned a hole between us, but it hardly seemed to matter; our accusations were minor compared with the other seismic currents that had stunned us today. We could apologize to each other later (if we wanted to), but in my exhaustion I couldn't see how we would overcome the mystery of this woman's murder in the new context of my identity theft, my arrest, his accusations about Julie. My body sank into the leather cushions, exhausted, and my mind ground away at all the fresh, grisly problems.

As we drove north Julie's GPS system electronically illustrated our progress; we were a little red dot that shivered forward on a jagged blue line. The image was strangely reassuring to me. Between the system's interactive mapping and Bobby's speed and precision as a driver, we would reach the house quickly. Bobby had once told me that when we were driving together and I was at the wheel, which was rare, he never felt he could close his eyes in case I veered off in the wrong direction or, worse, didn't notice a potential accident, and so he was always alert at my side. I had never suffered such vigilance when he drove and tonight, staring at the quivering electronic blip, I became hypnotized by our quiet and the drone of the road. Before I realized I'd closed my eyes, I was asleep.

Chapter 8

The driver's-side door slammed shut and I opened my eyes. It was eight in the morning and we were parked outside Julie's big red barn-house with its wraparound lawn, pale salmon rhododendron bushes and neat curb—a picture postcard whose perfection seemed to distance it from the murder that had taken place right out front, on the street, now rain-washed clean of Zara Moklas. Bobby was halfway across the lawn to the kitchen door. My rental car, which Julie had been driving in my absence, was not in her usual spot in the driveway; in its place was a gardener's pickup truck loaded with landscaping equipment. As I crossed to the house I caught the bright scent of freshly cut grass. The buzz of a lawn mower I couldn't see floated in the limpid morning air.

Bobby pulled open the outer screen door and waited for me. I dug into my purse for my key ring, a jangly amalgamation of keys from Lexington and Great Barrington that I had never taken the time to separate despite the growing bulk. When I reached the door I found him reading a note Julie had taped to the interior glass: *Mica, I'll be out all morning, so when you get here please get right to work on the lawn and the flower beds. If I'm not back by noon, I'll pay you next week. Thanks, Julie.*

I opened the door with my key. Immediately the alarm started its series of warning bleeps, the one-minute grace period before it went off. Ever since the malarm, the escalating bleeps had triggered anxiety and now, as I input the code Julie had taught me, my pulse hammered in my ears, the machine feeling again, turning me on for action. Then the red light turned green and my pulse slowed to normal. I pushed open the door and walked into the kitchen.

"Julie? I'm home!"

Bobby followed me in and disappeared up the back staircase. I could hear his footsteps upstairs as I walked through the dining room, sitting room and into the living room. The quiet—I could *feel* it. It was no surprise when Bobby came down the living room stairs alone.

"They're not upstairs," he said.

"I guess they went out somewhere."

"This early in the morning? Where?"

"Anywhere—errands, playground, both. Who knows?"

"I wonder if she saw the gardener before she left." And with that, he was out the door. In a moment he appeared in the backyard, framed in the living room window. Bobby must have called Mica's name, because he too entered the frame and they stood together, talking. Mica was a small, stocky Mexican man with a purple bandanna tied around his head. Julie had told me he came every other week, her only concession to hired help until her thwarted intention of asking Zara Moklas to take on the heavy housecleaning. Bobby was doing most of the talking while Mica listened and spoke just a little. Behind them a squad car drove past on Division Street, slowing as it reached Julie's, then picking up speed and moving on—the last phase of our security detail, I guessed. It reminded me that I was supposed to call the Great Barrington police to check in when I arrived. I called from the living room phone but didn't ask for Detective Lazare. I simply told the receptionist to please put it on record that I was officially here. Then I went outside to join Bobby and Mica.

I found Bobby on the stone patio, watching Mica push away a wheelbarrow full of pulled weeds.

"So?" I asked.

"He didn't see her."

"What were you talking about?"

"I asked him how long he's worked for her and what it's been like."

"Why?"

"Why not?"

"Oh, *Bobby*!"

"There was no harm in asking."

I couldn't argue with *that* old saw, but still I didn't like it. "You're being paranoid about Julie. Do you realize that?"

He didn't answer and I was too tired to pursue it. I plunked myself down in one of the canvas patio chairs and he sat down next to me. We were *both* exhausted. I didn't agree with him about Julie and the earrings, but in truth I understood why he had jumped to that conclusion. Diamond studs, though, were common, and so were white diamonds, which was probably why the crook had ordered them specifically: they'd be easy to sell. Bobby was as eager as I was to get answers about the felony warrant and the slow drain of my credit, but blaming Julie was way out of line. She was an intense person and yes, *yes*, she could be inappropriately flirtatious at times—I'd seen her in action, but *I'd* always understood the blurred boundaries even if others hadn't. The more I thought about it, the more I realized that Bobby had probably misinterpreted something Julie had said or done. It had never occurred to me before this moment to wonder what feelings Julie, my look-alike, stirred in him. Feelings he couldn't help, feelings that simply resided in him because of our own sexual relationship. I knew he could tell Julie and me apart, but when he looked at her what did he *see*? What did he *feel*? What involuntary sensations bubbled under his skin? I had always thought of Bobby as my very own and felt confident that Julie honored that, but I had not considered Bobby's side of things, not really. I would now. And I had to open my mind to the probability that he *had* been faithful to me all along, that the Lovyluv e-mails were somehow (but *how*?) part of the identity theft, my arrest, the whole rotten shebang. I rested my ankle on his knee, and in a return of my gesture he laid his warm hand on my bare skin. And then he breathed. We both did.

"So where do you think they went?" he asked.

"Maybe to the playground. Lexy discovered the baby swings recently and she *loves* to swing. Or maybe to the store. Or even both."

"She wakes up too early, doesn't she?"

"The minute the sun's up, so is Lexy."

"So you think Julie took her out on errands and stuff?"

"Of course," I said. "The note to Mica said she'd be back at noon—so they'll be back at noon."

"Actually, it said if she's *not* back by noon she'd pay him next week."

"Meaning she expects to be back but she might not make it in time. Same difference, Bobby, don't you think?"

He nodded, yawned. "Are you hungry?"

"Starving."

In the kitchen I brewed coffee and raided the fridge for eggs, bread, butter and jam while Bobby searched the phone book. This time he wasn't looking for a cybercafe; there were plenty of computers right here in this house. I *knew* what he was looking for: a jeweler. Before he said anything, I had a chance to think it through. What would be the harm of having an appraisal of my zircons? If that was what it would take to get him off the subject of Julie, then why not? We could go right after breakfast and get it done before Julie and Lexy got back at noon. By the time we sat down to breakfast, I had made up my mind.

"We can go for an appraisal," I told Bobby.

He smiled, put down his coffee, consulted his notes. "There's a jeweler on Railroad Street that opens at ten."

It was almost nine when we finished eating and piled our dishes into the sink. While Bobby showered, I went upstairs to the Yellow Room. Everything was exactly as I had left it except for the yawning absence of Lexy, her empty crib, the unusual quiet. I tried Julie's cell phone again and left another message (where *was* she?). There was a new voice mail, which I saw was from Clark Hazmat. I hadn't heard my phone ring and I wondered if his latest call had come in during the beeping as I'd turned off the alarm system; preoccupied by the mind-static of dread at another possible malarm, I wouldn't have registered anything. Why was Clark calling me, anyway? I had neither time nor energy for him, especially now, and so I ignored his second message as well. I then called Liz. She wanted to see our credit reports and I promised to fax them right over. I brushed my teeth, washed my face, gathered my hair into a ponytail and took the voluminous reports upstairs to the fax machine in Julie's office.

Ten minutes later, Bobby found me standing in front of Julie's desk watching the fax feed through. I had to stand guard over it, occasionally adjusting the pages so they wouldn't get stuck. Waiting with me, he glanced around her large high-tech office and I realized he had never been up here before.

"She *has* been successful," he said, looking at her Stevie and the other awards arranged on the shelf.

"Where do you think she gets all this money?"

He cocked an eyebrow, avoiding my rhetorical question, and crossed back over to the desk, where he watched my credit report (a work of fiction) thread through the fax machine. Picking up the pages that had finished, he neatened them into a stack and accidentally jostled the wireless mouse. The sleeping monitor popped to life and I was startled to see that Julie had changed her screen saver to a photo of herself and Lexy, one of the portraits I took last week and downloaded right before leaving for Manhattan. Bobby and I both stared at it. I wondered what he saw. Could he recognize Julie in two dimensions as readily as I could? What *I* saw was myself but curiously the self part was reflected in Lexy's image, not Julie's, and it struck me how much my center had shifted in having a child. The emotional negotiation of being with Lexy and Julie, the three of us together, had blunted that awareness before now, but suddenly it was clear. If I had to choose between them I would choose my daughter, not my twin—an impulsive thought I could never speak aloud.

"Why is the computer on?" Bobby sat down in Julie's chair.

"She never turns it off," I said. "She works really crazy hours and she likes to check her e-mail a lot."

I stood behind him, looking at the computer's desktop. The entire left side was covered with neatly arranged icons. It was impossible not to study them, given our argument last night. She had a zillion programs and Web links at her fingertips and even though I was no computer whiz I recognized them all: Excel, PowerPoint, Lexus Nexus, Money, and so on and so forth through the standard inventory of professional tools.

"What is all this?" Bobby's hand was cupped over

the mouse, but he didn't dare click anything with me watching.

"All the usual office stuff. You'd know half of it from the clinic, Bobby, if you ever used the computer."

"Please don't start that now, Annie. I never needed a computer in my life." He didn't finish the sentence: *until now.*

Just to satisfy him I double-clicked on some of the icons. Programs and sites filled the screen, with Julie's sign-on data loading automatically. Because we weren't marketers nothing looked more intriguing than anything else.

"Satisfied?" I asked.

"I didn't say a word."

My lips clamped and by his sigh I knew he caught my meaning. *You didn't have to.* The final page of the credit report exited the fax machine. Bobby clipped the pages together and left the report on my dresser in the Yellow Room.

We headed into town.

Five minutes along, turning off Division Street, I realized how close we were to the nursery school playground, the closest place to the house with baby swings.

"Take a right, just for a minute," I said.

"It's almost ten. Shouldn't we go directly to the appraiser?"

"Just drive past the playground."

When he understood my motivation he didn't question me again: maybe, just maybe, we would find Lexy and Julie here. The little schoolyard was busy with a dozen or so preschoolers laughing and running and climbing and jumping and chasing each other on the wood-chipped ground. A teacher in a blue skirt turned to watch us as we drove slowly past and with a pang of shame I realized how it must have looked, two strangers eyeing the children. I waved, but she just stared at me as we drove away. I realized what a dumb idea it was to look for Lexy here—Julie and I had never brought her during school hours, when the older children used the playground. I glanced at Bobby, staring ahead at the road, and knew he was feeling what I felt: shame, helplessness, an unnamable unease. No parents felt right, separated from their child; even without a solid reason to fear for her safety, we wouldn't relax until we saw her with our own eyes.

"Maybe she's at the public playground in Stockbridge," I ventured.

"We don't have time now, Annie." Translation: he didn't think they were whiling away the time at any playground. It wasn't hard to guess what he *was* thinking—*your sister took your identity and now she has our child and you're not even worried*—another impulsive thought that I willfully banished. There were more and more things I could not dare to think about right now, like why I had been arrested, really *why*, and what the charge against me could blossom into. My goal this morning was to reach noon with Bobby's suspicions dispelled and just stay balanced on what was feeling like a tightrope walk: one wrong move and I'd be in free fall. I *needed* to convince myself that they could turn up unexpectedly, anywhere, and so all the way to Main Street, in the thick springtime air that was beginning to feel like rain, I looked for them—on the library lawn, on the sidewalks of town, through the shadow-glazed shop windows on Railroad Street.

We parked at a meter and found the storefront jeweler. A small oval sign swinging on a bracket over the sidewalk read SIMONOFF ANTIQUE AND ESTATE JEWELRY. As soon as we crossed the sidewalk we saw that the shop was dark, and a handwritten note posted on the door told us that today's opening time would be half an hour later. So we walked down the street to Martin's restaurant, where the breakfast rush had lulled and no one minded if we sat over cappuccinos.

Our table, in the window, overlooked the quiet sidewalk. I spoon-sipped some of the fluffy cinnamoned milk from the coffee but couldn't drink much of it. I felt a little sick to my stomach from the mix of adrenaline and exhaustion that had been fueling me for a solid twenty-four hours now, ever since I saw the smile melt off the face of Emily Leary, director of human resources, at the hospital where I would very much *not* be working. The sharp memory of yesterday morning's encounter with the police made me cringe. Staring into my cup, I stirred the frothed milk all the way in to what was now a tepid café au lait. Bobby wasn't drinking his, either. What we needed, really, was a bitter cup o' joe, pure caffeine with no apologies.

There wasn't much left to say and so we said nothing, just stirred our coffees and glanced at our watches and waited for the time to pass. I kept expecting to see Julie whiz past with Lexy in her stroller, its handles festooned with shopping bags, but I didn't. Weekday mornings in this town were sleepy, with just a few people running errands, some stopping to chat in the street. A woman I didn't recognize saw me in the window and waved—she must have thought I was Julie— and I waved back. As our silence endured, Bobby's end of it began to agitate me. I *knew* he was holding back more layers of the onion-thoughts he had begun to unpeel back at the cybercafe in New York, that deep within him were stinging suspicions. The idea that Julie would try to seduce him was outrageous! I couldn't even *think* about it; and yet . . . against my will the emotional details of Julie's infertility floated to the surface of my mind.

Julie, a dozen years ago, walking across a vast lawn at the northern New England college we attended together. It was winter and the lawn was covered with mangy patches of ice left over from a big snow. I had just come out of the library when I saw my sister walking with Ian, whom I had a crush on at the time. Ian was a big bear of a boy, nineteen, pale and funny. Julie knew all about my hankering after him and yet there she was, *with* him, which in and of itself was fine (I guessed), but then she slipped on some ice, and he clutched her elbow, and she grabbed his shoulder, and he laughed—and they kissed. I stood there, paralyzed, holding a big art history tome that suddenly weighed three hundred pounds. They kissed again and he actually *licked* her cheek and they laughed with such familiarity I knew their intimacy was not brand-new. So . . . I gave up on my plans to seduce Ian. And Julie and I had it out that very night: she admitted they had slept together (twice!) and tearfully apologized for hurting (betraying! deceiving!) me and promised she would drop Ian immediately. Which she did. But the damage was done. The worst damage, it turned out (because my heart healed quickly and moved on to Rich, who was *much* nicer and better-looking than Ian), was that Ian had passed on to Julie more than his affections. Weeks later she discovered she had chlamydia, a sexually transmitted disease that can leave you infertile. Within a year Julie's infertility was confirmed by our gynecologist and my bitter feelings about the Ian Incident were swallowed by a stronger feeling: sorrow over Julie's inability to *ever* bear her own children. When you are an identical twin, your sibling's fertility in a way is your own and so I felt her prospective losses acutely. By the time college was over and we no longer lived in the context of this misfortune, we put it behind us and it became a fact-of-life stepping-stone after which Julie created a successful adulthood. When Lexy was born we shared in the elation of *our* daughter's birth; Julie was as overjoyed as Bobby and I. The earrings had been a gift to mark new motherhood: matching earrings, one pair for me, another for her.

"It's time." Bobby took both our mugs to the counter and we went back outside. Gentle cloud-dappled sunlight bathed the whole west side of the street and sidewalk as we returned to Simonoff Antique and Estate Jewelry.

A bell tinkled when Bobby opened the glass door. I followed him into a small but gracious space lined with wood and glass jewelry cases. A delicate clear-glass chandelier was suspended from the ceiling and the walls were covered in dusty framed prints of mid-century abstract expressionist paintings by Pollock, de Kooning, Rothko—obvious ones that I recognized as readily as anyone—as well as some Calder and, surprise, a Basquiat. In the back of the store a window had been carved over the jeweler's work area and we saw a gray-haired woman hunched over a table, squinting as her weathered hands manipulated the latch end of a necklace with the pointed tip of precision pliers. At the sound of the bell she looked up at us and I saw that her eyes, now relaxed, were bright, bright blue.

"Good morning." Bobby walked toward the back of the shop, smiling.

"Morning," the woman answered in a reedy voice.

"Glad to find you in," Bobby said. "We came by before and saw the sign."

"Yes," she said, "I'm sorry about that. My husband, Gaston, usually opens and I come along later, but he's under the weather today. How can I help you?"

"We were wondering if we could get some earrings appraised."

She pushed back her chair and vanished for a moment, then reappeared through a door in the shop's back corner. She was tiny, not even five feet tall, and I guessed in her seventies. She wore a long fringed denim skirt, battered Birkenstocks, a red long-sleeved turtleneck and not an iota of jewelry. Positioned now behind the counter, she introduced herself.

"I'm Ellery Simonoff. Do you have your appraisal item with you?"

"My wife's earrings."

I took them off and gave them to the woman. They looked like fallen stars in the earth of her craggy brownish palms. "They're only zircons," I said.

"Well, there are zircons and there are zircons and there are . . ." She squinted at the earrings and her voice trailed off as she set them on a worn velvet display board. We stood in front of her while her thickened fingers placed one earring in her opposite palm. She studied it through a magnifying monocle squeezed over one eye. Using a pair of steel pincers, she lifted it up and turned it around, inspecting it from different angles.

"This is what we call a bezel-set cubic zirconia—a very nice one—six millimeters, almost one full carat, set in sterling silver. The stone is white. The cut is round brilliant. You see the silver setting, how it encompasses the stone?"

Bobby and I both nodded, keen students. His expression was serious and a little disappointed (it seemed to me) at the detailed description of the zircon, whereas *I* could not have been happier at this news that my precious earrings were certifiable fakes. Winning a marital argument always felt like a reprieve, usually fleeting, but so much had hung on this one. The relief was so satisfying I could feel the tension melting out of me. So . . . my earrings were fakes; Julie was just plain Julie (no surprise there); she would have Lexy home by noon; and Bobby and I could put our ugly middle-of-the-night argument behind us and go in search of the *real* spendthrift thief who was pretending to be me.

Mrs. Simonoff continued. "It's a knockoff of a popular Tiffany earring designed by Elsa Peretti. I'd say that someone did a decent job with this one."

Bobby took the earring from her palm and held it up in the diminishing light from the window. Minute by minute, clouds were moving in. More rain was on the way. "It looks so real."

"Well, it would, to the untrained eye."

"What would it sell for?"

"Around thirty dollars for a pair."

He put the earring on the velvet board beside its mate, which Mrs. Simonoff now carefully picked up. It sparkled for a moment before the natural light from the window darkened completely and outside the first trickle of rain began.

"This earring?" She switched on a bright lamp and moved the earring beneath it. "Look carefully."

We bent together over her palm, bronze and vivid in the small spotlight. The second earring seemed to flash and flicker, almost jump out of her hand.

"Another white round brilliant, but this one's a full carat set in platinum. Color grade F, with an excellent clarity grade."

Why was she describing this one differently? "That one's set in silver and this one's platinum?" I asked. "Isn't that a more valuable metal?"

"Oh, yes, much more valuable." She picked up the first earring and paired it with the second in the deepest crevice of her palm. "Do you see the difference?"

As Bobby leaned closer his face seemed to awaken with recognition. He touched the second earring with the tip of his forefinger. "This one's a real diamond."

"That's right. It's a *real* Tiffany Peretti, valued

at . . ." Mrs. Simonoff pressed down both sides of her mouth in a thoughtful expression typical of the French, and I knew she had spent a lifetime with her French husband, Gaston, absorbing his mannerisms, just as I knew that at this very moment all my certainties were in reversal and life as I'd known it was *over*. "I'd say, about ten thousand dollars for a pair."

Bobby straightened to full height. "We paid eight thousand."

"We?" My voice was loud, unreal.

"My dear"—Mrs. Simonoff addressed me soothingly, but her attempt to calm me failed; my insides felt like an earthquake had hit—"you got an excellent price. It's a stunning piece. But why did you pair it with a zircon?"

I couldn't help myself: I was sick. I ran out of the store and made it across the sidewalk to a public trash can on the corner, where I threw up. Rain was pouring now and I was soaking wet, which was just as well. It covered the stench and the mess and ensured that no one was around to see me. No one except Bobby. It was a minute before he got to me—Bobby being Bobby, he wouldn't have left the store without first paying Mrs. Simonoff and attempting some kind of polite explanation—but finally he arrived at my side in the rain, holding a tiny envelope that must have contained the earrings. My ponytail had come loose, so he pried the wet hair off my face to free me as I heaved over the large metal can. Mrs. Simonoff, meanwhile, emerged under an umbrella, offered a handful of paper towels and then retreated to her store. I cleaned my face and my shirt and threw the soiled paper squares into the garbage. Then Bobby and I walked through the pouring rain to my sister's car.

"You're right," I said.

"I wish I wasn't."

"But you *are*."

"I'm really sorry, Annie." He opened the passenger door to let me in, then hurried around to the driver's side, but before starting the motor, he turned to face me. "Now what?"

"You're asking *me*?" Buckled forward in the seat, I wept into my hands.

My brain felt like an out-of-sync lightning storm, revelations flashing at once. If Julie had bought those diamond earrings it meant she had bought all that other stuff; it meant she had somehow engineered my arrest. When I was out of town. *When she had Lexy.* It meant she had planned this for a long time; that she probably *had* tried to seduce my husband when I was pregnant and vulnerable; that she had organized the demise of my marriage. That she had lured me to her; weaned my baby with my help; *prepared* for today. And if I hadn't inadvertently mixed our earrings the appraisal would have been for a pair of zircons; we would have relaxed a bit, gone home and waited for noon—giving her more time to run away.

Bobby rubbed his hand across my shoulders, warming me. His tone was gentle. "I think we should drive straight to the police station."

"No, let's go home first. Maybe they're back."

"*Annie.*"

He was right; they probably weren't at the house. No: *they weren't.* But even knowing what I now knew, beginning to understand it and recognizing the truth of what Bobby had first suggested at Twelfth Night, I still harbored a little seed of hope. Just a tiny one, which I would keep to myself.

"Okay," I said. "Let's go see Detective Lazare."

Chapter 9

Gabe Lazare leaned back in his swivel chair and listened. His desk was angled into a corner of the low-ceilinged, white-painted Detectives Unit of the Great Barrington Police Department. Bobby and I sat opposite him, soaking wet from the rain, and took turns talking. I could hear but not see the half dozen other detectives at their desks behind us: the clatter of typing on a computer keyboard, chair wheels rolling across linoleum, a phone ringing just once before being answered, the hum of unruffled voices. Under the fluorescent lights, Detective Lazare's pale skin contrasted ghostily with the dyed frazzle of his pitch-black hair. The large rectangular window behind him showed the rain-beaten bright green leaves of a century-old maple tree.

"You're convinced your sister bought the diamonds?" Lazare asked me. The identical-looking yet mismatched earrings lay on a clear space of his neat desk.

"I can't say I'm sure, but it seems she might have."

Just saying those words aloud, voicing my tentative doubts, felt shattering. The translation was so stark: my sister *hated* me. I loved her and she hated me. And she had Lexy. I was starting to feel sick again.

"I hate to say it, but it doesn't really surprise me." Bobby glanced at me, deciding how much he could say before earning a dreaded reaction from me. "I think Julie was feeling rejected by me—"

"Because you rejected her." Detective Lazare nodded. *Got it, move on.* Bobby smiled a little uneasily and agreed.

"Yes, I rejected her. I was really stunned when she came on to me. I mean, she's Annie's *sister*."

"With identity theft," Lazare said, "the wisdom is that it's often someone who's got access, someone who works in the home, a coworker, even a family member."

"That's right. I read that in the book I picked up." Bobby hadn't mentioned exactly that to me before, about it often being someone close to you, and I now wondered how much that notion had contributed to his thinking about Julie.

"Have you reported this yet?" Lazare asked.

"We put a fraud alert on our credit reports," Bobby said.

"I mean to the FBI."

"No," Bobby said. "We just found out last night. We drove straight to the house this morning, then went to the appraiser."

"You can reach the FBI twenty-four hours—"

I had to interrupt the detective. "It was my fault. When Bobby first said he thought Julie might have something to do with it, I wouldn't listen. We decided to get the earrings appraised first. I couldn't just accuse my sister of something like this."

"The thing is, *you* don't have to solve this, Annie." Detective Lazare's eyes smiled, seeming to forgive my hesitation. I had the sense that he comprehended my emotional plight, the delicacy of what was at stake for me. "The FBI has a Cyber Division—they've been bringing us up to Boston for conferences this past year to brief us on cyber crimes and offer help if we need it. They'll work with us. They know how to investigate exactly this kind of crime."

He picked up his phone and crooked it between neck and ear while searching for something on his computer. A phone number, presumably, because then he dialed. Waited. Pushed a few buttons, obviously navigating a voice-mail system. Finally telling some stranger that we needed help from the federal government.

"It appears to be identity theft," he said, "and yesterday she was picked up on a felony warrant she claims is false. In New York City. Bail bond, yes. Yes. I don't know yet. It's under review."

Claims was false? His choice of words shook me, but I kept quiet.

Lazare hung up the phone and opened one of his desk drawers, saying, "It's all set. They're sending us one of their computer fraud specialists this afternoon. I mean it when I tell you they're very serious about this kind of crime these days." He withdrew a sheet of paper from the drawer and set it on his desk: APPLICA-

TION AND AFFIDAVIT FOR SEARCH & SEIZURE WARRANT. As we spoke, he filled it out.

"That's what the book says." Bobby nodded. "That it took a while, but they're finally starting to put some manpower behind dealing with it."

"Have to," Lazare said. "It's running rampant."

Rampant? Well, it was almost a relief to hear that the criminal malignancy that was threatening to ruin my life was common, not rare, meaning that identity theft was already a contagion run amok (something I had unfortunately never paid much attention to). Was it possible that I had been chosen arbitrarily, that *my* thief could be any one of *many* invisible thieves stalking cyberspace? But then I thought of the earrings. I thought of Julie, felt her in my soul, and couldn't speak.

"They say you can only do so much to protect yourself," Detective Lazare said. "One thing that might make you feel better, Annie, is that once ID theft's been confirmed by law enforcement, the victim is pretty much off the hook for the damages when it comes to credit cards."

"Except," Bobby added, "according to the book, it supposedly takes years to clear your name. And a huge percentage of identity thieves are never caught."

When I had the chance I was going to rip up that book; I didn't think I could handle knowing much more about my personal demolition. Whoever said ignorance was bliss was right and I wanted mine back!

"So," I said, "jumping to the conclusion that my sister's behind this is kind of rash, then?" My voice sounded feebler than I'd meant it to and my words seemed to float away, untethered to reality.

I saw the pause in Detective Lazare's expression and felt it in Bobby in his chair beside me: amazement that I wouldn't accept what seemed evident to them.

"Sweetie," Bobby said, "Julie's got all the computer skills to do this, and she gave you those earrings as a gift, *lying* about them, and she's got so much money." I wished he wouldn't talk about Julie's money, as if we could safely assume that any woman with all that wealth had to be some kind of criminal (even though it *was* strange how all this was falling into place and she *did* seem to live very, very well). "It really does make sense that it was her—and that she's taken Lexy away because she wants her, too."

"Hold it, now," Detective Lazare said. "That is a big assumption. You left your daughter in Julie's care and she left a note saying she'd be back by noon, and it's only"—he flipped his wrist to consult his watch— "eleven fifteen."

But logic couldn't penetrate the evocation of my most devastating fear: that Lexy was *gone*.

"We need to find her." It burst out of me with so much volume that the other people in the room seemed to temporarily freeze—and then the shuffle of office noise began again.

"Okay, Annie." Lazare kept his tone smooth, to calm me, but I wasn't calmed. He steepled his fingers and I noticed that his squarish nails had been jaggedly clipped. "Julie's note said noon—I say we wait. If she's not back by then—"

"Wait?" How could we just wait?

"And they're not really assumptions," Bobby said. "Detective, you yourself called the FBI. Obviously you think something's wrong."

"Identity theft is one thing," Lazare said. "The FBI fraud specialist will be here soon and we'll start looking into that. Child abduction is a whole other ball game."

"Detective"—Bobby leaned forward—"Julie tried to get me to go to bed with her. She bought diamonds and charged them to a credit card in Annie's name, a card we didn't even know about. Something *she* did landed *Annie* in jail. She practically destroyed our marriage—and now she's off somewhere with our daughter."

"Let's try to calm down a minute—"

"No," Bobby said. "We don't care if she's at the grocery store. We want to find them, *now.*"

Bobby's anger was satisfying, even comforting. His persistence had transformed into a kind of emotional passion he rarely indulged in. *I* was usually the reactive one. My mind seemed to unclench; and then I thought of something.

"She's driving my rental car and it has a GPS system."

"Well, good," Lazare said. "That gives us something concrete. They provide those systems so they can keep track of their property—sometimes customers dump the cars. They'll have a tracking system. An individual unit doesn't even have to be turned on to be traceable. What agency did you use?"

I told him and he leaned abruptly toward his computer. He was a fast typist and in a minute he was dialing his desk phone. He recited his credentials and stated his case, then was put on hold. "They're checking me out, which is smart of them." Finally they came back on the line and his face lit up.

"You're sure?" He listened some more. "All right. Thank you." He hung up and said, "The GPS system shows them at the house."

I stood up and pulled my purse strap over my shoulder. If Lexy was back, I could have her in my arms in ten minutes' time and the worst of this would be over. Bobby also stood. Lazare folded his search warrant application and stuffed it into his shirt pocket, then he scooped up the earrings, slipped them back into the little envelope and handed it to me. I put it into my change purse as we all hurried out of the station.

"I'll meet you at the house," Lazare said. "I'm stopping at the courthouse to drop off this warrant application." He used his key chain remote to unlock his car and in the lot behind the station a silver sedan beeped and its rear lights blinked.

We had parked Julie's Audi out front. It had already stopped raining and then, as we reached the car, the clouds dissipated and sun poured lavishly onto the road. Bobby drove and I sat beside him, watching the bright greens and pinks and yellows and reds and oranges of springtime stream past, hoping with all my heart and soul that I would find Lexy back at the house. My feelings about Julie were too inchoate to classify, but I supposed I hoped to find her, too. Was it possible she had an explanation for all this? *Could* it be possible she was not the one wreaking havoc in my life?

We were halfway there when my cell phone rang in

my purse. I fished it out, hoping it would be Julie, aggravated that it would probably be Clark Hazmat again.

"It's Liz," I told Bobby when I saw her law firm's name on the caller ID.

"Hey, honey," Liz said. "How are you hanging in there?"

"Not so great." I told her about the appraisal. She listened quietly before plunging in to her reason for calling.

"Better hold on to your hat," she said, "because it gets worse."

"Tell me."

"The embezzlement charge?"

"*Fake* embezzlement charge."

"Yes, that's the one." I almost laughed, then I almost cried, and then she told me, "Almost twenty-five grand, in two parts, siphoned out of two different bank accounts belonging to your Kentucky prison."

My prison! "What do you mean, 'siphoned'?"

"Transferred into accounts owned by you," she said.

"You mean *not* owned by me, Liz—"

"Yes, Annie, I do mean that. But I have to convey what I've been told."

I was stunned. Speechless.

"Here's what we're going to do," Liz said. "I'm about to call this organization affiliated with the FBI called IC³—the Internet Crime Complaint Center—and start by lodging a formal complaint on your behalf. That's step one. Step two is contacting the Cyber Division of the FBI and requesting hands-on help with this *now*."

"The local detective here just did that."

"Great. I'll call anyway; it never hurts to reinforce a call for help. Where are you now?"

"On our way to Julie's house. The GPS system in the car she's driving thinks she's home."

"Good luck, Annie. Let me know what happens. And don't worry. I'll keep in touch, too."

My blue rental car was nowhere in sight when we pulled up in front of Julie's house. Mica's truck was gone, so we parked in the driveway and were standing on the lawn when Detective Lazare arrived. A heavy humidity hung in the air and for the first time this spring I felt claustrophobic inside my clothes. I had on the same outfit I'd worn to Manhattan two nights ago, jeans and a tight-fitting top that revealed my milky cleavage in a way that no longer felt daring, just sad. It was the outfit I'd changed into after my prison stay (the beige suit now hung in my father's city closet—I would never wear *that* bad-memory rag again). I was aware of a film of sweat clinging to every inch of my skin as the three of us—Detective Lazare, Bobby and I—searched the grounds of Julie's house, front and back, for the car.

It wasn't there.

"What now?" Bobby asked Lazare.

Lazare looked around, thinking. Then he faced me and said, "I have a hunch about something." He walked toward the house and we followed. At the kitchen door he stopped. "If I go in there before the search warrant's issued, and we find she's removed the GPS unit, and if this turns into something, we won't be able to use it."

I understood him perfectly: he meant *in court*. It

would be disqualified as *evidence*. Hearing it put that way sounded unreal. I just couldn't believe it would go that far.

"It's possible that, with Annie's permission, I could legitimately poke around inside the house," Detective Lazare said. "Possible, but not certain. Why take chances?"

"So you want me to do it," I said.

"That's right."

"Can Bobby come with me?"

"He's your husband. There's nothing unusual about him going into the house." Meaning *yes*.

So I unlocked the kitchen door and Bobby followed me in. Dust sparkled in a block of sunlight that fell from the window. The teal enamel wall clock read 11:45 and I *knew*, in the perfect quiet, that they weren't here and hadn't been here for a while and probably weren't coming.

We began in the kitchen, opening cupboards and cabinets. In the dining room and living room we checked in and under and on top of furniture. I took a flashlight from the downstairs coat closet and shone it into the two oversized ceramic urns Julie had picked up at a local antique shop, finding cobwebs and a mouse skeleton but no abandoned electronic devices. Upstairs, Bobby looked through the loft and the un- used guest room, while I looked through the Yellow Room and the Pinecone Room. We opened every drawer, looked into the corners and high shelves of every closet, checked under every bed. The longer we looked and found nothing, the more my rebellious hopes began to return. Noon arrived and I found myself pausing to listen each time a car drove past the house.

"I'm finding *nothing*," I called to Bobby. "How about you?"

"Nada," he said, joining me in the second-floor hall. He opened the door that led up to Julie's third-floor suite. "Shall we?"

"Wait," I said. Across from the Pinecone Room was another closet. When I opened the door, an automatic ceiling light showed a neat color code of linens: sheets below, towels above. On the floor were two stacked laundry baskets and an empty humidifier. I bent down to pull forward the baskets—and there it was, lying on the floor. The GPS unit from my rental car. The satellite-signal receiving device looked like nothing but a small hunk of black plastic surrounding a sleeping grayish screen. A single suction-cup leg extended from its back. It was a relatively inexpensive model, probably bought by the rental car agency in bulk and considered expendable.

"Here it is," I whispered.

Bobby joined me and looked at the unit, such an innocuous little thing. After a moment he took it from my hands and we walked down the stairs and out of the house. A band of sweat had formed down the back of his shirt and as soon as I noticed it I realized that my own forehead was damp, my temples dripping, my heart filled with cold fright.

The only reason someone would remove a global positioning system from a car was so they couldn't be easily found.

Detective Lazare was sitting on a shallow stone

fence twenty feet from the kitchen door. A neon-winged dragonfly had balanced on his bent knee and he appeared to be watching it. When he saw us, and stood, the dragonfly fluttered away.

Bobby showed him the GPS.

"You're sure that's the one that was in your car, Annie?" Lazare asked.

"Positive," I said.

Lazare flipped open his cell phone and calmly told us, "I'm requesting an Amber Alert. Is Lexy her given name?"

"Alexis," Bobby answered.

"What color are her eyes?"

"Brown."

"Any birthmarks?"

Bobby looked at me; he didn't know.

"Behind her left knee," I said. "It's maroon, small, like a lopsided triangle."

"The car," Lazare said. "It's sky blue, right? Toyota? Four-door?"

"Yes," I answered.

"Interior?"

"Pale blue."

Lazare scrolled down his cell phone's stored-numbers list and dialed. He announced himself officially, without any of his usual chitchat. "I need an Amber Alert *stat* for a baby girl. Alexis Goodman, goes by Lexy. Almost six months old, short reddish peach-fuzz hair, brown eyes, maroon birthmark in the shape of an uneven triangle behind her left knee. Presumably in the care of her maternal aunt, Julie Milliken. I'll e-mail a photo in the next few minutes."

It would be crucial to know what Julie looked like. There had to be thousands of blue cars on the road in which a woman might be driving a baby any number of places or just lulling her to sleep. It would be so easy for Julie to pass through the world as a mother, as *me*, raising Lexy. It could really happen: I could lose her forever.

Lazare followed Bobby and me inside the house and upstairs to the loft computer, where I opened the file of images I'd downloaded on Sunday night. He selected a picture of Julie alone, standing in front of a living room window behind which rain poured in an unfocused haze, facing me (facing the camera) with the blank expression of listening. A moment before the picture I'd asked her if she wanted chicken for dinner; a moment later she'd answered *yes*. In the end we went out to Rouge.

I typed my sister's name and clicked *send as e-mail*. Lazare put in an address, wrote a short note and zapped it away.

A car drove toward the house and my heart raced. *Was it them? Was this all a mistake?* The car passed.

Life without my daughter would be unbearable.

"This Julie's computer?"

"No," Bobby said. "She's got an office upstairs."

"Mind if I take a look?" Lazare asked me. More prewarrant permission, I guessed.

"Go ahead," I said.

Bobby led Lazare down the hall. When I didn't follow, they both turned around.

"I'd like to shower," I said. "I feel gross, and I need to pump."

"Okay," Lazare said. "I'm not going to touch anything. I'll just eyeball things until I hear the warrant's gone through." He smiled kindly and I wished he wasn't here. If only there had never been a reason for this wise, persistent man to have entered our lives.

They disappeared up to Julie's lair and I to my beehive yellow room. The buzzing in my head wouldn't stop. I was deliriously exhausted and anguished beyond anything I had ever felt before. I sat on my bed for about fifteen minutes, crying and pumping milk, then sealed a fresh bottle for Lexy and went to the kitchen to put it in the freezer. Back upstairs in my bathroom, I stripped naked and stood under the streaming hot water, wishing it could melt away my sense of weakness because what I wanted now was to be the strongest mother who had ever lived. *I never gave up hope*, I heard myself saying. *I always knew we'd find her.* When I came out of the shower I was clean but otherwise untransformed. I dried myself. Brushed my hair and my teeth. Rubbed cream into every inch of my skin. A look through my dresser drawers and closet offered nothing I wanted to put against my body; nothing from my old life, my life before yesterday, seemed credible. I wasn't really *me* anymore. And who was Julie?

Wrapped in a towel, I went upstairs to my sister's bedroom. The office door was ajar—I could see Bobby sitting at the computer, pointing and clicking, and Lazare standing behind him, watching—and I closed it. I slid open one side of Julie's closet and ran my hand along the edges of her hanging clothes. Her taste was simple, *classic*, and all the fabrics were top quality.

Who had bought these clothes? Had she paid for them, or had I? A few still had their tags attached. I didn't want to wear anything brand-new; I wanted something *she* had worn. When I saw a white-on-white gauzy outfit of baggy pants, loose Indian-style shirt and underneath camisole, I lifted the hanger off the rod. This one had caught my eye immediately during this visit's first closet inspection, but I hadn't dared borrow something so pristine, not around a baby. I slid the pieces off the hanger and put them on.

Clad in Julie, I moved slowly around her room, imagining what it was like to be her. I'd always thought I knew, that we were essentially the same person, but the last two days had taught me otherwise. I was going to have to face the probability that Julie was not who I had thought she was, which therefore meant—*didn't it?*—that neither was I.

I sat down on one of the black chairs and peered into the curio table at the merged families of glass cats. Which were mine and which were hers? Then I noticed she had added a few objects and they startled me: Lexy's red teething ring (her favorite!) and the other pair of earrings. Julie's pair, the other mismatched set. *There they were.*

I lifted off the glass top of the table and set it carefully on the floor. The stickiness of Lexy's teether soothed me a little, helped me to *feel* her, and I slipped it into a deep pocket of the white slacks. Then I picked up the earrings. They settled into the creased palm of my hand, innocent little chips of rock, identical except *not*, because one was real and the other wasn't. I couldn't tell which was which. Leaning back in the

chair, I lifted my hand to the window to bathe the earrings in light. After the rain, the sun seemed so raw;
but I couldn't see what Mrs. Simonoff had recognized
so easily. So I turned on Julie's bedside lamp, crouched
down and put my hand under its hot halogen bulb.
Here, one earring glittered magnificently, while the
other stayed as dull and predictable as always. That
one was *my* zircon.

I pressed the post into my pierced left ear and attached the backing. Then I put the real diamond back
in the curio table—rejecting the fleeting, painful notion that I could be tampering with *evidence*—and removed eight little glass cats. If not for these souvenirs
I would have thought that distant summer in Italy had
been a mirage. How could my parents have ever been
married? How could they have ever been *alive*? How
could Julie and I have ever been so close? Had the four
of us ever really been a family? I looked around Julie's
bright white room with its painted black rafter-spun
ceiling hiding so much space. Were our love and trust
of each other actually over? Until Lexy, our bond had
been the most significant force in my life.

Setting the top back on the table, I thought of the
other zircon. Apparently I hadn't worn them both together since the first night of my stay here—the night
of Zara's murder—when Julie and I had mingled our
glass cats, and removed our shoes and our earrings,
and talked late into the night. I felt myself sinking
deeper into a paralyzing quicksand of loneliness. As a
twin, especially an identical twin, I had never felt
alone before and I didn't like it. No, I *hated* it.

I padded barefoot downstairs to the Yellow Room

and my purse. I wanted to wear *my* earrings again. I wanted them together. I opened my coin purse, identified the real zircon under the bright bathroom light and slipped it into my naked ear. Here I was, all white and sparkling like a woman on a couch in a catalog: *page fifty, a complete room for easy living*. On a slick page it might have been a comforting image (*Julie's* area of expertise) saying *buy me, I will cure you of your doubts*; but in reality all the white linen and glitter in the world could never conceal the ins and outs, ups and downs of a woman's inner life.

My cell phone, still tucked into my purse, began to ring; and as it had every time it rang these past two days, my heart jumped. *Could* it be Julie, finally calling back to check in? To explain her absence? To assure me that Lexy was happy and fine? To promise they'd be back soon? (The rest of it, the money stuff, was such a complicated tangle, *not* a phone conversation.) I fished out my cell and at the sight of Clark Hazmat's name on caller ID my thin hopes caved dramatically and completely. Why wouldn't he stop calling me? That was it: I was going to finally tell him he'd have to leave me alone.

"Hello—" But before I could say anything, he jumped right in.

"Miss Milliken! It's me, Clark!"

"Yes, Clark, I know, but—"

"I've been calling you since yesterday. Maybe you didn't get my messages."

"I got them, but, Clark, I've been really busy."

"Yeah, I saw the papers this morning."

"It's in the *papers*?"

"Bad news travels fast. That's why I've been calling you. After I read the paper I couldn't help doing a little investigating, you know, since I've got my special computer skills."

Special skills. That was one way to put it. Clark had done seven years as a computer hacker. Maybe he was lucky to have sat out all that progress, when instead of reading potboilers in his cell he might have graduated from breaking into corporate networks to breaking apart individual lives. He himself might have become an identity thief.

"Clark"—I spoke carefully—"what are you saying?"

"I'm saying I dug pretty deep, hope you don't mind. You got some real problems, Miss M, but any schmo with half a hard drive can tell this one's a setup. You're just not the Jaguars-and-diamonds type and I never saw you once with a California tan."

I cringed. He really *had* looked me up. "How do you know all that?"

"I'm telling you," he said, "it's a hacker's paradise out there now. Good time to be new in the game, *bad* time to be an ex-con with no job, looking in the window. I wanted to give you a heads-up yesterday, but I guess by now you've figured out a thing or two."

"You're right. I have. Listen, Clark, I can't stay on the phone. Things are worse than what you can see on a computer. You have no idea."

"Actually," he said, "I think I do. The article? It talked about a murder—"

That word, coming from Clark, sent a chill through me—Clark, with his topiary hairdo and skull tattoo.

"And it talked about"—a rustle of papers, a pause—"Thomas Soiffer, the guy with the APB on his head. So I looked him up, too. And guess what."

"Did you *find* him?"

"Nah, Miss M. I found out *about* him. Guy got hacked, just like you."

It took me a moment to decipher that, and then I asked, "Are you saying that Thomas Soiffer is also a victim of identity theft?"

"Bingo."

"Who stole his identity?"

"Dunno. Wish I did. I always liked you, Miss Milliken. I'd really like to help you out with that one, but I climbed a few fences while I'm on the leash, if you know what I mean. I just wanted to give you a heads-up on the Soiffer thing in case the cops didn't figure it out yet. They're not the swiftest sometimes."

"Thank you, Clark," I said. "Thank you very much for calling me."

"You got it, Miss M," he said. "Listen, good luck with all that, okay?"

"Thanks."

"Maybe when things settle down, I'll give you another buzz. Freedom, well, I guess you know it can get lonely out here."

"Yes, call me," I said, and meant it. "I'd be happy to hear from you again."

I went straight upstairs and found Bobby still clicking away with Julie's wireless mouse. Lazare had pulled up a chair beside him.

"Detective Lazare," I said. He turned to look at me. "Do you remember Clark Hazmat? I told you about him yesterday morning after I ran into him in Manhattan."

It took a second for the detective to register my meaning. "The convict," he said.

"*Former* convict. He just called me, and I have to tell you what he said." I described Clark's claim about Thomas Soiffer being an identity theft victim.

"Interesting," Lazare said. Just: *interesting.* But for the first time since I'd met him I thought I saw his cool demeanor falter. If Clark was right, if it was true, it implied that Zara's murder and my identity theft might share a common denominator in Thomas Soiffer. I pictured him on Julie's road at night, stalking her, killing Zara instead. It made awful, perfect sense.

Lazare straightened a leg and leaned back so he could reach into his pocket for his cell phone. While he made some calls—checking into the whereabouts of the FBI cyber specialist, the status of the search warrant, the progress of the Amber Alert—I stood behind Bobby. He had managed to open multiple Web sites, leaving their names lined up along the bottom of the screen.

"You looked up her Stevie Award?" I asked.

He swiveled to face me, his expression clouding. "She never won one."

"You're sure?"

"According to everything I checked."

"But her marketing career—"

"It was real," he said, "and it looks like she really *was* successful, or *is* successful. It's hard to follow. There's a lot of information on her, but it's kind of random and the dates start petering out about a year ago."

A year ago: after Paul had left her and she'd dated a little bit, with miserable results. A year ago: when I married Bobby. *A year ago.* Was that when she stopped being *my* Julie?

Behind Bobby, the screen saver popped on and there they were, Julie and Lexy smiling together, recognizably themselves. Nothing was different on the surface. And yet everything had changed.

A little while later the doorbell chimed. Bobby and Lazare went downstairs together to answer it while I stayed in Julie's office. Through the window I saw an official-looking black sedan with a fat antenna parked just over the spot where Zara had left her vanished mark. Lazare had already told us that the FBI fraud investigator wasn't expected to arrive at the precinct for another two hours and would call first. So who was this? Could the Amber Alert have worked that fast? Three squad cars pulled up in quick succession behind the black car. And I stood there, and I waited, understanding the tidal pull in the hearts of military mothers who remain at the window, frozen in a private dread. When they came in person, wasn't it always with the worst possible news?

Chapter 10

Bobby appeared with a blond man whose weathered face appeared years older than his lean body. He wore black slacks, a crisply ironed white shirt and penny loafers, each with a shiny new coin. His voice was a melodious baritone. "Special Agent Rusty Smith, FBI. This the computer?"

"That's it," Lazare answered, coming up behind Smith. Then, to me: "Warrant's been approved. Agent Smith's going to take a look in Julie's computer before deciding whether he needs to take it."

"She have a laptop, too?" Smith asked.

"Yes," I answered, "but I don't see it. She must have taken it."

Smith sat down, positioned himself in front of the screen and cupped his hand over Julie's mouse. "Well, let's see what she's got here," he said in the easy, professional tone of a doctor saying *open wide* and searching for infection in places you yourself cannot see.

We stood behind him for a while, watching, but there was little that made any sense to me. He navigated the system deftly, discarding most of what he came upon. Finally he launched a search and sat back, arms folded, to wait while the screen filled with unrecognizable (to me) data. It appeared to be some kind of code. Smith reached into his back pocket and withdrew a small pad, then turned around to ask any one of us, "Is there a pen I could borrow? Forgot mine." Bobby leaned forward and nudged a blue ballpoint so it rolled in Smith's direction. His freckled fingers caught it before it rolled off the desk. He made a few notes, then shut down the computer.

"So what do you think?" Lazare asked Smith.

"Looks like it's loaded," Smith said in a tone that was matter-of-fact, even unconcerned. Like Lazare, he was at work, doing his job and probably (hopefully) doing it well. Julie's computer being "loaded" was just another development in just another case, nothing like the life-changing shift it was to me. Bobby took my hand and squeezed it as we stood there, listening to the cops chart their plans.

"I'll bring it with me to Boston," Smith said. "It'll take some time, but I can e-mail you a preliminary report tonight."

As soon as the screen blanked, Agent Smith began to pull out plugs and loop cords up and down from his elbow to the crook of his thumb, creating a stack of neat bundles, which he left on the desk. In fifteen minutes, he had Julie's hard drive and keyboard packed into the trunk of his car. Bobby and I watched from the window while Lazare shook Smith's hand and waited as he drove away.

In the light from the window, the skin beneath

Bobby's eyes was a translucent blue-green mottle. Exhaustion, *collapse*, had appeared in his face when I wasn't looking. I took his hand and he smiled at me.

"I don't think Julie would put Lexy in any danger," he said.

"Of course not," I said. "She loves Lexy."

I put my arms around him and for a minute or two we just held on, trying to keep at bay our worst fear: that our baby could be lost to us. I knew Julie would care for her lovingly, but we wanted more than that. We wanted Lexy back.

Downstairs, six officers from the Great Barrington Police Department were searching the house. Julie's catalog rooms with their pretty surfaces were now overturned and upended. Bobby and I didn't know what to do with ourselves. Everywhere we went we seemed to be in the way, so we just floated from kitchen to dining room to living room until we heard Detective Lazare's voice in the backyard. I opened the French doors in the living room and we went outside, where the early afternoon sun made mirrors of rain puddles on the slate patio.

When Lazare finished speaking with one of the officers, he turned his attention to us. Smiling a little, he said, "These waits are hard, I know."

"What about the Amber Alert?" I asked him. "How long do they usually take?"

"No good answer there," he said. "They take as long as they take. We've thrown a wide net—we'll find them."

But how could he be sure?

He pinched the bridge of his nose between forefinger and thumb, briefly closing his eyes. "This Thomas Soiffer thing has thrown me a little, I admit," he said. "I made a call and found out that your Clark Hazmat was right about Soiffer getting his identity stolen, too. But without the murder weapon, we've got nothing to check against Soiffer's prints on file, so we've just got to go with what we've got. Here's what I'm thinking: Soiffer, he was mad as hell"—Lazare paced back and forth, tracking wet footprints from the damp grass to the slate—"and he came here, right here, to Julie's house. He stalked her, waiting for the right moment. And Zara Moklas, poor kid, who happened to resemble you two in the dark, walks by and she gets it for all the damage your sister did to the wrong guy." He stopped pacing and looked at me. "How does that sound to you?"

"About right," I said quietly, despising the presumption that any of that could actually be true. Despite what Julie may have done to me, the possibility that Thomas Soiffer had really wanted to kill her was deeply painful.

"But what I can't get"—Lazare talked and paced— "is how your daughter factors into this."

"You're married, Detective," I said, "and so I assume you've been in love."

He stopped and looked at me. "Still am, actually."

"So you know how deeply love can move a person," I said.

He nodded. "Go on."

"Julie loves Lexy in a really special way, particularly since she's my daughter." I wiped nascent tears away with my fingertips. It was awful thinking this way, but too late to pull the thoughts back in. "Julie can't have children of her own."

"So she's jealous?" he asked.

"Yes," I said. "Essentially. Lexy's like the baby she can't have herself, but it's more than that. Lexy is *my* baby, and Julie wants what *I* have. When our parents died we were left very much alone together, and when I had my own family, I stepped out of our bubble. She wants Lexy, so she took her."

"And the rest of it?" Lazare stepped forward, his eyes pinned on me now. "Stealing your identity. Why?"

"I'm not sure," I said. "Maybe hurting me first would make it hurt less for her when she stole my baby. I really don't know."

"Or maybe it's just what she does," Bobby said. "If she did it to Thomas Soiffer, and she did it to Annie, then she probably did it to other people, too."

It was hard not reacting to that. Julie was still my twin and loving her, defending her, was sewn into my being. At this point I would have been willing to take Lexy back and walk away from the rest of it—but would I ever have that option?

"It's a wait-and-see game now." Lazare opened his cell phone and dialed a number from memory, saying, "Let's see what gives."

But nothing gave. The Amber Alert had netted no information and, more significantly, no Lexy. Once the police finished searching the downstairs, they worked their way through the bedrooms and finally went upstairs to Julie's suite. Lazare worked his phone. Bobby and I retreated into the living room and sat together on the couch.

"Now what?" I asked.

"We wait, I guess."

"For how long? It's torture just sitting here in this house, Bobby."

"Do you want to take a drive?"

"I do and I don't. If we leave, I'm afraid we'll miss something. And if we stay, I'm afraid we'll miss something. Every place I am right now feels like the wrong place."

He took my hand and squeezed it so hard it hurt. His eyes were full of turmoil when he looked at me and started to say, "Listen, Annie, I—" But he stopped when Detective Lazare walked through the French doors to announce that he was returning to the station but would be back soon. When we were alone again, Bobby did not finish his broken sentence. What had he been about to say? *I'm going crazy, too. I love you. I will move with you to New York when this is over. I want you to come home with me.* It could have been anything.

On the coffee table lay *Identity Theft in a New World*, the book Bobby had bought at the airport. I reached for it, stretched out on the living room couch, plunked my feet in Bobby's lap and opened to the first chapter. I was a fast reader and as the afternoon waned I was increasingly astounded by what I learned. It seemed that identity theft was more than just a new hazard to beware of. Its practitioners had, somewhat silently, multiplied into a small invisible army with potent, far-reaching tools that had already devastated a

growing number of victims. Because most targets of
identity theft never learned who had victimized them
and because the thieves usually got away, the victims
shared a sense of fragility, realizing that it could happen again at any time. You no longer knew who to
trust. Identity theft had destroyed careers, broken up
families, ruined lives. The book even went so far as to
liken it to a tsunami, whose imminence might come in
a warning but whose arrival could not be stopped once
it was set in motion.

As I read, I saw myself in every word, except that in
my case there was more at stake than financial losses.
There was Lexy. At every thought of her, panic blossomed in my chest. And so I read and read and read to
pass the time and fill my brain with something other
than raw worry. Up until now, I had shouldered every
burden life had thrown me. I could even handle the
theft of my identity—but not the theft of Lexy.

Bobby rubbed my feet as I read, disappearing occasionally and then returning, dozing at his end of the
couch. As twilight swallowed the last of the afternoon,
I fanned the book open on my chest and closed my
eyes, too. It was Tuesday evening and we hadn't slept
more than a few hours since Sunday night. I thought
about Lexy, recalled the bright lines of her face when
she smiled, the incredible softness of her skin, the
powdery smell of her neck, the salty taste of her tears
when I kissed her cheeks as she cried. It was the smiling face I settled on as I drifted off to sleep. When I
awoke, hours later, the night outside the windows was
solidly black and Bobby was gone, no longer at my
feet.

I got up and saw that the police were gone, too, and had left everything more or less in place. Then, nearing the kitchen, I heard voices.

Bobby and Gabe Lazare stood together in front of the microwave, which was elevated above the stovetop; something inside slowly rotated and the appliance's feeble light cast them as Vermeer milkmaids at a window, somber faces aglow. Lazare was holding a piece of paper, with Bobby reading along.

Beside them, on the kitchen counter, lay Julie's sleek pink cell phone. I felt a lump in my stomach when I saw it—this explained why she hadn't answered any of our calls—and when I saw my wallet next to the phone the lump dissolved to bile. I swallowed it back. Why should it be any surprise that Julie had abandoned her phone or stolen my wallet? Why should I feel shocked by the sight of these two objects? I flashed back to Gatsby's, where I'd last seen my wallet on Thursday. When had she taken it from me? Somehow I had missed the significant event of my sister stealing from me, over and over and over. Had getting my driver's license and Social Security card been Julie's final step in *becoming* me? Had leaving her phone behind been a step in *un*becoming herself?

I picked up the wallet—*mine*, but its discovery held no comfort for me. Opening it, I found exactly what I now expected: nothing. All my ID had been removed, even the little photo I carried of Bobby and Lexy.

"Where was it?" I asked.

In a strange, choreographed movement, they looked over at once. They seemed surprised to see me. I must have slept longer than I'd thought.

"Buried under one of the slabs of slate on the patio," Bobby said. "The police tracked the cell phone's satellite signal and found the wallet with it."

"Heard from Agent Smith." Lazare rustled the paper in his hand, which I now saw was a printed e-mail. "He's been busy. Seems it *was* Julie who wrote those love letters. And she was tracking the GPS in the Audi, so she knew you were on your way back. Wonder if taking off like that was a change of plans—maybe she couldn't face you, knowing you had been arrested, that it went that far."

I couldn't know what Julie was thinking, not exactly, but his hypothesis felt right. "Or maybe," I said, "taking Lexy was never a plan at all. Maybe she just did it."

"Maybe," Lazare said.

I put the wallet down and joined them in front of the microwave so I could read the e-mail. It was littered with acronyms, words and phrases that would have seemed like another language if I hadn't just read that book. She had amassed a collection of identities, not just mine or Thomas Soiffer's, by way of parts and pieces of information. She phished for suckers, keylogged for PINs, sent Trojan horses into private kingdoms. She had encrypted lists of MMNs (mother's maiden name); cobs (changes of billing capability with a PIN included so you could get at someone's bank account or credit card by using the PIN to change the mailing address); dumps (a credit card number); drops (a safe address, such as a post office box, to collect statements and deliveries); and algos (algorithms for encoding the magnetic strip on the back of a credit card). Smith's sign-off suggested that Julie might have even been a rather large fish in a growing sea, saying that it looked like she might have "successfully hit an aggregator."

"What does that mean?" I asked, touching my fingertip to that last line.

"Aggregators are companies that collect consumer data," Lazare explained. "Cyber thieves love them because they don't have to work so hard to gather all the information they need; it's all in one place. Remember that scandal a couple of years ago? When that company, ChoicePoint, actually sold information to con artists posing as marketing executives?"

I not only remembered—I had just read about it in the book. When ChoicePoint's data bank had been compromised by the thieves, the sensitive information of hundreds of thousands of people, both credit and personal, was suddenly *out there*. Data-aggregation companies collected information on individuals, including birth certificates, DMV records, credit and medical histories, court records and consumer transactions to create database reports on billions of individuals. They made money by selling the data to direct marketers to help them target products to consumers— so that people like me, lovers of *stuff*, could browse and dial or point and click from a consumer menu that had been designed just for us. According to the book, the government wasn't exactly on top of it, evidence of which I had now experienced more personally than I could ever have imagined.

The microwave buzzed and its light turned off.

Bobby opened it and, using oven mitts, removed a no-longer-frozen pizza.

"It isn't much," he said, "but we'll split it three ways."

"Not for me, thanks," Lazare said. "Remember that wife I told you about?"

"Of course," I said. "Good night." I kissed his cheek and he pulled back, startled.

"Good night." He folded the e-mail into his pocket and quietly left.

Bobby and I split the pizza onto plates and poured ourselves glasses of wine. We ate across from each other at the kitchen table, listening as the whir of Lazare's car engine melted into the deep silence.

"So," I said, "I guess that's why we never saw those other bills."

"Must be."

"I'm having trouble believing this. *Julie?*"

He put down his wineglass and reached across the table to touch my arm. I reciprocated with my palm over the back of his hand. I felt so *stupid*. I had followed Julie right into the trap: leaving Bobby, running to her for shelter and support, trading clothes like we were little girls and, worst of all, agreeing to wean Lexy. I had just begun to recognize Julie's envy, but not the *strength* of it. How could I, when all our lives we'd been better-than-best friends? How could I have foreseen that she would plan all this, set the stage, make me her puppet? There I was—*here I am*—jerking and dancing on an invisible web she wove just for me. *Cobs* and *dumps* and *drops* and *algos*. Okay, she'd proven she was smarter than me, but that was no

big surprise. I was the one who was supposed to have
emotional intelligence and now she had taken that
away from me, too. She had siphoned off my identity
so slowly and cannily I hadn't noticed. And she had
my baby. *My baby.* Julie had taken my *soul*.

The phone rang just before seven the next morning.
The caller ID read "GBPD"—Great Barrington Police
Department.

"Yes?" I answered, hoping for the best and fearing
the worst. *We found your daughter. She's here and
she's well*; or . . .

"Detective Gabe Lazare asks that you turn on your
TV," a woman's voice said.

Bobby and I had slept chastely beside each other
and now I woke him. We rushed downstairs to the living room and turned on the TV that hung over Julie's
living room fireplace. The local news station held their
camera steady on a microphone-festooned podium on
the police station's front lawn. Tying the belt of my
robe, I realized my hands were shaking.

Bobby sat down on the couch and I joined him. I
forced myself to breathe deeply, and again. Finally Detective Lazare arrived in the screen's limited perspec-
tive, walking through shadows thrown by overhead
branches that obscured the golden morning sun. He
settled himself behind the podium and cleared his
throat. The dark swaths beneath his eyes told me he
hadn't slept and I noticed that his badge, which he usually didn't wear, was positioned front and center on his
lapel.

"As you know," he began, "a week and a half ago

Zara Moklas was murdered on Division Street in Great Barrington. Now, for those of you from out of town, that's a quiet country road, a residential area. Her body was found in front of a house from which a baby was abducted yesterday."

"Baby Lexy?" a pretty television reporter asked.

"Yes."

"Any news on the baby, Detective?" asked a walnut-faced reporter holding a small pad and a pen.

"Nothing substantial, but we're following every lead, so to the folks out there watching: Please keep on calling."

I let out an involuntary moan and Bobby wrapped his arm around my shoulders, pulling me close. On the screen, a reporter in a plaid shirt raised his hand. Detective Lazare nodded at him and a slim audio recorder was lifted between them.

"Detective, do you think Zara Moklas's killer abducted the baby? Do you think the killer was after the baby in the first place? The press has already reported that Zara looked a lot like the owner of the house—"

"Hold it, now. Let's not jump the gun," Lazare said. "I'm only stating facts. The house is a common denominator in both cases and so we're looking at that. Period. Let's not jump to conclusions."

But the more Lazare denied that one overshadowed the other, the more the shadows overlapped. You could practically see the excitement in the reporters' eyes, in the tension and silence as they took their notes.

"Any new suspects, Detective?" Pen poised to write. "Have you lost hope of finding Thomas Soiffer?"

"We have *not* lost hope of finding Mr. Soiffer,"

Lazare answered. "We're as interested as ever in speaking with him right now." Soiffer's face filled the screen, taking me by surprise. It was the same mug shot I'd first seen last week. "As I've said before, Mr. Soiffer was known to be in the area shortly before Ms. Zoklas was killed. In light of this new development, we're hoping he might be able to provide us with some information that could help us in our search for Lexy Goodman."

A different television reporter, another woman, stepped forward. "Are you saying, Detective, that you want to question Mr. Soiffer specifically in connection with the abduction of the baby?"

"That's what we're hoping."

"Does that mean he's now also considered a suspect in the baby's abduction?"

A thin smile stretched across Lazare's face, the kind of blank-slate response that was no more promising than discouraging. "I'm saying he's a person of interest."

Person of interest. The media knew as well as I did what that overworked phrase meant: suspect without enough evidence for an arrest.

"One more question, Detective." Plaid shirt, recorder raised. "The owner of the house, Julie Milliken, is known to have an identical twin sister who is the mother of the missing baby. Is it possible that Mr. Soi—that *someone* who killed Zara, if they were after the baby—thought they were killing the sister? To get the baby? And why would they be after *this* baby, Detective? What is the significance of her abduction?"

"No use guessing, is there? We want to find Mr.

Thomas Soiffer and ask him a few questions. That's it for today. Thanks for coming out, folks. We're hoping the media attention will help us find the baby. Thank you." Lazare waved and thin-smiled as he turned his back on the reporters and walked away. Calmly. The way that man could hold himself together was disorienting.

Bobby picked up the remote and clicked off the TV. "What was that all about? Why didn't he at least warn us?"

"Last night he seemed convinced *Julie* had her," I said. "What changed? Does he really think that man has our Lexy?"

The phone rang again and this time it was Detective Lazare himself. Bobby answered the living room extension and I went to the kitchen phone so I could join the conversation.

"If Julie thinks we're after Thomas Soiffer for Lexy's abduction," Lazare was already saying when I picked up, "it just might make her feel safer and it might bring her out of the woodwork. She might increase her movements, which would increase our chances of finding her—and your daughter."

"Okay," Bobby said. "I can see it."

"So you *do* think Lexy's with Julie?" I said, jumping in.

"I suspect so," Lazare answered. "I'm using the media to set a trap. When we don't find someone right away, we try to jolt them out of their hiding place. I'm sorry I didn't tell you my plan, but you have to understand that time is not on our side."

I couldn't argue with him; he was trying to find my

baby. But a media blitz terrified me because of how it might shock Julie, and it seemed to me that Lexy's safety depended on Julie's equilibrium. What also frightened me was his comment about time, because if you really thought about the nature of time—how there was too much of it when it didn't matter and not enough when you needed it—you'd realize how perilous it could be, at life's worst possible moments, to wait even a minute too long.

By early afternoon, Detective Lazare appeared at the house to hand-deliver two important pieces of news. He came through the kitchen door and sat us down at the table so we could hear him out.

"We found Soiffer's van," he said, pacing, "behind an abandoned barn in New Hampshire. Now listen closely to this next part. A preliminary inspection found nothing of Lexy in that van. *Nothing.*"

Bobby and I glanced at each other. Something more was coming.

"The van had a lot of blood in the back part. It's already been typed, and the type does not match your daughter's. It *does* match Zara's, so that's where we're going with this. Unfortunately DNA analysis can take a couple of weeks, and we won't know for sure until then, but we seem to be heading in some direction now."

"Where's Soiffer?" Bobby asked.

"Good question." Lazare stopped at the far end of Julie's kitchen counter and appeared to contemplate her squat black espresso machine, but I knew his mind was deep in the morning's developments and the satisfaction that his plan, on some level, was working. "We've heard from Jason Soiffer, Thomas's son, to broker the safe emergence of his father."

It was incredible news. As Lazare spoke, it became apparent that negotiations had been going on for hours.

"Son's a straight shooter," he continued. "No record, avoided his father's criminal path completely. Jason Soiffer is a plumber, union guy, hard worker, salt of the earth. He is adamant that his father has nothing to do with Lexy's abduction. *Adamant*. I sat back and let him talk and he told me all about his father's problems. Said the identity theft took Tom by surprise about a year ago, and by the time he discovered it, he was on a mudslide, hitting bottom. Said his father was doing his best to keep out of trouble and rebuild his life on parole. He'd been out of jail almost two years and was doing well. Even the ex-girlfriend he'd assaulted was talking to him again—not the brightest move on her part, but the point is, the guy was hanging in there. He went to his local police about the identity theft, but they did nothing for him." Lazare paused at that and shook his head. "Local police departments only started getting trained on ID theft recently, ours among them, so I believe these people that they didn't get the help they needed. No one knew *how* to help. So Tom hired a private investigator, who found Julie for him, and then he lost it. He started stalking her. Jason said he'd known about it since late winter and tried to convince his dad to try the police again, but Tom refused. He was convinced the police wouldn't work too hard to help an ex-con. He felt he had to deal with it himself. Big mistake. With all the new attention, and now with the van being found, Tom figured he couldn't hide anymore. Jason says he can't explain the bloody van, but he believes that his father knows nothing about Lexy's abduction and that he did not kill Zara Moklas—but he was there, and he saw it."

"He saw it?" I leaned across the table and reached for Bobby's hand. "What did he see?"

"We don't know yet." Lazare pulled out a kitchen chair and joined us, finally coming to rest. "He'll come forward if we get him immunity. I said I could look into some kind of limited immunity, pending the results on that blood, if he agreed to be photographed with me. I want Julie to see that we've got him. Jason said his dad wouldn't like the publicity, but he'd see what he could do. We're waiting to hear."

"So it's working," Bobby said. "Just like you hoped."

One side of Lazare's mouth crooked up. "Looks like it, so far. I'm calling another news conference for eight o'clock tonight in the hope I can get him out of hiding that fast."

The eight p.m. news conference—this one held outside Julie's house—came and went with nothing but a tepid update on the case in which Detective Lazare basically stated that nothing had changed. The reporters seemed only mildly disappointed; apparently Lazare had succeeded in making Lexy's disappearance a top story of the day and any exposure of the players was grist for the hungry media content mill. That was a bonus for us, because now the whole country cared and was watching for Lexy. At the end of the news conference, as planned, Bobby and I joined Lazare in the glare of lights so we could beg and cry in public. We did. I hated for Julie to see us this way, since I suspected she would feed off our weakness, but Lazare promised that it was part of his plan. When Soiffer eventually emerged, so would we, again, relieved and hopeful that this person of interest could offer information that would lead us to our daughter. And then, if Lazare had his way, in the relative safety of misdirection, Julie would shed a layer of caution. Or would she? The Julie I knew had never been careless and the Julie I *didn't* know was turning out to be exceedingly calculating.

At two o'clock in the morning Thomas Soiffer arrived at the Great Barrington Police Department in a sea of artificial lights. It was a carefully brokered moment; there was no talk, just the image of Soiffer being escorted into the station between his son and Detective Lazare. Half an hour later, senseless with exhaustion, Bobby and I faced a splinter group of reporters who had traveled back to Julie's house.

"I'm so grateful." I wept on camera, Bobby pressed to my side. "Now they have Thomas Soiffer in custody. If this man knows who killed Zara Moklas, then maybe he can also help us find our baby."

And so the night passed, hour after hour, while Detective Lazare kept Thomas Soiffer to himself in ominous silence at the police station. The reporters and TV crews camped outside the Main Street entrance occasionally defaulted to reporting on themselves with another "live update on the situation in Great Barrington, Massachusetts." Bobby and I kept the TVs on throughout the house so wherever we were we would hear the news bulletins. Soiffer's appearance and our on-screen plea were continually repeated, but there was nothing new. I started to wonder if we'd have better luck getting information from *our* reporters—the small clutch of them huddled in vans out front or pacing Julie's lawn to stretch their legs—but I had already cried twice on camera and Lazare had coached me not to overdo it and not to let them catch me off guard. He preferred scheduled, controlled news conferences. Every half hour or so there was a woodpecker-like burst of knocking at our kitchen door, which we ignored. Until Lazare announced the results of his interview with Soiffer, or until Julie made a move, there was nothing more to say.

Finally, in the pitch-dark hours of early morning, Bobby and I retreated to the Yellow Room—and bed. It had been over a month since I had made love with my faithless husband, but now his faithfulness had been rebuilt by a pile of rotten facts. He had never cheated on me; his denials had been accurate all along. Julie had systematically stripped me down and ripped us apart. I felt a kind of angry sorrow that I didn't recognize and felt as if, no matter what happened now— if Lexy was back with us, unharmed, in an hour—I had lost something forever. Our marriage would never be as innocent as it once was. I put my hands under his T-shirt, pulled it over his head, unbuckled his belt and zipped down his pants. He pulled all the white cloth off my body. His skin felt warm and familiar and yet there was a sense of urgency in our lovemaking, as if it was the first time—or as if we'd never have another chance. I loved him. But something was still wrong. I couldn't detach my mind from Lexy. Nothing could blot out her absence, the empty crib in our room. Nothing.

Dawn arrived, bracing the house in its usual chilly mist before spreading fresh, clear light across the sky. Peeking out the window of the Yellow Room, I could see individual dewdrops clinging to blades of grass and had to resist the urge to run out there barefoot and feel the dampness for myself. I hated being shut in the house like this, sleeping in helpless bursts, waking again and again to the sharp realization that my baby was still gone.

Bobby slept deeply and I tried not to disturb him as I turned on my camera, positioning myself at the window. I shot straight through glass and screen, wondering how these barriers would translate the outside view, how exactly they would distort the plain reality of grass. As my camera clicked and whirred I imagined Lexy, a little girl, running into the frame, her bare feet feeling the damp grass. I could *feel* her life. If Julie succeeded in keeping her, would her sensations of me as her real mommy eventually be erased? Would the two mommies, the double vision of me and Julie together in her buried memories, blur into one? I took a dozen shots before capping my lens and zipping the camera back into its case.

I dressed and went downstairs to the quiet kitchen, where I made coffee, then carried my mug into the living room and turned on the TV. Just as I settled into the couch, the phone rang. This early, in such total quiet, the sound hit me with the impact of a full-scale malarm and I stood abruptly, the seed of panic planted, before realizing that it was only the phone. A pretty television

reporter I recognized from yesterday's news conference, a blond woman in a pink suit, appeared on the
screen. She was standing outside the Great Barrington
Police Station, holding a microphone to her mouth,
and at that moment I knew it was Lazare calling the
house and that this time his preemptive warning had
failed. The phone stopped ringing—Bobby must have
answered upstairs—and I watched with the rest of the
world for news of my child.

"It seems that Julie Milliken, who is being sought in
the abduction of her niece, whom the world has come
to know as Baby Lexy, is also under investigation in a
just-developing case of identity theft. The victim: her
identical twin sister, Annie Milliken-Goodman, Lexy's
mother. It was in front of Julie Milliken's Division
Street home nearly two weeks ago that this woman"—
*a picture of Zara Moklas, smiling, appeared on the
screen*—"was brutally murdered. Just last night,
Thomas Soiffer, who had been sought in connection
with that case"—*a replay of his surrender*—"turned
himself in to the police. And now the police are on
their way to Barton, Vermont, where early this morning a motel owner reported renting a room to a woman
and baby resembling Julie Milliken and Lexy Goodman. Barton police are already at the scene."

Bobby, fully dressed, came running down the stairs
into the living room.

"Come on," he said. "We're meeting Lazare. If
we're not there in ten minutes, he'll leave without us."

Chapter 11

A sign reading NORTHWEST KINGDOM MOTEL & CABINS stood at a turnoff from Route 5 in Barton, Vermont. Bobby and I sat in the backseat of the squad car that had met our helicopter at a local airfield; Lazare sat up front in the passenger seat. Our car kicked up dust all the way down the long road bordered on both sides by towering pines. Half a mile along we were forced to stop. The road was blocked by four different camera crews, each with its satellite tower reaching skyward from vans that seemed too small to hold it. In the near distance I could see a clapboard motel. To its right, attached cabins, each with its own porch, staggered backward into the woods. Lazare thanked the cop who had driven us and got out. Bobby and I exited opposite doors of the squad car—and we ran.

About a hundred feet ahead, two men talking with each other stood out for their lack of uniforms: one a middle-aged man with close-cropped red hair, in baggy jeans and battered work boots, the other a tall man with a shock of white hair and a full beard, also in jeans and work boots. Beyond them, at the farthest end of the asphalt parking lot, outside the last cabin, I saw my pale blue rental car. The trunk and all four doors were wide open. An unmarked van was parked at an angle beside it and some kind of technician in a green jumpsuit was leaning into the trunk.

The two men turned around when they noticed us running toward them. Closer, I saw that the red-haired man was holding a walkie-talkie. He said something to the other man and walked to meet us.

"Detective Lazare?" He must have recognized him from TV.

"That's me," Lazare said. The two men shook hands.

"Detective Andy Phipps. Pleased to meet you."

"These are the parents, Annie and Bobby Goodman." Lazare introduced us. "Baby girl here?"

"Not now, but she was," Phipps answered. "Come on, meet Leo Brook, owns the place. You can hear it from the horse's mouth."

Brook greeted us with a nod of his bushy chin. This close, I noticed the bulbous nose and bloodshot eyes of northern solitude. I knew his kind from my New England college winters. They were the *locals*, men and women skilled at hunkering against the bitter cold year after year, spending too much time alone, maybe drinking too much, emerging in spring older than a single season.

"Like I was telling the detective"—Brook's voice was coarse yet gentle—"they checked in early this morning, using the name Erin Garfield. Wanted the farthest cabin. Said she didn't want the baby to wake

anyone in the night. I told her there's no one else here
right now, but she said that's what she wanted. I'm not
one to quibble with a paying guest. Had no reason to
doubt her until I opened the newspaper over breakfast."

"They're not here now?" It was all I cared about.

"Like I told the detective, they went out a while
ago." Brook's voice rose with distress, as if his lack of
vigilance, when he had been unaware that it was required, had failed us all. "Didn't see where exactly.
Kicking myself but good, I can tell you."

"You couldn't have known, Leo," Detective Phipps
said. "You got us here—that's what counts. If we have
any more questions, we'll look for you in the office."

Brook nodded, glanced at me and Bobby, then left
us with the long, reaching strides of a very tall man
who seemed to buckle with every step.

"All their things are still in one of the rooms,"
Phipps said. "My guess is they don't know they're
missed here and they'll be back."

"But the car," Bobby said.

"Left on foot, probably. Leo said there was a stroller
parked outside the door this morning, but we can't find
it anywhere. I think they went out for a walk."

"A walk?" I looked all around. The compound was
nestled in forest and the driveway was long, feeding directly into the main road. It didn't look like good walking territory, not for a set of wheels unsuited for rough
ground. But Lexy must have needed a nap and Julie
must have decided to lull her with a ride in the stroller,
which often succeeded in calming her when I, and my
breasts, were unavailable.

"Leo gave you a cabin to use while you wait."

Phipps threw Lazare a key. "I'll be here if you need me."

Bobby and I followed Gabe Lazare across the parking lot. The doors of two neighboring cabins were wide open. One must have been ours and the other, directly in front of the blue rental car, must have been Julie's. Outside the second door a uniformed officer was posted and inside was a moving shadow, someone searching. I paused, longing to enter the cool darkness of their room, to see and smell and feel the place where my baby had only recently been, as if any sensation associated with her might wipe clean my worry. I could see the curved ends of two twin beds with brown-striped mustardy bedspreads. As I neared the cabin a cop shook his head, warning me not to come any closer.

I turned to Bobby, wondering if he shared my frustration, if he also wanted to get inside that room. But his attention was caught on something else: the car, the *trunk* of the car, out of which the green-garbed technician unfolded his body to standing. In one gloved hand he held a paper bag and in the other—Julie's kaleidoscopic sweater.

Lazare hesitated, glanced at the sweater and nodded at the technician, who slid it into the bag. I wondered if the detective remembered me wearing the sweater to Julie's the night I arrived. He must have, since he'd commented on it at the time. I remembered being struck that he would notice a piece of clothing when a woman had been killed. I remembered thinking, wearing the bright sweater, how Zara's blood looked even brighter, how I had not known that an abundance of fresh blood could be so vivid, bathed in artificial light. I had forgotten all about the sweater since that night and now wondered how it had gotten into the trunk. For all I knew, Julie had worn it when she took flight with Lexy. I could just see her standing at her closet, deciding what to wear, and I instinctively agreed with her that because this brash garment was impossible to hide in, it was perfect for an escape. Opposite Day, we used to call it as kids, delighting in how easy it was to defy people's expectations.

Bobby and I looked at Detective Lazare at the same time. Deflecting our questions with his practiced silence, he put his hand on my lower back and guided us into our waiting cabin.

It was like a rustic suite with just the basics: a bare-bones living room—nubby couch, upholstered rocking chair, two-seat table, TV—and a small bedroom tucked away at the back. Even on this bright spring day the inside light was gritty and dim, struggling through two meager curtained windows. Lazare sat on the rocking chair and folded his hands over his middle. Bobby and I sat together on the couch. I realized that until our impromptu helicopter ride that morning when the only thing on our minds was zeroing in on Lexy, we hadn't seen the detective since his TV image escorted Thomas Soiffer into the police station in the middle of the night.

"What did Soiffer have to say?" I asked. "Where is he now?"

"We're holding him on a parole violation." Outside, a cloud shifted; the room brightened and the fine lines on Lazare's face came into focus.

"Was he charged with murder?" I asked.

"Without his blood analysis and without a murder weapon, we don't have any case. No evidence, no arrest."

"But—" I started.

Lazare clapped his hands on his knees and stood up. "Let's just leave it at that for now." He crossed the room, turned on the TV and sat back down in the rocking chair.

I felt the injustice of a censured child and wanted to shout at the man, shock him into telling us more. It was *wrong* of him not to tell us. Our daughter was *missing*. We had seen a woman, *dead*, outside my sister's house. The sight of Zara Moklas came back to me, her body eerily still, throat sliced open, oozing the final essence of her life. I looked at Bobby, hoping to engage him in my frustration, but like Lazare he had shut down, checked out, and was watching (or pretending to watch) Oprah interview a young actress who intermittently giggled.

It was an unbearable wait, worse even than my night in prison. Despite the shock and humiliation of that, I had believed, at least, that Lexy was safe. I had believed I'd be reunited with her quickly and that somehow my wrongful arrest would get sorted out. I thought of Liz; our conversations since the morning when I'd returned to Great Barrington had convinced her beyond a doubt that I would be easily vindicated of the embezzlement charges, but that was hardly the problem anymore. The problem was that I had lost my baby and my sister, all in one fell swoop. I had lost my *heart*. Who was I without them? As my mind lit on that question—the problem of boundaries of experience and meaning, all the implications of *self*, not so much as a series of experiences but perceptions, beliefs and feelings that define what we think of as a person's *soul*. I sensed myself drifting. Who *was* I? Who was *I*?

And then, suddenly, I heard Julie outside. "*Stop it. Don't touch my baby!*"

I ran to the cabin door and there she was, gripping one of Lexy's stroller handles while one cop held the other handle and another tugged her elbow, trying to pull her away.

"*Your* baby?" I hurried down the porch steps. When she saw me, her mouth dropped open. She was mute. For the first time ever, I had rendered my twin speechless. She had no answer before the question, no end to my sentence. She had *nothing*.

I went straight to Lexy—*my* baby—who was groggy but awake in the stroller and clearly alarmed by all the turmoil. As soon as I saw her my milk dropped, soaking the front of my shirt. Bobby ran ahead and helped the officer detach Julie from the stroller while I knelt down in front of Lexy. Balancing on the balls of my feet, smiling and crying, I unbuckled her straps. She stared at me. I noticed that she didn't reach for me as she always had before, so I leaned in closer and whispered, "It's Mommy! Come here, my sweet angel." One little hand reached out to touch my face and she started to cry. Leaning forward, she searched behind her for Julie, then looked at me and cried harder.

"Annie, you're scaring her," Julie said.

"*I'm* scaring her? Why are you doing this to us?"

"Doing what? Did you forget? I told you I was taking her to the house."

"*What* house?"

"In Maine," she said. "The house I rented. I told you all about it."

"You're a *liar*." Bobby released her to the cop, who manacled one of her wrists, then the other. "You *bitch*."

She looked shocked at that and even *I* felt shocked, automatically defensive of my sister's dignity. But I got over it quickly.

"Embezzlement of federal funds?" I said.

"What are you talking about?" Her tone was incredulous, and her eyes—the eyes I knew so well—challenged me. There was something new in them, a hoax I had not been let into.

"I was arrested in Manhattan," I said. "I spent a night in *jail*."

"Jail?"

"Oh, Julie, *don't*. The FBI's got your computer all decrypted, so there's no way to deny it."

She paused a moment before her eyes clouded over and she looked really scared. "I have no idea what you're talking about, Annie. Please, *please* help me. This is all a misunderstanding . . ."

Misunderstanding? *Help* her? I couldn't believe my ears.

Lexy was sobbing now and I lifted her out of the stroller. I held her and rocked her and *loved* her with every iota of my being. In the bubble of privacy in which I greeted my baby, I became aware of cameras clicking, reporters talking to video lenses, Julie being read her rights. Without looking back, I carried Lexy into the cabin.

We settled down on the couch, her skin so very soft against mine. She looked healthy and clean and she was *safe*. It was an unrivaled joy to have her back in my arms. But I could see that she was restless, confused. I thought it might help us both if I nursed her, so I lifted my shirt, unhooked my bra and offered her my breast. She turned away. Tears gathering in my eyes, I tried again. It took a while, but finally, tentatively, she latched on—and drank.

The cabin was beautifully quiet while Lexy nursed, pressing her chubby little hands into my swollen breasts, realizing—or remembering—that I was *me*, her real and actual mommy. I could have sat on that couch with her forever. Outside, voices crescendoed, lulled, spiked again. Finally, cars began to drive away. I had the relieved feeling that I'd been forgotten and would be allowed a long, luxurious seclusion with my child.

But then I heard two voices—Bobby's and Detective Lazare's. They were standing outside the cabin, talking about Julie.

"What now?" Bobby asked. "Will she actually be released?"

"If she can post bail, yes."

"You know she'll be able to post bail. I can't *believe* this."

"We have enough evidence for a federal charge of computer fraud," Lazare said. "It's a *charge*, not a conviction. After she's processed, the legal case will begin. Everyone has the right of innocence until proven guilty."

"What about kidnapping? That's a felony."

"Annie left her sister in charge of Lexy. She had permission."

"Julie *disabled* the GPS and *buried* her cell phone," Bobby said. "She made a deliberate effort not to be traced."

"*Someone* did those things, yes. But you see the difficulty—without a witness we can't substantiate that it was Julie who hid the GPS and the phone. In the eyes of the law it could have been anyone."

"That's *ridiculous*."

"You heard Julie," Lazare said. "She claims this was a planned trip. If she can find a way to prove it, then it may not technically be kidnapping."

"Annie didn't know anything about a house in Maine. Julie made that up."

"But we have to investigate first."

"This is fucking unreal!"

I could picture Lazare in the thick silence that followed Bobby's outburst—his taut non-smile, his infuriating patience.

"Okay, what about Thomas Soiffer?" Bobby asked. "Are you telling me he didn't witness Julie killing Zara Moklas?"

"I'm not telling you anything right now."

"*Julie* killed her, Detective. I bet that's what Soiffer told you. It's part of everything that's happened so far—our breakup, the identity theft, Annie's arrest, the kidnapping, *everything*. Just tell me: Am I right?"

"A significant amount of blood matching Zara's

general type was found in Soiffer's van," Lazare said, calmly, coolly. "If it isn't her blood, he'll be eliminated. If you're right about Julie, we'll get there in time."

"How much time? She'll cut and run, Detective. I know her."

"Your daughter's in there," Lazare said. "Don't you want to see her now?"

And suddenly, as their footsteps clomped up the outside steps and across the wood porch, I knew something terrible: I *knew* what Thomas Soiffer had told Detective Lazare. He had witnessed Zara's murder—that was already established—but naturally Lazare had his doubts. That was why they had taken as possible evidence the sweater from the trunk. And that was why he wouldn't arrest Julie for murder.

Soiffer had reported seeing Julie kill Zara—which meant he might have seen *me*.

PART THREE

PART THREE

Chapter 12

First thing Monday morning, a full week into this nightmare, there was a chill in the Great Barrington Police Department's Detectives Unit. It was too late in the season for heat and too early for the sun to have penetrated the windows and worn away the nighttime country cold. Through the window behind Lazare's desk I watched the leaves of the big maple tree shiver as light bounced off their undersides, flashing like thrown coins. Before leaving me alone here, Lazare had brought me a mug of hot coffee, which was nice-ish of him. I had been told to wear jeans and a plain short-sleeved shirt for the lineup and my arms were covered in goose bumps. I'd been here ten minutes and he hadn't said much, just the usual pleasantries, but today his über-calm was anything but reassuring. For all my questions this morning, he had offered a single answer: "No." No, the blood test results from Thomas Soiffer's van were not finished being analyzed. No, Soiffer was not being arrested, at the moment, for Zara's murder. No, a murder weapon still had not been found.

Why wouldn't Lazare *talk* to me, just tell me what was going on? It was an *outrage* that I was here at all, waiting, while he went about the business of making sure all the other Annie-look-alike women were gathered so we could stand there being scrutinized by, presumably, Thomas Soiffer. *Person of interest.* Ex-con. Victim. Witness. The man was so many things, my head was spinning. Was *I* being put in a *lineup* based on *his* word? Not just me, but Julie too. She was to be put through the same paces, at a different time, so our paths wouldn't cross as we were *processed.* Since our return from Vermont, she had been arrested for fraud, grand larceny and a long list of other crimes all related to the identity theft. Posted bail and been released. (Incredibly, her grand larceny charge did not automatically erase *mine*, which continued to wend its way through the legal system.) We hadn't laid eyes on each other, nor would we anytime soon. We were officially severed. But Julie—*oh, Julie*—how I missed her! I still couldn't believe this was happening or that I might actually have lost her, or lost who she used to be. And now, for us to be compared by the police in this light, to be studied with the implication that one of us may have committed murder. I knew *I* hadn't. Which meant . . .

No. I couldn't go there, couldn't think that, couldn't plant that rotten seed in my heart. To save my sanity, for now, I would stick with the probability that Thomas Soiffer had killed Zara. Because *that* was what made sense. I had to assume that Soiffer had lied about witnessing but not committing the murder. That Lazare was just covering his bases by putting us in lineups, crossing us off his list, saving time, on the off chance that Soiffer was telling the truth. A very *remote* off chance. Obviously, the only thing a lineup would reveal was that people couldn't tell me and Julie apart. At most, identifying *me* would discredit Soiffer's statement that it was *definitely Julie* he saw slicing the poor woman's throat (assuming that's what he'd said—and why wouldn't he try to point fingers elsewhere? *His van was full of blood*). Maybe that was all Lazare was after, discrediting Soiffer. No, not all. He also wanted *our* blood. He had me and Julie scheduled for blood tests; mine was to take place later that day at a local clinic.

The coffee had warmed me somewhat and when I finished it I wanted more, but the pot was all the way across the room. Was I allowed to walk over and get some for myself? I swiveled around to look for Detective Lazare—he wasn't here—and saw that a few other detectives had trickled in to start their day. All three avoided looking at me, much as the New York City detectives had ignored me in their own precinct. Once again, they were *us*, I was *them*. I was a *suspect* now, a person being readied for a *lineup*. I noticed that one of the detectives, a woman about my height and with my coloring, was also wearing jeans and a plain T-shirt. I guessed she was part of the lineup, too. I tried to catch her eye and smile, just to see what would happen. She put her purse on the desk, took out a small appointment book, set it by the phone and flipped it open. I stared at her, but she wouldn't look at me, not even a glance, though I knew she knew I was sitting right here.

I got up, *invisible*, and carried my empty mug across

the room, making a beeline for the coffeepot. Filling my mug with the steaming coffee, I saw that someone had brought a box of blueberry muffins. I took one, curious to see if *now* the detectives would react. Nothing. I spread open a paper napkin on the edge of Lazare's desk, set my muffin down and had broken off just one piece of the top edge when the room's far door swung open and Lazare waved me over.

"Okay," he said. "We're ready now."

I stood up, chewing my single bite of muffin, a blueberry bursting tartly on my tongue—delicious. I smiled. Now they all glanced at me, just for one quick moment, but there was no satisfaction in this meager attention, just a flush of humiliation as I followed Detective Lazare out of the room.

Down a bright, clean hall. Up a narrow, painted-cinder-block staircase. Directly into a white, white room where three other Annie-and-Julie-sort-of-look-alikes were lined up shoulder to shoulder against a bare wall. The fifth and final one, the detective from downstairs, now joined us at the end, right next to me. It was even colder in here and I hugged my forearms over my middle until Lazare, turning to shut the door, said, "Arms down, please." I dropped my arms and smoldered. The chilliest thing right now was the brevity of his words, the crispness of his tone. I *hated* being here.

White women, white room, gray linoleum floor buffed to a high polish, fluorescent lighting that hid nothing and a large panel of one-way glass in which I saw my own reflection multiplied by these strangers who resembled me only on the barest terms. Who *were* these women? I wondered (other than the detective, fifth on the right).

We stood there for about five minutes before a disembodied voice filtered commands into the room.

"Number two, please step forward. Thank you."

"Number one, please. Thank you."

"Number four." That was me. "Turn to the right. Thank you. To the left. All right. Thank you."

And then, a minute later, it was over. Detective Lazare opened the door, thanking each of us in exactly the same tone as we filed past him. I couldn't look at him. The women seemed to scatter as we made our way down the stairs, then along a hall that branched in two places. By the time I reached the front lobby, there were only three of us left, and in the parking lot I was alone.

It was still early and there was time to get back to our new, temporary home at a local inn (how could I ever set foot in Julie's house again?). My appointment at the clinic was at noon, which meant I could do Lexy's midmorning feeding at my breast and Bobby could give her some cereal and a bottle at around one o'clock, before her afternoon nap. I hadn't realized just how tense I'd been about the lineup until now, when it was over, and I found myself sitting in the driver's seat (my replaced license snug in my wallet) of my new silver-gray rental car, the old rental car having been impounded by the police. Still parked in the lot, I wept into the steering wheel. It took ten long minutes to cry myself out, and then, finally, I headed to the inn.

A few miles outside of town, the Weathervane Inn was the only establishment that would have us, as none of the others took children under twelve, especially noise-making smell-issuing babies. It was perfect—big enough to have some privacy, small enough to feel comfortable. They served a full, filling breakfast and, for lunch and dinner, pointed you in the direction of the many excellent local restaurants, which I had never really noticed, as we'd done our eating mainly at Julie's house. The innkeepers, Mr. and Mrs. Boardman—a long-married couple who had raised a family in this very inn—allowed guests use of the two living rooms, one of which was kind of a family-den-cum-kids'-game-room, which made it a perfect place for us to hang out. All the weekenders had fled the night before or early this morning and when I returned from the police station I found Bobby alone in the den with Lexy on her play mat on the floor.

On a side table next to the couch was a bouquet of lilacs. The fragrant and vaguely purple clusters relaxed over the lip of a glass cocktail shaker filled with water and I couldn't resist leaning over and taking a deep whiff of the tiny blossoms. The lush smell filled me, *warmed* me, replacing the chill of the police station, and I took another breath of it. Then I kissed Bobby and snuggled next to him on the couch. Together we watched Lexy.

Even after two days, it still felt like a miracle to have her back. I didn't know if I'd ever trust anyone with her again—except Bobby, of course. Maybe I would be one of those mothers who never used a babysitter and never let her kids out of her sight. Bobby and I had already decided to return to Kentucky together when Detective Lazare was through with me here and when Liz had sorted out the embezzlement charge and we could buy back the bail bond. Kent, amazingly, had softened up and had stopped hassling Bobby about all the time off (wisely, since the Family Leave Act allowed Bobby ample time to care for his family without loss of his job, and if Kent had persisted in his harassment it would only have meant a lawsuit). So we would go home. But I would not return to work at the prison—I would *never* set foot in any prison again. I would stay home and be with Lexy full-time until I figured out my next move. In a year, once Bobby had earned his pension, we would relocate somewhere that we both agreed on. That was our new plan.

"Liz called," Bobby said after a minute.

"And?"

"She's asking around for recommendations for a criminal defense lawyer, either from around here or the Boston area."

"Do I really need another lawyer? And why Boston? It's so far."

"It's not really that far—and yes, Liz says you should have a lawyer who knows Massachusetts criminal law."

"But I'm not a criminal!"

"I know that." He kissed my forehead. "And Liz knows that, and Thomas Soiffer probably knows that, and, let's face it, *Julie* knows that. But still, Liz said that because they're putting you through all these paces, you need representation. Just in case."

"In case of what?"

"I don't know, Annie. Just *in case*."

"What about Julie? She's probably already got the best lawyer there is."

"Probably."

Bored with her toys on the floor, Lexy started to fuss. I bent down and brought her to my lap, running my hands along her soft, soft arms and kissing her sweet-smelling peach-fuzz head.

"Listen, Annie." Bobby raised his eyebrows and set his mouth in preparation for this: "Liz told me something else. She said she spoke with the police in Lexington, and they told her they'd confiscated our computer, from home."

I stared at him, speechless.

"They sent our computer to the FBI in Boston."

"*Why?* Do they actually think *I* started all this? Like I'm some kind of madwoman hell-bent on self-destruction—"

"Annie." Bobby's tone was firm. "Liz said not to waste time getting upset about it. I think she's right. Rusty Smith's probably checking to see how Julie's viruses and stuff got into our files, something like that. The important thing is that Liz thinks she should be able to have the embezzlement charge dropped in the next couple of days, and as soon as that happens, buying back the bail bond won't take long."

"Two whole days?"

"She said Thursday at the latest."

"But Thursday's *three* days away."

"*Annie*, it's really in our best interest to cooperate. Once the blood results come in, the criminal stuff will work itself out. And remember, Lazare's dealing with Julie, too. He may need to talk to us some more. It's important we stick around for that. Three days isn't that long if you look at the larger picture."

"Fine," I said. "We'll stay and talk to him, and I'll meet my new lawyer, but I want to go home by the end of this week. If anyone has any more questions, can't they talk to us on the phone?"

Bobby's smile showed hints of mischief. It really was tempting, even for someone as disciplined as he was, to slough off our fast-multiplying shackles just by deciding to go. He could get what he'd wanted all along: I would go home with him. "Well," he said, "we'll try to leave by Friday—or sooner, if we can."

Lexy grabbed at my shirt and I got her latched on for her midmorning feed, then settled my head on Bobby's shoulder. With one extended finger, he stroked his daughter's supple cheek while she sucked away at me. When she was finished, I handed her to him and he paced the room, patting her back in hope of a burp. I leaned across the couch and sank my nose into the lilacs to drink some more from their glorious scent. The lilacs had bloomed weeks ago in Kentucky, where it was warmer. So you see, in some ways I was lucky: this year, I got lilacs twice.

A blue-green vein fattened in reaction to the tight rubber tourniquet, the needle pierced the skin of my inner arm and I could feel my blood pulsing out. I watched as the technician, a tiny Korean woman, capped one vial and attached a second to the needle. All my life, I had never looked away when blood was drawn, and, in fact, today it strengthened me to watch my blood fill the glass vials. That was a difference between Julie and me: during any medical procedure, she blanched and looked away. Not I. Nearly every drop of blood that had ever left my body had been observed by me. All our adult lives Julie and I had donated blood as a matter of conscience, and every time it was the same: I would focus on my blood's journey from vein to tube to vial; she would focus anywhere else. When Lexy was born, I had screamed and fought and even watched, at moments, through a mirror I had insisted Bobby hold up at the end of the hospital bed. I remember him cringing a little at the suggestion of the mirror— he thought it was "gruesome"—and I had to explain my strange relationship with blood, as a twin. It was a matter of my own body and where it ended; blood that came from my body belonged only to *me*. Julie had her own blood and her own reaction to it.

This fascination had started when I was a child, when a teacher had explained that during gestation some twins shared a sac, while others had their own individual sacs; likewise, some twins shared a placenta, while others did not. And to further complicate the possible variables, twins sharing a placenta and a sac sometimes also shared circulation: that is, *blood*. One's blood would circulate through the other and back again, to the extent that some fraternal boy/girl twin pairs soaked up each other's hormones, blurring gender-based behaviors later on. So the question of whether or not I had my very own blood, or some combination of mine and Julie's, felt significant to me.

Because we were identical twins, I was attuned to any differences. For instance, growing up, I'd thought I was served a greater dollop of bravery (what my

mother called "impulsiveness" or, in frustration, "fool-
ishness") than my sister, but I now realized that my curiosity about my own blood was about an *urge* to see
evidence of my*self*. Because we were so much alike, it
was impossible to know exactly how much we
shared—where she ended and I began. Did the blood
that came from my body also flow through hers? Were
we *really* identical twins or did we only *look* identical?
It was something I'd always secretly wondered
about—secretly because our parents had never allowed
us to broach the possibility that we weren't actually,
verifiably, genetically *identical*. We'd looked so cute in
matching dresses and played so nicely together and
everyone mistook one for the other. What other proof
did you need? And what did it really matter? Before
we got old enough to insist that our parents tell us (if
in fact they knew), they both died.

My blood left my body, entered the tube.

I looked at the technician. "My twin sister and I
never had the blood test, to find out if we're really
identical."

"You want it?"

"Yes."

"I'll take some extra, then."

She twisted off one filled tube, plugged it, and attached another. In the end she had four tubes of my
blood upright in her tray. I felt a little dizzy, so she
gave me some orange juice and a cookie and told me
to sit for a couple of minutes before getting up. I drank
the juice and ate the cookie, but I didn't want to stay.

I was still a little dizzy on the way home, so I drove
slowly, but mile by mile, I felt better. It was a magnif-

icent spring afternoon, greenery and flowers bursting in every view, and the road back was quiet. The sense of peacefulness I had abandoned on my way to the clinic began to return to me. By the time I pulled into the small gravel parking lot of the Weathervane Inn, I felt practically happy—done with the lineup, done with the blood test—like a child who hated camp X-ing days off a calendar. By the end of the week we'd be *home*.

Before I was out of the car, my cell phone rang. I saw it was Bobby.

"Where are you?" he asked.

"I just pulled up. I'm right outside the inn."

I got out of the car, slammed the door and there he was, slipping his cell phone into his jeans pocket.

"Lexy still asleep?" I asked.

"Listen, Annie. Bad news."

I froze. I didn't know if I could take any more. "Better just tell me."

"Gabe Lazare called," he said. "It turns out Julie *did* rent a vacation house in Maine. It agrees with everything she said before."

"But she never said anything to me about that! She says I *knew* she was taking Lexy there, but I *didn't*."

"Shh. Calm down." He reached out to stroke my arm, but I yanked it away.

"I can't calm down. She's lying, Bobby! Does this mean they're not going to arrest her for trying to steal Lexy?"

"I think that's what it means. I really don't know. Lazare won't tell me much. But he said we had to stay until he gets the DNA analysis from the blood tests. He said it could take up to two weeks, but he would get this one expedited."

"Why can't we go home while he waits for the tests?"

"I don't know."

I steeled myself. "How long?"

"A week. He *promised*."

Another week in this town, staying at an inn like tourists, while my sister lived, a free woman, in her luxurious house. What if we saw her in town? Would we have to travel to distant counties for our meals just to avoid Julie?

"Forget it, Bobby. We're going home *now*."

"Annie—"

I left him standing on the path, went upstairs to our room and packed up all our stuff. When Lexy woke up I changed her diaper and nursed her. By then, Bobby had gathered up the last of his personal toiletries. He checked us out and drove the car to the airport in Albany. On the way, he confessed that he'd made two calls before joining me in our room while I was packing.

"Lazare said that if you leave the state, you'll be jumping bail. That simple. Liz agreed with him; she said she'd try to reach the judge and see what she could do, but she couldn't guarantee anything."

"This is nonsense, Bobby," I said. "They can't keep me here."

"Actually, Annie, they probably can." That was all he said. Clearly he had made up his mind not to try to stop me. But didn't he also want to go? I knew that if he was really dead-set against it, he would have said so. As for the potential consequences of flight, I was so upset I couldn't think about them right now.

We drove in silence the rest of the way. Even Lexy was fairly calm in her car seat in the back. I looked out the window at the highway connecting Massachusetts and upstate New York, the ribbon of road pulling us in, bringing us closer to the airport and our home in Kentucky. It probably *was* a stupid idea to run home, but how could I resist? I was frantic for all this to end. I wanted to breathe my own air, walk my own floors, sleep in my own bed. I was as desperate to be home now as I had been to leave home two weeks ago. I couldn't wait a week or more.

We arrived at the airport and returned the rental car. Bobby carried our luggage into the terminal while I pushed Lexy in her stroller. There was a flight in three hours and we booked it—using our very own credit cards, which had finally started to reach us at the inn. We were standing on line to check our baggage—and I felt so close to normal, to *home*—when I turned and saw Detective Lazare come in through a revolving glass door. When he saw that we'd spotted him, he attempted a smile. He *had* to be kidding.

"Fancy meeting you here," he tried to joke, but no one laughed. Then he just tossed out his lasso. "Can't leave, folks."

"You really don't need me here," I said. But Bobby looked nervous, and that shook my confidence, so I added, "Do you?"

"I spoke to your lawyer," Lazare said. "Her motion to modify your bond is still in effect, but your permission to leave New York State extends only to Massachusetts."

"I went to Vermont and nothing happened."

"You were with an officer of the law—me. And there were extenuating circumstances."

"So, come to Kentucky," I said.

"It's a secured bond, Annie. You could lose your house if you get on that plane. Are you sure it's worth it?"

"Annie—" Bobby's forehead was damp; a droplet traced an uneven path down his temple. "He's right."

I *knew* he was right. They both were. Standing here, about to send our luggage to Kentucky and board the plane, it suddenly seemed like a very bad idea. Most impulsive acts could be overcome, but clearly this one would have serious consequences that would affect not just me but Bobby. Even Lexy's future well-being would be affected if I took off and jeopardized our house. I felt like a greedy child caught with her hand in the candy dish. Greedy and stubborn. I would give it up, but not without a show of pride.

"*Why* do you need me here?" I asked. "I did the lineup and I gave blood. Can't you call me if you need anything else? I'll come back."

"I'd like an explanation about that, too, Detective." Bobby let go of the suitcase he'd been rolling along the line. "It isn't really logical for us to stay if there's any chance the bond can be modified again."

A couple came hurrying up behind Detective Lazare, passing in a rush to catch a plane, and he moved closer to us, speaking in a low, confidential tone.

"Okay, I'll tell you why I need you to stay, Annie."

"Finally—"

"Just *listen*, please." He paused a moment before saying, "Thomas Soiffer saw Julie kill Zara Moklas. It happened very fast, but Soiffer is adamant that he saw Julie do it."

That was exactly what I had assumed. No real surprise there, and yet hearing it from the detective brought home with force the horrifying turn this could take if Soiffer's blood test eliminated him from suspicion. If Julie had actually *killed* someone. Soiffer *had* to be guilty; it was the only explanation that made real, deep, true sense to me. The only explanation I would be able to live with.

"He says he saw Julie," I said. "Not *me*."

"Well, Annie, that's just the problem," Lazare said. "How can he tell you two apart?"

"Obviously he can't."

"He picked you out of the lineup. He also picked Julie."

"So the lineups were useless. That's a no-brainer. You still haven't told me why I have to stay."

"I want to investigate this carefully," he said, "without wasting time chasing you down."

"You know where I'll be," I said. "Right there at home."

"There's too much at stake for you to go. With a witness saying—"

"I don't know why you even listen to Thomas Soiffer," I interrupted. "*He* probably did it. There's no reason to even discuss it, is there, until you get back his DNA? It's *all about* the DNA, Detective. Am I right?"

"Exactly, Annie." His expression stilled. He didn't

blink at all. "It's all about the DNA. I'll just tell you, then. Soiffer's results came in this afternoon."

"And?" Bobby asked. His face had now broken into a full sweat.

"Thomas Soiffer did not kill Zara Moklas," Detective Lazare said.

"But the blood in his van?" Bobby asked.

"Of course he killed her!" I said.

"Stop, both of you. Listen carefully." Lazare lowered his voice so it was barely audible, as if whispering would lessen the impropriety of revealing secrets in the middle of a busy airport. "He did kill someone, but not Zara. We matched the blood to a prostitute who was found murdered two weeks ago in Beartown State Park in Monterey."

"So the other blood with Zara's—" Bobby began.

"Was not Thomas Soiffer's," Lazare finished. "Which increases his value as a witness."

"A murderer?" The sharpness of my voice made Lexy cry. Bobby took her out of my arms, paced away a few steps and bounced her. I lowered my voice. "Are you telling me a judge and jury would actually listen to what one murderer says about another?"

"That remains to be seen," Lazare answered.

"The sweater that guy took out of my rental car in Vermont," I said, recalling the flashy sweater I'd worn the day I first arrived at Julie's. "There was no blood on it—Zara's or mine or Julie's or anyone else's. Am I right?"

He stared at me, keeping completely still. I felt the grip of frustration and plowed forward despite his unwillingness to respond.

"Everyone from the Lexington airport to the Albany airport to the pit stops I made along the highway that night *saw* me wearing that sweater, and you say Soiffer saw Zara get killed. He couldn't have missed that sweater, Detective. Did he describe it, too?"

Before Lazare could answer, if he was going to, Bobby returned with a now-quieted Lexy. He had wiped his face and his skin was dry. In the pause of calming Lexy, he had also calmed himself. "If you mishandle this case," he told the detective in a new, flinty tone, "we'll sue you, personally. Do you understand me?"

Lazare nodded.

"Did he?" I asked again about the sweater.

"You were very right before, Annie," he said. "DNA is the *only* way we'll know who was there that night with Zara. Now that Thomas Soiffer is eliminated as a suspect, that leaves us with your blood tests—yours and Julie's. And both of you claim innocence."

"And you believe her over me, after everything else?"

"The identity theft is a separate matter at this point," Lazare said.

"But it's not separate," I said. "How can it be?"

"We're going to piece everything together, Annie, and find out. In the meantime, we *all* have to wait."

"What if our blood's identical?" I asked. "*Then* what?"

Lazare gave me one of his half-baked smiles, which infuriated me because I expected, or *wanted*, so much more from him. And he said, "We'll see."

We re-rented a car and Detective Lazare followed us

all the way back to the Weathervane Inn. Thankfully
Lexy fell asleep in her car seat. I was so glad she
wouldn't remember any of this when she grew up and
I wondered what, in the future, we would tell her. It
was so strange to think that we could simply leave it
out of her life story—and that she would never know
Julie.

The silence in the car was stifling, so I rolled down
a window a few inches to let in some air. When we left
the highway for the smaller roads, the wayside displays
of bright azaleas, forsythia, roses, marigolds, lilacs,
daisies, the regiments of newly planted impatiens—
reds, pinks, oranges and whites—made me think about
the sweater with its vivid colors, announcing *I am
here*. It was what I had originally liked about the
sweater and what I now detested: you couldn't fail to
see it. My mind kept replaying the memory reel of the
rubber-gloved technician taking it out of my trunk and
dropping it into a paper bag. What had Julie done to
the sweater she'd stuck in the car on purpose for the
police to find? *Did* it have blood on it? And if our
blood turned out to be as identical as our faces, how
was I going to prove that the blood found on the
sweater, if it *was* ours, wasn't *mine*?

It was late afternoon when we pulled into the parking lot of the inn, first Detective Lazare, then us. He
didn't get out. He just sat in his car and watched us
carry our baby and our luggage up the curving path
bounded by bushes of blue pompoms. Watched us
skulk back into the inn. I paused just inside the door,
listening to the detective's engine drive away, leaving
the road empty and quiet. Apparently he trusted us

enough to stay put. At that thought I looked at Bobby, who was standing at the dining room entrance calling out for one of the innkeepers. I felt like a fly stuck in a sticky web and, seeing a way out, I blurted, "Bobby, wait—let's just go."

He seemed to droop. "Oh, Annie."

Mrs. Boardman just then came through the dining room from the adjoining kitchen. "Welcome back! I saved your room, just in case." I wondered now if he had suggested to her that we might be back, if he had thought all along we would never get on that plane. She handed him the key and I marched past them, up the stairs, struggling through an unexpected sensation that I was standing in the middle of a live firing range and couldn't tell who was shooting blanks. That was isolation: when you wondered if *anyone* trusted you. I thought of my blood, the DNA that was my body, and I realized that it would have to speak for me now as Thomas Soiffer's had spoken for him.

In our room, which had been cleaned and neatened, I tossed my purse on the chenille bedspread, kissed Lexy's cheek and set her in the borrowed crib with the yellow bunny Julie had given her and to which she had become attached. *Bunbun*, we had named it. The lace curtains had been drawn open and sunlight blazed into the room. After a few minutes Bobby came up and unpacked for all of us while I sat in the wingback chair, remembering, with inchoate longing, a winter trip Julie and I had taken with our parents to Florida: Mom unpacking in our large hotel room, Dad brushing his teeth in the bathroom, while Julie and I improvised hide-and-seek by sealing ourselves into the cigarette-smoke-smelly closet. We sat beside each other on the scratchy carpet, holding our breath and clasping hands, thrilled by the possibility that our parents didn't know where we were.

Bobby zipped the empty suitcase and stashed it in the closet.

A whole week went by.

A week of sleeping, meals, minor errands, books, phone calls, conversations. A week in which Liz engineered the acquittal of the embezzlement charges against me and the repayment of the bail bond, which freed our house and my future. A week when no sooner was I officially a free woman than I met my new criminal defense lawyer. Elias Stormier was a wiry man with a halo of gray hair, who listened gravely to my story and believed me when I told him I had nothing to do with Zara Moklas's death, and who asserted nonetheless that a good defense was a good offense, and who joined the wisdom-chorus advising me to stay put and wait out the blood test results to avoid *an appearance of flight*. It was a week of squeezing my eyes shut at the peaks and valleys of a roller-coaster ride of worries and relief and sorrow—I missed Julie. I *missed* her. A week of facing grim realities.

But it was also, miraculously, the week Lexy started crawling, first tentatively, then daringly over every floor. She was young to crawl and her relative independence surprised us as much as it empowered her. Her determination to master her new mobility was thrilling, and it helped take our minds off *the wait*. The blood test results loomed, casting shadows everywhere, and Lexy dodged and darted them. I began to understand that regardless of what happened to me, to *us*, Lexy would forge ahead. She was unstoppable. This inkling of hope offered its own form of happiness that no new piece of information could completely destroy.

When Lexy wasn't wearing us out chasing her around the inn, we were reluctant tourists. We haunted the Mount, the house where nearly a hundred years ago Edith Wharton had written some of her most famous novels (in the gift shop I bought *Ethan Frome*; I'd finished *The Talented Mr. Ripley* and needed a new book); traipsed the gardens and climbed the famous blue steps at Naumkeag; visited the Norman Rockwell Museum in Stockbridge (*not* stopping in town at the creepy caterpillar playground even though Lexy let out a cry of desire when we passed the dangling baby swings). Then on Monday, a full week into *the wait* and after a drizzly morning in the car (because we'd *had* to get out of the so-called house), Gabe Lazare phoned to say the blood test results were in.

We'd just walked into the red-velvety back room of the Helsinki Cafe and were settling in at a table. It was already late for lunch and Lexy was getting cranky, but I wanted her to eat her jar of mush before breast milk and back-into-the-car and back-to-the-inn for a nap.

"I'd like to speak with you," Lazare said.

"You *are* speaking with me."

"No, Annie. I want to *see* you, to speak with you in person."

The waitress came over, holding a pad and pencil, ready to take our order. As Lazare spoke, I heard Bobby ordering for both of us; he knew I loved the falafel platter they made here.

"I was right. It was her, wasn't it?" I didn't ask it as a question.

"Where are you right now? I could come to you."

"We're in town, eating lunch." The truth was, Helsinki was so close to the police station we could walk there in five minutes.

"When you're done with your lunch, I'll see you here." He hung up before telling me exactly where he was, assuming I would just know, which of course I did. He was at work, *on the case* as usual. No one could fault this man for not trying his hardest.

"It was Lazare," I told Bobby. "He has the blood test results."

Water from his glass sloshed out on the way to his mouth. He set the glass down without drinking. "And?"

"After lunch, we'll go see him."

"Don't you want to go right now? Don't you want to *know*?"

"Of course I do, but I'm hungry and we have to feed Lexy before we do anything else."

So I fed her. And we ate. But nothing tasted good; adrenaline killed my appetite and I think Bobby's, too. We finished and he paid while I struggled to change Lexy's diaper in the bathroom. On our way back to the car I saw that the cloudy, drizzly day had brightened. *Yes.* The news would be good. The blood would tell the story. It would be neither my blood nor Julie's. Zara's killer would be someone else entirely and Lazare would have to broaden his search. I would send Liz flowers (and a check) and give Elias a bottle of good wine (and a check) and Bobby, Lexy and I would be on our way home to Kentucky. Then, on the drive over, the clouds returned and with the disappearance of that brief spate of sunshine went my optimism.

"What if—" I stopped myself.

"What if what?" Bobby turned the steering wheel, pulling us into the parking lot of the police station.

"Nothing."

After that we kept quiet—what was there to say? Lexy had fallen asleep almost instantly upon leaving the restaurant, so Bobby sat with her in the car while I went inside for the news.

Detective Lazare was standing in the station lobby, staring out the window with his hands clasped behind his back. He was calm, thinking. Two armed officers got up from a snack table as soon as they saw me, handcuffs dangling off their belts.

"I'm sorry, Annie. I really am," Lazare said. "But now we have an eyewitness *and* evidence."

I guessed I knew then, but *still* I didn't fully believe it.

One of the officers approached me as he snapped open a handcuff. *No*, I thought, and against my will I started to cry.

"That really isn't necessary, is it?" I asked.

"It's the law," he said, and the officer bound my wrists behind my back while Lazare spoke:

"Anais Milliken-Goodman, you are under arrest for the murder of Zara Moklas. Anything you say can be held against you in a court of law . . ." The rest was a blur until he stopped reciting the legal catechism and paused to search for words. "Annie, listen, I'm—"

"*Don't* say you're sorry!"

He sighed and didn't say it again.

"The blood tests," I said. "Tell me, because I don't believe this is happening. *Tell me*."

"The blood is yours."

"So what you're saying is that Julie and I aren't identical?" I didn't really believe that, either; nothing in me had ever truly questioned our inherent sameness. "Go ahead, Detective. Lay it on. *Tell* me."

"Actually, you and Julie *are* identical. But your blood shows a vital difference: lactation hormones."

"And you think you found *my* blood—"

"No, Annie, we *did* find your blood—at the crime scene, and on the sweater with traces of Zara's blood, and it's conclusively yours."

My brain was whizzing through a maze, looking for entries and exits, desperate for release from this illogical knot. How had they found *my* blood at the scene of a crime I didn't commit? How had *my* blood gotten onto the sweater? I thought of the moment, as I was leaving Bobby, when my elbow buckled the stained glass on our front door . . . but the glass itself hadn't broken . . . I hadn't gotten cut from that. It made no sense. *How?*

"Wait a minute, Detective." My wavering voice rose an octave; it was someone else's voice, not mine. "Soiffer never said anything about a sweater when he saw Julie kill Zara, did he?"

"So you took it off and then put it back on," Lazare said. "There are various explanations for that."

"I didn't kill Zara," I said. "Please listen to me: I did not kill her."

"Those are only words, Annie."

"What if you're wrong, Detective? I mean, people

get sentenced to death on conclusive evidence that *isn't* conclusive in the end."

"This isn't wrong. It was double- and triple-tested. I didn't want any mistakes."

"Detective Lazare," I said, my shackled wrists burning, "before you go through with this, I want you to think about something really carefully: Why would *I* kill Zara Moklas?"

"Good question." The thin smile, the cool eye. He nodded to the cops to take me away.

Chapter 13

When I first stepped into my cell at the Berkshire House of Correction in Pittsfield, Massachusetts, all I saw was hard surfaces: concrete floor, cinder-block walls, a low stainless-steel toilet with no seat, a tiny stainless-steel sink, bars on a slit of a window, a concrete slab with a thin, stained mattress that was to be my bed. But little by little I began to study the cell's details and was surprised by how much I found. *People* had been here, proving that I was not really alone; and as the hours passed the ghosts of my cell kept me company. Their smells: sour, musky and a little sweet. Their stains: on the floor by the bed and in the corner near the toilet. Their scratches: on the sides of the sink, the corners of the slab-bed and every single bar. Especially their wall etchings: *I will be stronger when this is done*; *I am a gif in a box, when they unrap me they will no I am good*; *pls forgive me mama*. What had these women been accused of? This was a holding cell in the Department of Corrections, like the clipboard on your computer that holds the cut before the paste, or the garbage can before it's emptied.

Correction. Department of. Who named it that? Never before had I thought about that term: *correction*. I had worked in a prison and never really thought it through! No one was perfect and in every society there were mistakes, errors, and these errors (these *people*) sometimes needed correction. Sometimes the wrong people were corrected. Sometimes the uncorrected were released still riddled by error. Sitting here, I kept thinking of my father's old typewriter and how its individual keys leapt at the page to strike a blow that left the imprint of a letter. A had a broken leg. P, a broken face. U always struck with a shadow. Dad would carefully correct his stories with a black pen and a bottle of Wite-Out. I hadn't thought about that typewriter for many years and remembered now that Julie and I had let the liquidator sell it when the house was emptied in preparation for sale. We had walked out of that house one day, not really *knowing* we would never return. We had moved from there to here on a wave of time, and now another wave had overtaken us and I was hovering on the crest, waiting to see where it would plunk me down.

Here in jail the nature of waiting was completely different from last week's wait at the inn. This wait was bottomless. *Endless.* It was amazing how fat and long and droopy individual minutes could become. You sank into them, grew paralyzed in your state of waiting. Sitting on your thin mattress. Or standing, feeling the cold floor soak through your thin plastic sandals. Everything had been confiscated from me, even the flow of time; I had no watch, there were no clocks on the walls and the guards thought it was fun to keep us in temporal darkness. All I had was the sun sliding up and slipping down my window strip. I stopped counting hours after lights-out. It didn't matter anyway: *time*. Thinking of time. Speaking of time. I *couldn't*.

I didn't eat anything, either, because the food was so bad. Now I understood something the prisoners back home used to joke about, how you knew how good prison food was once you spent a few nights in jail waiting for your trial. Jail food was awful—I hadn't known meat could be that tough or how nimbly human hair stuck to undercooked potato. Twenty-four hours on the inside and I could feel I'd gotten thinner, making my recent efforts to diet really absurd. Even my breast milk went on strike, to the point that I didn't even bother requesting a pump.

No sister, no baby, no milk, no body, no time, no *me*.

Bobby visited after lunch the second day, and mercifully he brought Lexy. He had to know how much that meant to me. I admit I had worried that he would keep her away from the correctional facility in case floating errors might randomly insert themselves into her psyche and mysteriously screw her up for life. (As if being wrenched away from her mother, now twice, would not leave a scar.) So when he showed up with her, I felt renewed confidence that he had my best interests at heart.

We were given a private visiting room. I don't know why (though I could guess why, since the room was in a cell that locked up tight: it must have been for violent offenders, you know, really scary people *like me*). Four stools were affixed to the base of a round stainless-steel table and the room was brightly lit. A boxy in-house phone hung off one cinder-block wall.

As soon as the guard locked us in and turned her back, I took Lexy into my arms. I didn't offer my breast and she didn't try to nurse; it seemed wisest to let her adjust exclusively to the bottle since I had no idea when I'd be out of here. She had grown more restless than even yesterday and could not be contained in my arms for long, so I put her down and watched her crawl around, grateful that Bobby had dressed her in long pants so her knees wouldn't get chewed up by the concrete floor.

Bobby had thoughtfully brought a few family pictures for me to keep in my cell (I was allowed up to ten): shots of the three of us taken by Julie and a couple of him and Lexy taken by me. He set the pile on the table. Looking through the photos, I saw he had also brought one of Lexy and me, but on closer inspection I saw that it wasn't me—it was Julie. Weeping, I ripped it in half, fourths, eighths.

"I'm sorry," Bobby said. "It was a stupid mistake."

"Can't *you* tell us apart?"

"Yes, I can." He leaned from his neighboring stool to hold me and I could smell him: spicy, warm, familiar. "You're depressed, sweetie," he said, stating the obvious, but I forgave him.

"Don't I deserve to be? Julie's destroyed me, Bobby. She's really done it."

"You won't be in here much longer."

"But neither of us ever thought it would go this far," I said, "so what does it matter what we think?"

"Elias is working really hard."

"Yeah, right."

"He is, Annie, but these things take time."

"Do you remember that guy at the prison—Ernesto, the lifer? He always said he was innocent. No one listened to him. *We* didn't listen to him." Ernesto had briefly worked as an orderly in the PT clinic until his constant talk about his innocence got on everybody's nerves and we had him replaced.

"I remember him." Bobby sighed. "This is going to change us. When I go back, things are going to be different."

"I?"

"*We*. But I meant, specifically, back to the prison—you said you weren't going back to work there."

"I'm never setting foot in that place again."

Lexy then crawled her chubby little hands up my leg until she grasped my knee, standing.

"Look at you! My big girl!" I lifted her up and swung her in the air. Her riotous laughter made me smile.

Footsteps of a guard approaching and a rough male voice: "Time's up!"

I held Lexy, kissed her, drank her in, whispering, "Come see Mommy tomorrow, okay?" Then I looked at Bobby: "Okay? You'll bring her?"

He smiled at us and kissed me. "Okay."

But the next day he came alone.

"Mrs. Boardman offered to watch Lexy at the inn." He handed me the copy of *Ethan Frome* I'd bought at the Mount, then said, "Bad news." He faced me across the cold steel tabletop, holding both my hands in both of his. His palms were sweaty and I wanted to pull my hands away but didn't. "I don't know how this happened," he said. "It came out of left field."

"What, Bobby? You haven't told me *what*?"

"I spoke with Liz—"

"I thought she was finished—there's no more grand larceny charge. Bobby?"

"It was reinstated." He pulled one hand away to run it through his hair in a gesture like something off TV, I thought, something not completely genuine, not *real*. His other hand gripped mine so hard it hurt and I instinctively drew away, laying both palms flat on the table. Panic ripped its way up my spine and I told myself: *No*. I would come at this head-on.

"Why?" I asked.

"The FBI's been going through our home computer. They said that all the identity theft activity was 'ghosted' in Julie's computer—generated by someone else. They said she might have been set up. They said it started in *our* computer, Annie, with *us*." His pupils shrank to black dots. Was he afraid of me now? *Me?*

"Say it, Bobby. You want to."

"Okay." He looked at me with those wary eyes. "With—" But he couldn't say it and we were left with silence, coldness, four stone walls, a steel table, a man and a woman and a single, unspeakable word: *you*. He couldn't say it and I wasn't going to say it for him because I couldn't believe he would think it at all. How could he think *I* had started all this!? Why *would* I? For what purpose? To land myself in jail?

"It doesn't make any sense, Bobby."

"Yes, I know it doesn't. I *do*." He slumped into folded arms, smaller than I'd ever seen him. Shaking, crying. I reached over to touch the back of his neck. His hair was tacky, like he hadn't washed it in a couple of days, and a film of sweat seemed to have ground itself into his skin. "I'm *sorry* this is happening to you. It was never supposed to be like this."

Of course it wasn't. We had been a normal, happy family; bad things were never supposed to happen to *us*. And yet somehow they had, one thing after the next—and it wasn't over yet. As he cried, my anger cooled. I wasn't the only one Julie's lies had fouled. I *had* to be here, but he *didn't*. Before I released him, though, I had to ask him one more time:

"Are you *sure* you believe I didn't do any of this, Bobby?"

"I'm sure." He lifted his face from his arms to look at me. His eyes seemed sunken in dry, creased skin that didn't belong to him; I had never seen him so exhausted. "But the *computer*—"

"Computers lie," I said.

He nodded. Our lives these past weeks had demonstrated *that* more than anyone should ever know.

"Listen, Bobby, I've been thinking that you and Lexy should go home. You were right when you said this whole thing was going to take a while and you sitting in that inn isn't doing us any good. The day care will take her back—I'm sure they will—and you can get back to work. Both of you could use the normalcy, I think."

"I don't know." He nodded, shook his head, cried

harder. "I don't want to leave you here." And then we were quiet, leaving unresolved the possibility that Bobby and Lexy would go home without me.

A minute later, when the guard told us our time was up, Bobby kissed me and left; and I went back to my cell, where loneliness grew out of all proportion. Finally, in the late afternoon, with the outside sun throwing a vivid pattern against my cinder-block wall, I opened the Wharton novel. I hadn't realized when I'd bought it that Ethan Frome's story took place right here in the Berkshires: a turn-of-the-last-century farmer falls in love with someone not-his-wife and his conflict over fleeing his doleful marriage drives him, with his beloved, to near suicide. At the end of the story, the now-crippled farmer lives in poverty with both women: one a martyr, the other an invalid. Another triangle to contemplate. Or not. I closed my eyes, wishing I hadn't read it, and tried and tried and tried to sleep.

Elias Stormier came the next day. He was tall and lanky, with short gray hair ringing a pale, domed head. His forehead was unusually large and this comforted me, as if the size of his head was an indication of intelligence; if anyone needed a brilliant lawyer, *I* did. He wore small round glasses with a distinct bifocal line halving top and bottom. But what I liked most about this plain man was his Burl Ives voice: a medium-tenored tone that seemed to glide out of him.

"The reinstatement of the grand larceny charge is bad news," he said, "and to be honest, it doesn't help our case."

Our case; I liked that. We would be partners on a sinking ship.

"On the other hand," he said, "that charge relates directly to the assumption that you are your own identity thief"—his unblinking eyes, bluish and watery, smiled into mine—"which is a real mind-bender."

"It's ridiculous is what it is."

"Yes, I agree: it's absurd. Why would you have staged that kind of crime against yourself?"

"I *didn't*," I said. "Julie must have done something to my computer, rigged it somehow. Maybe when she visited me last winter."

"The FBI recognizes that as a distinct possibility," he said, "and they're looking into it. Anyway, you weren't charged with computer fraud, so they can't hold you for that. All that does for us right now is muddy the waters." He flipped the top sheet of his yellow pad to consult something on a previous page. "The real reason for my visit today is that I bring good news."

"You have *good* news?"

He nodded, smiled.

"Shouldn't you give the good news *first*?"

"Not if I want you thinking positively when I walk out of here."

"Please, spare the drumroll," I said. "What is it?"

"Your blood from the crime scene and your blood on the sweater?"

The blood that couldn't be mine because I didn't kill her.

"It had been frozen," he said.

"What?"

"Frozen."

"So I really am a cold-blooded killer?"

He laughed. "I'm glad you haven't lost your sense of humor."

"Actually, I have," I said. "What does that *mean*, it was frozen?"

But even as I said it, and as he began to answer, it fell together in my mind. Why hadn't I thought of it before? Last March, during Julie's most recent visit, we had gone to the American Red Cross in Lexington to donate blood. It was something we had done all our adult lives. Bobby had stayed home with Lexy while Julie and I gave blood; first me, then her. Afterward, we went out to lunch.

My attention returned to Elias, in midsentence: ". . . and Bobby directed me to the Red Cross and it didn't take very long to find out that Julie had donated two vials of her own blood, while you had donated only one."

"No," I said. "I also gave two."

He noted that, saying, "Which is what we suspected."

Meaning Julie had stolen the second vial of my blood sample that day. And stashed it in the freezer at my house. And carried it home with her to the Berkshires, where presumably she then stored it in her own freezer (where all during May I had been freezing another bodily liquid, my milk, for Lexy to drink). Now I understood why I had been unable to find one of the three small freezer packs I used for cooling Lexy's stored breast milk in transit: Julie had taken one of the packs to keep my blood cold during her flight home.

"She planned it for so long," I said. Voice cracking. Stomach quavering. Brain spinning. "Since March."

"At least," Elias said. "She planned every aspect of this quite carefully, it seems. Another development is that apparently she had made an appointment with Zara the night of her death. Zara mentioned in an e-mail to a friend that she planned to see about a new cleaning job on Division Street before running an errand at a store that closed at eight o'clock. The e-mails were in Hungarian and had to be translated. No specifics about the appointment—no name or address—but the implication is there."

"I didn't get to Julie's house until eight, but she expected me sooner. I told her seven . . ."

"Which would have placed you at the scene of the crime," Elias said. "Or close enough."

"But why Zara? Why hurt this innocent person?"

"I suspect, in Julie's mind, that Zara's resemblance to you both played into it somehow. Look-alikes are often stand-ins for the real target of enmity. But that's just one guess."

Enmity. That word was a deep, cold, echoing well. And the way he'd said it—like a fact, not a riddle. I could not understand how Julie could feel *enmity* toward *me*.

"Did I tell you," he broke my silence, "that she voluntarily submitted to a psychiatric examination?"

"No," I said. "*I* wasn't asked."

"A sign, my dear, that her lawyer doesn't think an examination of you would yield any benefit."

"Little does he know!"

Elias smiled. "Most psychological diagnoses are

relative. Julie's—*sociopathic, narcissistic*—could well be applied to half the people I know. But her so-called conditions are *why* she agreed to the exam at all. She was convinced her powers of deception were that good."

"But even that's circumstantial, isn't it? Psychology isn't exactly a tangible science."

"No, it's not. And you're right: it's circumstantial, at best. But the diagnosis still weakens your sister's claim of innocence when it comes to Zara's murder. If—let's hope *when*—the FBI concludes that she tampered with your computer last March, well, that together with the frozen blood, the missing vial, the psychiatric diagnosis and Zara's appointment on Division Street, and the spotlight shifts decisively from you to Julie."

"None of this makes sense to me," I said. *"None of it."*

"No crime is truly logical, despite how well it's planned. Criminals typically hurt themselves as much as they hurt anyone else, if not more."

"If they get caught," I added.

"Precisely."

"Julie's going to get away with this," I said, feeling it, *believing* it. She had gotten this far and *I* was the one sitting in jail.

"No, dear, she's not." Elias's slender, wrinkled fingers drummed the yellow pad as he spoke. "I've been down to Lexington and I've got a deposition from the technician who took your samples that day. She corroborates that she drew two vials of blood from both of you. She was embarrassed that she hadn't noticed one of yours was missing when she delivered them for storage along with the samples of five other donors. But the donation records show that only one was received. So that's our first smoking gun."

"Is there another?"

"Not yet," he said, "but chances are there will be, sooner or later, when the murder weapon surfaces. If Julie left fingerprints on the knife, it will place her at the scene. So this, the frozen blood, will get you out of jail. And that, the knife, may just put her here in your place."

"But it's still missing," I said, "and they looked everywhere for it. It might never be found, Elias."

"Possibly not. But I hope it is. It will strengthen the case against her in court."

"Has she been charged?" I asked.

"The police are weighing the evidence. The problem is, it's all circumstantial. No one saw *who* took the blood sample from the Red Cross. No one saw *who* froze it. Or *who* sprinkled it at the scene. We have *no* murder weapon with fingerprints or fibers or any other telling evidence. We have *no* vial that held the blood sample. And of course the only witness to the crime was Mr. Soiffer, who can't say exactly *who* he saw, and even if he could, frankly, the jury probably wouldn't trust him enough to carry a case of this gravity. So there we are: if the police charge Julie with what we've got now, it wouldn't hold up in court. Remember, Annie, the benchmarks the state has to meet for a first-degree-murder conviction are not taken lightly: premeditated malice and extreme cruelty."

Premeditated malice and extreme cruelty. Well. Regardless of whether or not she would ever face a judge,

I knew she had met those appalling tests. I knew and I would always know. Everyone could punish her endlessly and it wouldn't change a thing; and it wouldn't change the fact that already, in one significant way, we had already shared a punishment: we had lost each other. And yet . . . I had to admit that, in my heart, I felt no craving for her to spend the rest of her life in jail. Even if she deserved it. Even if she was dangerous. Even if she hated me. *Even if she had killed someone.* Julie was my twin; *love* didn't even cover it. Our entwinement was unassailable and indefensible, as fixed as history; and my mind couldn't bend that, because it was simply true. As Detective Lazare and I had agreed, it was all about the DNA.

"What now?" I asked Elias.

"Tomorrow we go before the judge. We present the new evidence. And we request that the charges be dropped in light of the new evidence." He gathered his papers, stood up. "The judge will see how weak the state's evidence is now, considering you have an identical twin."

"Why tomorrow? Why not today?" My plaintive tone seemed to echo through this room of cold, hard surfaces, uselessly, joining the ghosts of all the other voices that had asked the same question right here, every day, over the years.

"Scheduling," he said. "I'm sorry."

And he was gone.

For all the minutes of all the hours of the rest of that day and night, I paced my room or lay on my cot, letting the inertness of my body calm my racing mind. Julie: a murderer. I recalled my photos of Zara's fading outline on the street in front of Julie's house—*here she lies*, the last shadow of a woman's life—and wondered what *her* final thoughts had been. She was the one person who knew everything about her death and the only person who could not be asked.

In the morning, a guard brought me a breakfast of watery gray oatmeal, which I nibbled at, and half a plastic cup of canned pineapply-tasting orange juice, which I sipped at. I was hungry. When the guard returned an hour later to pick up my tray, she told me that my lawyer would be by for me at eleven o'clock and left behind a bag containing the clothes I'd arrived in: jeans, sneakers and a black T-shirt that smelled as if they had been stored in a damp cave. I could only imagine what the judge would think of me in these smelly, wrinkly clothes, but I had nothing else to wear. (I'd never thought I would wish for my beige suit, still hanging in the Manhattan studio, but I *did*.) Then, just before eleven as I waited impatiently for Elias to come and *spring* me, the guard reappeared with a box.

It was from a women's clothing catalog, it was addressed to Julie's house and it had been opened. When I peeled back the tissue paper I found a crisp envelope with a card showing a long-limbed woman at a cafe table. Inside, the card read *I'm sorry* in Julie's writing. *She was sorry.* I knew she was. Tears formed in my eyes as I read and reread those two words, her terse apology that was like the Dutchman's finger in the dike. *I'm sorry.* So much was packed into those two little words: guilt, sorrow, regret, loss . . . it was a definition without end.

I was sorry, too.

Inside the box I found chocolate brown linen pants and a pale pink blouse. Beneath the clothes was a slender box with hammered-silver button earrings and a matching necklace. At the bottom of the box were Julie's own cowboy boots, wrapped in tissue paper. She had even included a bra, underpants and a pair of socks. *Sundance catalog: everything on page seven, please.* It was pirate's loot, was what it was. If I wore the outfit, wouldn't I be consorting with the enemy? But it was clean and mostly new and better than what I had on. And it was more than just clothes: *Julie* had sent it over; she was saying good-bye.

I stuffed my old sweaty clothes into the box and put on my new duds. Elias arrived promptly on time and escorted me to the judge.

The courtroom was cavernous and austere, with no wooden paneling or scrolled details to comfort you or make you feel connected to history or even the idea of justice. It was all *here and now*, a place of business. Broad linoleum floors, gated windows, rows of fluorescent lights—all the bright, chilly atmosphere of a megastore.

Bobby was waiting at the aisle end of the spectator benches, beside a slender woman with a pitch-black chignon and a bald man in a pressed denim shirt buttoned to his Adam's apple. When Bobby saw me, he smiled so eagerly it made me a little nervous. (Lexy, I assumed, was with Mrs. Boardman again at the inn.) I waited with Elias in a group of cordoned-off seats toward the front of the courtroom. The edges of my metal chair were sticky with spilled soda and the air smelled, inexplicably, like roses. I watched the judge dispense justice with razor-sharp efficiency to man after man, woman after woman. Nine defendants preceded me and all but one were sent back to prison accompanied by a guard. When a teenage boy with white-boy dreadlocks and a snake tattoo rising out of his shirt collar was turned back to his cell, the tidy couple beside Bobby left the courtroom in tears. After forty minutes my name was called and I took my place at Elias's side before the bench.

Judge Leonard Hersey seemed young, about forty, with thin blond hair, aviator glasses and a blond goatee. He towered over us behind his large, elevated desk. I heard the shuffle of his quick perusal of some papers—presumably my file—before he looked over and down at me with Aegean blue eyes.

"Anais Milliken-Goodman?" He pronounced my name correctly.

"Yes, Your Honor."

"Good morning, Mr. Stormier," the judge said, addressing Elias.

It was already past noon, I thought, willing myself to keep quiet by fixing my eyes on a jagged scratch that ran horizontally about six inches across the front of the judge's wooden desk.

"Good morning, Judge Hersey," Elias answered.

The judge glanced at his watch. "Proceed."

Elias laid out the facts one by one, then deftly connected them like pieces of a puzzle. He concluded by flicking on a proverbial light so you could see the puzzle's picture: "Either one of the sisters could theoretically be guilty of the murder, and with nothing but circumstantial evidence, the charge against my client will not prove tenable before a jury. It will waste the court's time and the state's money. Therefore I request that Your Honor consider the immediate dismissal of this case."

Judge Hersey looked from Elias to me to my file and back to me.

"What do you say, Ms. Milliken-Goodman?"

"I'm innocent," I said, "of everything."

"So you think your twin sister is guilty—of everything?"

My eyes found that safe, deep, comforting scratch—that burrow in the wood that was indisputably *there*—and with all my strength I brought them back to the judge's vivid eyes. I nodded.

"The transcript needs a spoken word," he said.

"Yes."

"Are you prepared to testify against your sister in a trial, if so called?"

And here, I admit, I lied: "Yes." I knew that if a case against me wouldn't hold up in court without tangible evidence, it wouldn't hold up against Julie either. In truth, I didn't know if I would be capable of bringing myself to testify against her. Though if it came to it, *if I had to*, I supposed I would.

"All right, then," Judge Hersey said. "Dismissed. Next!"

The whole thing took about four minutes. *And I was free.*

Bobby greeted me with a hug and kept one arm around me as he shook Elias's hand, saying, "Thank you. *Thank you.*"

"All I did was sort out the facts," Elias said, but he was smiling, victorious, even a little proud. "And don't thank me too much. I'll be sending you a bill."

We all laughed. Elias said good-bye and left us alone in the wide hallway outside the courtroom. Well, not alone—Gabe Lazare was waiting for us near the elevator. I hadn't noticed him in the courtroom; he must have slipped in and stood in the back by the door.

"Congratulations," he said.

"Gee, thanks." I disengaged my arm from Bobby's and pushed the DOWN button.

"I'm sorry," Lazare said.

I jabbed the button again and looked at him. He was just one man, standing there in a cheap blue suit with badly dyed hair. It was hard to blame him for getting so excited about doing his job.

"Because of the blood and the witness," he said, "we had no choice."

"Why didn't your forensics people notice sooner that the blood had been frozen?" I asked. "That's what I keep wondering."

"I have the same question," he said, "but you were a flight risk and so we arrested you as soon as we could. This is a complicated case because you and Julie look so much—"

"Don't say it." I stepped closer to Lazare and kissed his cheek. It was the second time I'd kissed him, but now, instead of stiffening up, he gave me one of his half-cocked smiles. "Apology accepted," I said. "Good-bye."

"We'll find her," he said.

I looked at him. "Does that mean she's gone?"

"You didn't know?"

"I was locked up." I turned to Bobby, who looked as surprised at this news as I was.

"When?" Bobby asked.

"This morning, apparently," Lazare said. "She was seen at the prison, dropping off the box—you look very nice, by the way. Then she, well—"

"*Eluded* you, Detective?" I smiled.

"Not *me*, exactly. One of my men."

So Julie was gone. She must have heard about the frozen blood. She must not have done her research well enough; otherwise she would have taken that into account. She really had no choice but to run if she didn't want to be charged with murder on top of identity theft. Once she crossed the state's boundary, she would have jumped bail. I wondered if she had put her house on the line for her bond, or used some other collateral, or just come up with cash. My guess was that she put up her house; she wasn't coming back anyway, and knowing what I now knew about Julie, I realized she probably had bank accounts all around the world in other people's names. Well, to be honest, if *I* were her that's exactly what I would do at this point: run. She was all alone now and in my heart I believed she understood her mistake. She would carry her prison with her.

"She won't get away with any of it, Annie," Detective Lazare said. "We'll find her, and when we find the knife—"

"*If* you find it, Detective," I interrupted, realizing that he finally believed *I* had not killed Zara Moklas.

"I'm sorry, but you haven't found it yet and it's not like you haven't looked under every stone."

"We'll find it."

"I hope you do," I said. "I'd like this to be really over." Another lie: if it's being *over* meant the end of Julie, I could never want that.

The elevator dinged and the doors parted. I nodded at Lazare, looked at Bobby, smiled. "Let's go home."

Chapter 14

Home was as exquisitely *there*, plainly and solidly *real*, as when I'd left it one month ago. The house itself was a little dustier on its surfaces and grimier around its edges, but that was nothing. The differences, the real changes, were between Bobby and me. No matter how erroneous or misleading the reasons, you can't leave your spouse without breaking something. It's far too easy to shatter trust and confidence in a marriage, but what we'd been through went beyond those emotional delicacies. Personally I felt lost and rudderless in a brand-new way, and I think Bobby did, too. Without the drama, the challenges, the quests to peel back so many accusations to find the truth, having *found* the truth we were faced with a strange emptiness. We had to locate each other again in that vast space, to build anew, and we immediately started working on it.

We arrived home at the beginning of June in unseasonable heat, turned on the central air-conditioning, got Lexy to sleep in her very own crib in her very own room, and crawled naked and exhausted into our marital bed. Bobby put out the light and we turned to each other.

Kissing me, he said, "Let's make another baby."

I immediately knew it was a good idea, for us *and* for me. I wanted nothing more than to build a family with this man, to surround myself with the love and purposefulness of children. We made love that night, free and clear, and afterward Bobby wept in my arms. "It's over," I whispered to him. "Over, over, over." But he kept crying and I understood: he was still releasing emotional poisons. So was I. Our healing would take time.

The other rebuilding we had to do involved my name: my trampled credit history had turned it to mud. Clearing up *that* mess became a full-time job—phone calls through mazes that often landed me back at the starting point, letters, endless follow-ups. I became a vigilant bureaucrat on my own behalf. The discipline was good for me, though, as a tool to train my mind away from the deep ravines of personal loss that had reshaped my inner life. I *couldn't* let myself sink into those pits; I *had* to move on.

Bobby went back to work the second week of June in the lingering heat wave while I hunkered down in the cool indoors with Lexy. Lexy at almost seven months was crawling like a demon and struggling to cruise any handleable surface. Since she was my first baby, I had no one to compare her with, but everything I could find in books or on the Internet about developmental stages said she was too young to start walking and then, as likely as not, contradicted itself with examples of babies walking as early as nine months. *Early walker, late talker*, they said, and vice versa. Lexy exulted in her physical competence and I was proud of her, proud and tired, as I followed her in and out of rooms.

In early September, Julie was arrested in Rome, Italy, and extradition proceedings were begun. I experienced her downfall from a passionate distance. I couldn't quite purge her from my system and even now, after everything, her capture pained me, though I told no one of my deepest feelings, not even Bobby. I thought of her (and *felt* her and *saw* her) sitting in a jail cell in Italy. *Italy.* Of course. It was where our parents had taken us for the most memorable summer of our lives, when our family was still whole.

By mid-October, as the first brushstrokes of autumn touched our yard with a golden-hued palette of impending changes, Lexy was walking like a champ, I was spending less and less time chasing paperwork— and I discovered I was pregnant. Everything started coming into focus as we made our plans: Bobby would retire in the spring with a full pension and we would move to Northern California, where our new baby would be born. Eventually I would go back to work, preferably starting a private practice, and he would stay home with the children.

But then, as October blended into the nauseated days of early winter (whoever called it *morning sickness* had never been pregnant—it lasted all day!), things changed. *Life is what happens when you're making other plans*, or so the saying goes, omitting the equally true: *and so are unexpected endings.*

It was a Saturday morning. We had finished breakfast and I was lying on the couch, staving off the latest urge to vomit, with Lexy playing on the living room floor and Bobby upstairs fixing a gimpy hinge on the bathroom door. I could hear the squeaky push-and-pull of the door as he tested it and I could hear Lexy's sweet babble as she played. And then, suddenly—or it seemed sudden to me—the house was terribly quiet. I had closed my eyes for just a minute. When I opened them, Lexy was gone and I realized with horror that I had actually fallen asleep. I got up and started looking, calling her name:

"Lexy! Baby! Where are you?"

The quiet persisted, that *awful* quiet when you know something's wrong. I started to run through the house.

"Bobby! Where's Lexy? Did you see her?"

There was no answer, no sound, just the expanding sensation of a quiet that was *wrong*.

Through the living room window I saw Bobby standing on the front lawn, talking with our next-door neighbor. The front door was closed and I could see that Lexy wasn't with him.

"Lexy?" I called. "Lexy!"

Then, *then*, I noticed that the basement door was open. We always kept this door locked—it was a dank cave of a basement, completely unfinished, where Bobby had set up his makeshift carpentry workshop. Just half an hour ago he had gone down for a screwdriver. He must have forgotten to lock the door behind him. I raced down the rickety wooden steps into the dark.

"Lexy?"

There was a sound of truncated movement, a quick scramble like a frightened mouse.

"Honey? Mommy's here!"

Two high, shallow windows that had probably never been washed let in a bit of murky light, and as my eyes adjusted, I was able to see her. She was sitting on the floor, in a corner, under a porcelain utility sink. The whites of her eyes shone at me, and she blinked.

"Baby! What are you *doing* down here?"

On my way to her, I pulled the chain of an overhead lightbulb and the grungy basement came into better focus. It really *was* a pit in here. And the smell! The sour, lifeless smell of old dust and settled-in grime.

I crouched down to kiss Lexy and she tightened her lips. When I realized she was holding something in her mouth, the panic instantly returned. What nasty, treacherous basement thing had she been about to swallow?

"Give it to Mommy, Lexy. *Let go.*" I pried a finger between her lips to release her jaw and get out whatever she was trying to hide. Sweeping my finger over her tongue, I felt it: cold, round, flat, metal. A coin. She struggled against me as if she wanted to swallow it. When I managed to pry it free, I saw that it was a gunked-up dime.

I balanced her on my hip and slipped the dime into my pants pocket. Then my eyes settled on the sink: for an old sink that no one but Bobby used, it was surprisingly, freshly clean. I cranked open one of the faucets and held my fingers under the cold running water, then leaned Lexy in and repeatedly splashed water into her mouth, saying, "Let's get that yucky dirt out of there, sweetie pie."

Lexy laughed and opened her mouth wide. As I

cupped a handful of water and dribbled it into her mouth, the sink began to fill. A clogged drain. It was old and hardly used, so it was no surprise, but then the drain burped up a chunk of red. Crimson rivulets bled through the rising pool of water. Smaller flecks of dark red continued to pump up from the clogged drain.

It had to be paint. Red paint. But what in this house was painted red? My mind cataloged the rooms: whites, cantaloupes, yellows, greens—but nowhere *red*. I turned off the faucet before the sink overflowed. Had Bobby painted one of his carpentry projects red? I glanced around the dim basement and saw the up-ended chair he had been constructing for over a year now: raw, unpainted wood. And then, as my eyes swept from the shop floor to the neatly organized workbench, I saw it.

Among the tools on the top tier of his fanned-open toolbox, wedged lengthwise between a hammer and a short level: my long-lost kitchen knife. For months I had repeatedly searched the butcher-block knife holder and the kitchen drawers and had never understood where my best knife could have disappeared to. It was barely visible, but I recognized its ebony handle with the round steel screw that I was always tightening. Aside from the unreliable handle it was my favorite cooking knife; its ten-inch blade sharpened better than any of my others. A good cook can do just as well with *any* knife, but you formed special attachments to certain ones, and this one was *mine*. I was irritated to discover that Bobby had borrowed it for his carpentry projects, and on top of that he hadn't returned it.

I carried Lexy over to the toolbox and nudged away

the level so I could get my fingers around the knife's handle. Just as I picked it up I heard Bobby upstairs, calling me. Then his footsteps came thumping down the basement stairs.

"Annie?" He stopped halfway down, his attention caught on the red-filled sink.

"I found my knife." I picked it up. *My knife.* I'd had it over a decade and had used it to make some of my best meals. "I wish you hadn't brought it down here," I said. And then I saw the filmy red streak edging the knife's spine.

I looked at the sink. The knife. The red. And then I looked at Bobby.

His forehead dripped sweat, which he wiped with the back of his hand as he came all the way down the basement stairs. His other hand gripped the screwdriver.

"What *is* this, Bobby?" My voice seemed to float out of me. My stomach clamped. Breathing stopped. I held tighter to Lexy. The earth was shifting, I *felt* it. "Is this paint?" But it was a stupid, hopeful, *hopeless* question.

He was three feet in front of me now. Shaking. The color had drained out of his face.

"I'll take that," he said.

Instinctively, I pulled back. Shook my head. Angled Lexy away from him, toward the wall. "No."

"If we put it back—" he began, but I stopped him.

"Is this blood?"

"I washed it," he said. "It was clean. Some must have dripped down from under the handle."

My brain reeled back to the moment when I saw

Zara lying there in an expanding pool of dark blood that glistened in spasms as the police lights flashed over it. The violent pivot of her head away from her body. The unnatural skew of her limbs. Her eyes like blank screens. *Her red blood spilling around her, out of her, emptying her, draining the last living part of her onto the street.*

My fingers wanted to open, to drop the knife, but I resisted the urge to run away from this. He had to tell me. *I had to know.*

"You killed her," I said.

"No. I never lied to you about that, Annie."

There I was, holding my first child, pregnant with my second, and survival for all of us was the only possible choice. *We had to get out of this basement.* I looked straight into his eyes: I would keep him connected to me, get him talking.

"Okay," I said. "Do you want to tell me what happened?"

The words seemed to rupture out of him, like he'd been holding them back with the flimsiest of wills: "*It was Julie.*"

"But why"—I tried to steady my trembling voice— "do *you* have the knife?"

"If we unclog the sink, and clean the knife better, and put it back, no one has to know."

Outside, a car passed the basement window and dragged a shadow across his face, blotting him out except for a gray shimmer that surrounded him like fog.

Agree, I told myself. *Just agree.*

"Okay," I said.

"Annie—" He stepped abruptly closer. Lexy's lower

lip jutted out and her eyes searched my face for a signal. I kissed her, pressed my cheek to hers, rubbed her back. "You have to understand. Julie was just so—"

"I know what she is," I said. "I loved her, too."

He came closer, so close I could smell his sweat, the sharp, earthy smell of panic. If he thought he could bring me over to his thinking, convince me to trust him, get me to stay, *he was wrong*. But I had to pretend I was open, that I was listening carefully enough to maybe change my mind.

"The minute I drove up to her house," he said, "and saw Zara lying there *dead*, I knew the whole thing was insane. It was a nightmare, and I woke up. I thought Zara was *you*, and it just hit me how much I love you, and I couldn't go through with it."

"So you and Julie—you planned it? To kill *me*?" Was it even worse than I had come to understand? Had they actually wanted me dead? *Julie and Bobby both?*

"No one wanted to kill you," Bobby said, and his tone grew urgent, speeding like a reckless train, and I recognized this burning insistence from childhood, trying to convince my parents of something-I-hadn't-done-but-actually-*had*. "She wanted to make it look like *you* killed Zara. It was all planned out. She wanted you in jail and out of the way so we could . . ." And then his voice trailed off.

"Why didn't you two just run away, Bobby?" It seemed so obvious. "Why go to all that trouble when you could have just left?" As I asked this simplest of questions I felt myself shattering like a million pieces of broken glass barely holding the shape of a woman. But I could not, *would not* fall apart. I had children. I had my *self*, beneath the broken outside layer of what had been my life.

"It was never an option." He stared at the grimy, pocked cement floor. "It was Lexy she wanted, really. Not me." He looked at me and I stared into his weak, filmy, nothing eyes. "All this was *her* idea," he said. "Never mine. You have to believe me."

"I *don't* believe you!" My voice was loud and hard, like a rock through a window. Smashing it. I didn't care.

"It's true."

"You're lying."

He steadied his eyes on me. "She hates you."

"No, she doesn't."

"She does."

"But *why*?"

"Annie . . . how can I explain this?" His forehead tightened as he sought the words. "When Julie looks at you, she sees a better version of herself, and she can't stand it."

"What about you? Do *you* hate me, too?"

"No."

"But you went along with it. You gave her the knife."

"She took it," he said. "Last March, when she was here. She took it right after you used it, so it would still have your fingerprints. She said identical twins didn't always have the same fingerprints"

"You knew, all the time, what she was planning? What you *both* were planning!"

"Not me. *Her.* I tried to stop her, but she wouldn't

back off. I didn't believe she would actually go through with it."

What could I possibly say to that? He had participated in everything that had happened leading up to my walking out of this house last spring *and he hadn't believed it was for real*?

He stepped closer, and closer, until he was only a foot away from us. Lexy was silent, frightened. I squeezed her to my left side. My right hand gripped the knife. Sweat now coated Bobby's face like oil and I could see in his eyes that some kind of calculation was taking place.

"I made her give me the knife so I could bring it home and clean it, so I could protect you. I told her if she didn't give me the knife I would tell the police everything."

"Which would have screwed you, too, Bobby. You saved yourself, not me."

"You're wrong," he said. "I love you. *Please.* Wash the knife with me, help me clean out the sink. We'll replace the pipes. This can be over."

I would do it, if I had to, to survive the next hour. But there was one thing I had to ask first: "Bobby, what does Julie expect from you now?"

"Nothing. I broke it off that morning, under the tree, when you were photographing us. That's why she took off with Lexy."

I could still see his photo-frozen look of vexation that morning. Had she threatened to take Lexy? Had he not believed her? *The fool.*

"Okay," I said, "I'll help you clean it." The knife was covered with my fingerprints. *My* fingerprints, and a tangible shadow of my blood mixed with Zara's—frozen blood, but still *mine*. "Let's do it upstairs, in a bucket, with some bleach."

"All right." He smiled, softened. "That's a good idea."

I edged past him through the dark, grim basement, aware of how risky it was to have my back to him now. I heard him following me and when we came up the stairs into air and light—windows and doors, avenues *out*—I started to breathe.

He locked the basement door behind us and I set Lexy down on the floor. Still holding the knife, I leaned down and opened the cabinet under the kitchen sink, got the bucket and set it under a fast stream of hot water. My hand shook as I poured in a copious amount of bleach. I set the open bottle on the counter, thinking *I could throw it at his face, blind him, and get out of here*—but there was Lexy, crawling between the kitchen and the dining room, pulling her toy dog on a long string as it clacked across the linoleum.

"Put the top back on the bottle," I told him. And he did it, just like that. In that moment I understood how afraid he was and that he wanted to be told what to do. Bobby's passivity had often annoyed me, but only now did I comprehend its hidden danger.

I dropped the knife vertically into the bucket and angled it so the whole thing was submerged in the bleachy water. The pinkish residue that had edged the spine of the knife vanished. I rinsed my hands and dried them on a dish towel.

And then I turned to my husband, who was leaning on his elbow, looking into the bucket like it was a well deep enough to bury secrets. It wasn't, because *now I knew the truth*, and that hard kernel of knowledge would grow and blossom in my mind for the rest of my life. In the natural light of the kitchen Bobby's skin had taken back its healthy tone and he looked weirdly confident, as if everything would be fine between us now that the problem of the knife had been cleared up. He looked almost handsome, almost kind, almost right; almost my Bobby—but not him. What came next was what I *had* to do; it was the most strength I could pull out of myself to build a simple bridge—a bridge to safety—for me and my children.

"I'm going to ask you to do one thing for me," I said. "Only one. But it's very important."

"Anything." He touched my arm with what was supposed to be affection but felt like assault. I didn't flinch.

"I won't turn either of you in. Just don't stop me from leaving and don't try to find us."

His eyes clouded with surprise, panic, disappointment, a parade of emotions too cacophonous to control. He looked as if he might cry, but he didn't. He nodded. And that was the last communication between us, ever.

Just as he had last spring, he stood by and watched as I loaded Lexy's and my suitcases into the car and buckled her into the car seat. She didn't like being strapped down. She wanted to roam free and fast every waking minute, but today she had no choice. I started the engine, put the car into Drive, and inch by inch, mile by mile, devoured the road away from him.

It was all over now. Over. *And I was gone.*

ONE COLD NIGHT

Kate Pepper

One cold night she disappeared....

New York Police detective Dave Strauss is haunted by the one case he couldn't solve. A schoolgirl vanished off the streets of New York, with only a trail of blood and a series of untraceable phone calls from "the Groom" hinting at her fate. Now the cold dark night has engulfed another young girl—but this time she is part of Dave's family. He and his wife, Susan, know fourteen-year-old Lisa has not run away, and they know her disappearance is not just a tragic coincidence. And once the first phone call comes, they know she's not alone....

0-451-41214-1

Available wherever books are sold or at penguin.com

SEVEN MINUTES TO NOON

KATE PEPPER

In a comfortable Brooklyn neighborhood, Alice Halpern waits for her best friend, Lauren, at the local playground. But when Lauren doesn't show up, and then fails to pick her son up from school, Alice watches her own life turn into a nightmare.

As the police desperately search for Lauren, who is nearly nine months pregnant, Alice, herself pregnant with twins, realizes she's being followed and has the creeping fear that she'll be next. As the investigation intensifies, Alice is shocked to see her familiar world turned upside down by the list of suspects. And as two new lives grow within her, she must fight to save them, her family—and herself.

0-451-21579-6

"A new force to be reckoned with in...suspense."
—Donna Anders

Available wherever books are sold or at penguin.com

FIVE DAYS IN SUMMER

Kate Pepper

The Countdown Begins Now...

Before the long drive home from vacation, Emily Parker made a quick run to the grocery store...and disappeared. But as her husband and a retired FBI profiler scour the Cape for her, Emily's thoughts are not on her own safety. Kept helpless in a madman's lair, she watches him prepare a five-day countdown that will bring him to his real victim-her seven-year-old son...

0-451-41140-4

Available wherever books are sold or at penguin.com